To Catch a Hummingbird

A Miller's Creek Novel

MINDY STEELE

A patient man holds the
strong, the wild, and the beautiful,
whereas a man without patience
will be empty handed all the days of his life.

To my amazing children,
may you always believe in second chances
and that life is filled with happy endings.

CHAPTER ONE

If Lydia Rose Miller knew anything, it was that no matter how hard one tried it wasn't always enough.

"We're moving?" Her voice echoed through the two-story farmhouse and traveled into every dark and lonesome corner. She had never raised her voice to her mother before, but she had to be certain. Unfortunately, the words hadn't changed. *Moving*. Miller's Creek had always been home; they couldn't just leave. Yes, things had been hard since *Daed* passed away. Bills piled high on his desk were daily reminders of that, but moving? How had it come to that? *You failed again, that's why.*

"Calm down, Lydi. We both knew this day would *kumm*," Hazel, her *mudder*, said as if it had been up to discussion. After spooning dumplings into two separate bowls for their supper, Hazel found a seat at the kitchen table.

Watching her mother carry on as if the day was just any other, Lydia grimaced. Her stomach wasn't sturdy enough to eat a thing now.

"But this is our home. We cannot leave it." Frustrated, Lydia paced, her black shoes thumping against the hard wooden floors. *Mudder has lost her senses.* Lydia shook her head. Hazel Miller had become a bride in this house, borne three daughters in this house. Was she seriously just going to walk away from it?

The scent of wood smoke from the fire had always been warming, cozy, and welcoming. Now Lydia felt she just might choke on it as her breaths grew more rapid.

"We are not just leaving it." Hazel scoffed. "I had an offer for the farm and *haus*."

"You've had offers before." Lydia couldn't suppress her irked tone. When her father, Joseph, had been called home after three months in a coma, her mother had had offers. Why not? It was the most adored home in the area, with the best soil, many claimed. She flared her nostrils, recalling how many others wanted them to sell so soon after *Daed* died. It was disrespectful to assume two women weren't capable enough to handle things. Lydia stopped pacing. It appeared *they* had been right because they weren't handling things and were moving now.

April rain pattered down outside, bouncing off the tin porch roof, which wrapped the house like a welcome quilt on a winter's morn. Lydia loved the sound of rain, but tonight, the pings matched her mood. One by one they hit every nerve she had left with life in general. She ran her hand along her chilled arms, more for holding herself together, and collected her racing breaths. They had received two offers for the farm to be exact. Either one would have cleared their debts long ago. But there was that hope, a plan to hold firm to what little they had left, and if they worked hard enough to erase the medical debts, all would be well. Lydia wasn't sure hope even existed at this point in her life.

"It is time, Lydi. *Gott* has helped me realize this," Hazel said. "I need a new window to look out."

Her mother looked drained both mentally and physically. Lydia let out a long sigh. Who could deny the melancholy that filled their home? It was felt equally between them. *Daed* had been the heart and soul of their family, but regardless of his absence, Lydia couldn't imagine leaving the home she and her sisters had been born in, and she certainly didn't deserve a new window to look out after what she had done. No, Lydia deserved reliving her mistake every morning when the sun rose on the far pasture. She deserved seeing the life she'd once cherished crumble because of her weakness.

"I cannot leave." Lydia's words came out on a heavy sigh.

"Do you plan to marry and take over this farm yourself?" Hazel stared at her from the opposite end of the table.

"You know I am not." Lydia ducked her head. The only boy she had ever considered marrying was five years gone and two hundred miles away. He hadn't even written once since he'd said goodbye under that walnut tree at the end of their drive. She was done pining over a man who didn't love her enough and was too busy to consider the prospects of marriage and family. She didn't deserve either. Not when her mother had been robbed of the love of her life. With both her older sisters married and with lives of their own, *Mudder* had only Lydia left in her life. No, marriage was not an option for Lydia Miller.

"We must accept we cannot do this no more," Hazel said in a weary breath. Her mother was tired. Tired of long hours at the bakery and tired of tending to a house too big for only two women. Plain tired.

Lydia glanced at the bowl of warm dumplings with a soured appetite. Between randomly helping Hannah at the school, three days working at the bakery for her mother and grandmother, and tending to her *Aenti* May, she too was stretched far enough that she collapsed on her pillow early in the night. Right now, she felt that same weariness that met her each evening after collecting what money she could from wherever she could.

So much for making a dent and keeping things going.

Her shoulders slumped downward. "Where will we go?" Lydia plopped down in the chair, the only odd one at her family table, and tried absorbing her current reality.

Hopefully moving in with one of her two married sisters was not an option. She had been teased enough throughout childhood by the perfectly plain pair. Loving Gracie and Martha Sue was one thing, tolerating their constant badgering for her to be more like them, and married, was another.

"We are not going far. You remember Rebecca Byler?" *Mudder* lifted a brow and slowly took her first bite.

"*Jah*." Tiny hairs on the back of Lydia's neck bristled. Rebecca Byler was a crabby old spinster that tended to her nephew's children after their mother passed away years ago. She never wore a smile and always looked as if she had just woken from a long, restless night. She was an untidy sort from her lopsided prayer covering to her worn-out old black shoes. Even among the Amish, a people who dressed commonly the same, she stood out like a fly in cream. Frugal was one thing, neglect another.

"What about Rebecca Byler?" Lydia held her breath. *Please don't let us move in with Rebecca Byler.*

"She returned to Ohio last week. A *schwester* in need it was told." Hazel ate another spoonful of dumplings not mentioning what Rebecca's sister needed. *Mudder* was certainly beating around the bush. Not uncommon, but Lydia wished she would just say what she needed. After a full minute of delicate chewing and a slow swallow, Hazel continued, "I have been given an offer for a place for us to live in exchange for us helping someone who is in need."

Lydia perked. Charity was her weakness. Helping others gave you purpose and kept you busy all the same. With so few jobs in the area, it was volunteering oneself to others that helped her days to be full. Like Ben, the elderly widow Lydia often tended to on days she wasn't already consumed with other tasks. Ben had no other family to speak of. It was a shame some people grew old without children to help them.

"You help run a bakery six days a week. Where will you find time to spare for another anything?" Lydia's concern was well placed. *Mudder* baked from sunup to sundown. *Mudder* passed a soft, appreciative smile her way, and Lydia studied it for a moment. With all this talk of her marrying, had no one considered *Mudder* was plenty available of remarrying if she so chose to?

Hazel's soft cheeks, plump and barely traced with hardships, barely traced with hardships still held a beautiful complexion. Brown hair lightly threaded in silver coiled tightly under her *kapp* flickered in the late evening lamplight. Her stout frame was huggable, loveable, and that of a woman who tasted her goods before she sold them. It was her seal of approval. She had always said with a laugh. She was a treasure and still had more than enough to offer anyone lucky enough to notice.

Hazel sighed and watched the late evening sunlight being swallowed up by the night out the kitchen window. April had held on to its chill longer than usual. That was Kentucky weather for you, full of surprises, just like life.

But where will we plant our garden now? Lydia followed her mother's gaze.

"I love this house. The memories we have all made here. I shall never forget them." A tear ran down Hazel's cheek, and Lydia went to her side.

"What can I do? How can I fix this for you?" Lydia bent a knee and kneeled before her and then cupped her mother's worn fingers with her own. Who could bear watching their mother cry? Lydia most certainly could not.

"Nothing you can do. I cannot stay here any longer, Lydia. *Gott* says to not dwell on the past but a future with Him. I am tired of fighting for what is already lost. I miss the sounds of laughter in my life more than I want to sit here in this quiet surrounded by all that is familiar." Hazel wiped her face with the back of her hand and cradled Lydia's cheek. "*Gott* has a plan for us. We have been blessed in our time of need."

Blessed? We are selling our home! Lydia's insides screamed, but her expression remained tender for her mother's sake.

"Silas Graber is offering us a home in exchange for helping with his *kinner*. He is taking work outside of the farm
with the others working on the new building in town with
the *Englisch*. He needs our help now that Rebecca has left.
School will be out in a couple weeks, and all three *kinner* will
be underfoot."

"Silas Graber?" Lydia knew little of Silas Graber other
than he'd lost a wife, seldom spoke, and never smiled. *Daed*
had purchased a buggy horse off him years ago, but after
Jana Graber passed away, he was like a shadow, always
standing in the background any time she saw him at church
or picking up his boys from school on the days she volun-
teered.

"Bishop Schwartz came to see me last week."

"Again?"

"He worries for us." Hazel confessed the recent visits
had led up to making this decision.

"We have managed so far. He needn't worry," Lydia still
felt a bit raw.

She did appreciate the bishop's concerns. Joshua
Schwartz was a kind man who always considered others first.
Lydia found his company as well as his service impeccable.
If only his beard would lay down and not bounce every time
he spoke, she would give him the true attention the man deserved. But it was hard to hold a laugh trying to force its way
out, especially when the bishop got excited.

"It is his job to worry about those in the community."
That was true. "Thomas and Silas spoke with me yesterday
at the bakery."

Lydia's eyes narrowed at the mention of her *onkel*'s name.
Of course, Thomas had a part in all of this. He had tried
more than once to get *Mudder* to sell the farm. Thomas only
thought of Thomas. It was apparent his concerns were more
of a selfish nature when tending to his brother's widow and
daughter than it did for their true well-being.

Lydia inhaled a deep breath, calming her nerves for the third time in only an hour. Apparently, this was the plan? Leave their beautiful farm and home to help a widower with his children? Silas Graber had been widowed a good many years by her account. The man had one expression each time she saw him. Stone-faced. Who could blame him really? Losing a wife and raising three small children alone. As much as Lydia liked the idea of helping care for three children, spending every day in another home filled with loss felt like they were trading one dark storm cloud for another one.

"I have prayed long on it, Lydia. Do not look at me that way. This is *gut*." Her mother tried to sound encouraging.

Lydia swallowed back her heartbreak. *Trust your mudder; don't overreact.* It was a reminder to herself more than once in the last four years. Lydia hadn't said anything when Mother sold all their hogs to an *Englisch* farmer when they assumed *Daed* would wake from his coma. She too believed they could start over once he was to rights again. It had also lessened the workload for two already busy women to not tend to a hundred swine each morning and each night. Lydia did become a bit concerned when Mother sold the equipment and leased the crops and fields to Martha Sue and her husband, Adam, but she still trusted *Mudder*'s decision.

Her gaze rifled over the room. The home had slowly grown wider and emptier, bare of the furniture that had been purchased by the local community to help pay more on the medical expenses. She would never admit it aloud, but as the house began to hollow, it stopped feeling like home. No longer did Father's laugh linger within the halls where memory had held them for a spell. No longer could his scent be found within the cushions of the couch or the coat hooks on the wall by the door.

Working so many jobs made it easy to adjust. By the time she made it home in the evenings, she was too tired to think about what was lost. And that was when Lydia grasped what a blessing being busy was in a person's life. Loss could penetrate the heart like a well-aimed sword—if one had time to deal with loss, that was. And she was determined not to deal with it.

"You've already agreed to this, haven't you?" Lydia lowered her head, already knowing the answer.

"*Jah*. I think I will enjoy *kinner* under foot again." Hazel smiled and something in her pale gray eyes flickered with fresh life.

Mudder was excited and hopeful. Lydia couldn't deny her one second of that. "But you must do your part. We will work out a schedule." Hazel straightened, patted Lydia's hand, and then gave it a light squeeze. "That way the *kinner* are always under our care? And there is the matter of visitors." Her mother shrugged.

"The visitors?"

"According to Silas's mother-in-law, Francis Peachy, since Rebecca left for Ohio he has plenty of visitors offering help any way they can." Hazel's lips flirted with a grin.

"Oh, you mean those seeking a husband, don't you?" Lydia shook her head. Hazel nodded. "Then why can't he just let them? Can he not just pick one and marry? He will have his help, and it is only expected one marry for the sake of his *kinner*," she said.

Problem solved, and we won't have to move.

"He does not wish for that. Some do not re-marry. Silas is like that, for now at least."

Mudder sported a familiar smirk that Lydia recognized but hadn't seen in a while. It was no secret her mother and grandmother had a habit of playing local matchmakers. Well, if she was thinking of trying her hand with her, Lydia would have a thing to say about that.

"He cannot work the horses, for as soon as one comes with a pie or casserole, another is on the way. He only had peace because Rebecca was present. She had a talent for order that even your *Onkel* Thomas would be impressed with." Hazel chuckled at the comparison of Rebecca and Thomas and their strictness. Didn't sound like a problem to Lydia. It sounded like Silas Graber was a prickly and picky sort.

Onkel Thomas had become Miller's Creek's new deacon, just recently, and he was taking the role a bit too seriously as far as Lydia was concerned. As opposite from *Daed* as the night was from the day. His little talk with Lydia the day of her father's funeral concerning finding a husband and supporting her *mudder* was not appreciated, and she'd let him know just that on the spot. He didn't take kindly to her disproval of his plans for her, and that red-headed temper of his lashed out against her defiant tongue. She no longer considered Thomas the fun-loving *onkel* who carried her around on his shoulders, but one who felt he needed to determine her family on their every move without lifting a hand in help. Of course, he'd had a hand in *Mudder*'s decision. Just because he looked like *Daed*, Lydia wasn't about to let him think to fill shoes he could not fit into.

"*Mudder*, how will I get to work? Silas's farm is farther from town. That road is not very bike-friendly." The little side road on the opposite end of Miller's Creek wasn't buggy or car-friendly, either. Lydia stood and paced the floor again, letting the images of the Graber homestead come into her mind's eye.

It had been years since they had held a church Sunday, the last being just months before Jana Graber died giving birth to her daughter. What Lydia could remember was the road was narrow, full of holes, and far from everything and everyone. Maybe Silas and Jana liked that sort of solitude, but it just wouldn't work out for two women who held employment in town.

"It will work. You will see. And maybe you will forget your worries and start using the buggy. *Kinner* might be too big to fit in your bike basket."

Now *Mudder* was cracking jokes.

Lydia snorted. "*Mudder*, it is not a worry." *It is a fear,* she wanted to say.

"Even so," Hazel teased with a grin, "we will be living with a man who knows horses better than any. You help with his *kinner*; he can help you face that fear. You need to get over this. They are not all beasts."

Turning from her mother's view, Lydia rolled her eyes. Was she talking about horses or men? Lydia wasn't sure. In her way of thinking, beast or man could neither be trusted. Andy Weaver had spoken of love and marriage—and left her. Horses were fleshly animals that could throw you without warning. Silas Graber, a man and a horse trainer, would be teaching her nothing. That much she did know.

Lydia clenched her dress into both hands and stiffened. Images of her father flashed before her. *Daed* knew she was afraid of the horses and still insisted she help steady the large beasts while he tended to the plow. She'd begged him to not depend on her, and she had been right that he shouldn't have. When the two Belgians startled, she'd panicked and let go, permission for them to let go, too. She could still see *Daed* being dragged the length of the field before the animals stopped at the fence line.

I let go.

That place in her heart where guilt hid whispered to her as a cold, lonesome shiver of regret ran down her spine. No one blamed her for what happened that day, but no one knew that she had let go, either. If they only knew, no pity would have come upon her in those sorrowful eyes in her community, and no amount of working to help her mother would ever be enough for taking her husband away.

"We shall start packing *kumm* morning. We have just a couple days to be moved. Silas needs to get working. He does not want to ask the others to help with the *kinner*, and you know his youngest isn't in school yet." *Mudder* stood and collected her bowl. "He worries too many faces upset the *kinner*, and he will wait for us before heading to work for his brother-in-law."

"How can we pack up our lives and move in a couple

days? Who will help us?" This was happening whether she wanted it to or not. Panic rushed through her veins like a floodwater in spring. There would be no talking her mother out of any of this now. "I have to be at the bakery in the morning and *Aenti* May's by noon to help check the hives. You know she can't do it alone at her age."

"We can start after you return," Hazel said calmly, never one to easily get overwhelmed. "The Browns will deposit the money in the morning, and there are papers to sign."

"You mean Karen? Karen is taking our farm?" Lydia's inside voice vanished yet again. Karen Brown was a local woman who often filled in as a driver to their small Amish community. Lydia adored her. *Had adored her*, she amended, clenching her dress in frustration. Her head went dizzy as reality offered a hard slap to hopes to change her mother's mind.

"The Browns are not taking. She and her husband are paying well for it," Hazel said with a serious expression. "Adam will still lease the land until he and Martha can afford it outright. Bishop Schwartz and Thomas will *kumm* for me forenoon and help handle the paperwork and tend to Joseph's medical bill at the hospital. We will finally be done of that." Something akin to relief sounded in her mother's voice. "You will not have to work so many jobs. More time with the *kinner*." Hazel said it like it was all wonderful and well thought out.

Lydia couldn't disagree more. "But I like my work. All of it. I like having much to do."

"Oh, you will be." Hazel chuckled as she started the running water into the sink. "The Graber *kinner* need us. It is not about what we want, Lydia. A heart of charity, remember?"

Lydia nodded. *Mammi* Rose said she was the heart of charity among their kin and always encouraged Lydia to see this was her gift from God. Seeing a need and tending to it, wasn't really a gift, and if they only knew how easy it was to hide behind that veil of purity, that her helping others was more selfish than good, they wouldn't be so pleased with her. The busier the better, that was her way to face each day.

Surrendering to the day, she sank back into her seat again. The dumplings had already gotten cold. *Just as well.* Lydia closed her eyes, brushing away any negative thoughts. Anything her mother wanted, she would have. Even if it meant helping a middle-aged bachelor she barely knew with children marred by loss. Surely three children would keep her hands full.

Lydia didn't need easier, she needed every minute of her day occupied, or else she would have the time to think, and thinking led to a whole slew of things she wasn't ready to face. *Daed*'s absence had left a gaping void that still needed to be filled. Three children might do that, she hoped.

"Okay." She inhaled deeply, accepting this wind of change that she hoped wouldn't blow them both over. "So we are moving then." Lydia swung her hands into the air. A little dramatic, but *Mudder* was used to her antics.

Lord, I know nothing about motherless kinner, but Mudder needs this. Help me not spoil it.

CHAPTER TWO

Two days later, Lydia had whittled her belongings down to two small boxes and one unnecessary hope chest. The wooden chest served her better holding recipes, scraps of material, and books that *Daed* would have never approved of her reading. Most young Amish *maedels* filled their chest with linens and hope, things important for the home and family God would one day bless them with. God wouldn't be blessing her for nothing, now would He?

Evening sun claimed the front of the house as Lydia stepped out onto the porch to take a break from dividing household goods needed from those wanted into piles. A short rain shower had cooled the air. It was crisp and clean, nothing like the way she felt at all.

Mudder had been all too content tearing down what was left of their lives. Her vibrant humming echoed through the house as if nothing was wrong. If only she knew what Lydia had done, or not done, maybe she wouldn't be humming as she cleaned out the food pantry.

This was all Lydia's fault. *Daed* would still be here, the farm would be full of life and prospering, and *Mudder* would not need any new windows to look out. With one cowardly mistake, a downward spiral had consumed their lives, and there was nothing she could do to fix it.

Her eyes lingered to the right field, the fence of white where Dan and Doug, *Daed*'s two work horses, had finally come to a stop that day. It was a kick to the gut every time she stopped long enough to look at it. Part of her deserved to look at that pasture every day for the rest of her life—a reminder. Part of her, the part she kept hidden, hoped to never look at it again. The sound of buggy wheels pulled her out before she sank too deep into the horrid memory that changed their lives forever. She immediately straightened and tucked a loose strand of hair back under her *kapp*.

The buggy slowed to a stop in the yard. Lydia twisted her dress into her fist, a force of habit when she needed to become still or rein in a quick temper. Watching Silas Graber and Thomas Miller step from the buggy, she knew there was no going back. However, the sight of the two overly serious-looking men coming to take her and her mother away from their home sent a rush of anger through her.

When Silas reached Thomas's side at the bottom of the porch steps, Lydia gave him a hard look. This was the man she was to live under and help and try not to hate while she made his life easier.

Silas's jaws shut, clenched tight with no signs of relaxing, the moment their eyes locked. Conflict warred on his face. Regret maybe. She glanced at Thomas and forced herself to keep her composure. He had a way about him to bring out the worst in her. The men who were taking her life away were now standing in her front yard or what used to be her front yard. She should say hello but was mute, rigid, and brooding under a weakening sun.

"Where are the *kinner*?" Hazel asked, all too peppy, stepping onto the porch, a child over one shoulder as she most always had accompanying her.

Silas removed his black felt hat. Incredibly thick dark hair, needing cut long before today, sprang to life as if just freed. A lump lodged in Lydia's throat when she took careful measure of his heart-stopping hazel eyes as they went from her to her mother. She couldn't deny he was handsome. No wonder single *maedels* jumped at offering him help with his home and children. He didn't look as old as she'd believed him to be during church services. She had never taken time to notice. Another habit she should wrangle soon. What else had she been missing?

"Thomas's Libby is spoiling them with *kichlin* right now." Silas smiled half-heartedly at the mention of his children getting their fill of Libby Miller's much-sought-after brown sugar cookies. His short, thick, darkened beard didn't mask a small, low-set dimple on his left side. His gaze shifted from mother to daughter as if weighing each woman's current notions. He would do well to not concern himself with her current thoughts.

His soft-timbered voice suited his strong structure. Silas was the same height as her *Onkel* Thomas, but it was obvious the man labored longer and harder than Miller's Creek's new and meddling deacon.

"Silas has everything ready, and we have *kumm* to move your things," Thomas said and bounded up the porch like a man of twenty. "Let's not dally around."

"*He is thoroughly enjoying this.*"

"But—" Lydia spouted in defense. She wasn't ready for this. Was she? Hazel's hand rested on one of her firmly crossed arms, encouragement for her to stop her tongue from moving further.

"It is time, Lydia," Thomas scolded.

Why does everyone keep saying that?

Her gaze moved on Silas, who was taking in everything with a sorrowful expression that almost said, "I'm sorry I am here and taking you away from the only home you ever knew." She tightened her arms firmer around her middle, narrowed her gaze, and with a stomp of her foot stormed inside.

The last of the boxes were being unloaded into the small, gray metal addition built for Silas's aging parents years ago. The *dawdi haus*, as it was referred to, was attached to the back end of a much larger white clapboard farmhouse. The only good in this day was even though the Graber farm was almost seven miles from town, the old narrow lane she'd feared riding her bike on was now widened and covered in asphalt.

Silas's parents had been gone a good many years, but he had done a fair job cleaning the *dawdi haus* for their coming. A strong stench of bleach and furniture polish hit her the moment the door opened. Lydia took in the look of the rooms. Scanning the small dwelling with a scrupulous eye, she saw that it was quaint, with shelving and cabinets and handmade furniture. There were two small bedrooms and a smaller kitchen. It was suitable and not too stuffy, but still not her home.

"You can have that room, Lydia." Hazel pointed before stepping into the room opposite of hers. As Silas and Thomas carried her *mudder*'s chest into the house, Lydia slipped into her new bedroom. Avoiding them would be hard, but she was determined to get this day over with and see them gone.

Laying two handmade quilts onto the single bed, she paused and took measure of the tidy area. Then she caught sight of a small dresser sitting in the corner. Drawing closer, her fingers traced over the scratch on the left upper drawer. She remembered the scratch; she'd made it herself. This was her old dresser, sold to help *Mudder* pay medical bills more than two years prior. Silas had obviously been the one who purchased it on the day many had come to rifle through their things. A tear slipped out as she recalled the moment *Daed* had given it to her. He'd smiled with loving blue eyes and given her a hug. He called her his sunshine. She pressed a finger to her forehead where he had placed a tender kiss.

"This is like a bad dream. Please wake me, *Gott*. Wake me from this dream," Lydia muttered alone in the little back bedroom.

The bedroom had a single bed and hooks on one wall for hanging her things. Lydia sucked up her hurt and began removing those things from her wooden chest. She hung the four dresses she owned on one hook, her aprons on another. She was glad for the space, having been able to keep more of her own belongings than she had previously assumed she could when her mother first told her they would be selling most of what they had. This was all considering the Graber home was equipped for their practical needs.

"You best mind yourself. Only crazy people talk to themselves."

She flinched but refused to turn and recognize Thomas. Hope chest opened, Lydia hurried to cover her books with a small box filled with old cards and returned letters. A loud thud smacked the cool concrete floor causing her to squeak out a small surprised yelp. Thomas had dropped her only belongings instead of treating them with the care she'd given them as she put them into the box. Turning, she shoved two small fists on her hips and shot him a glare.

"You think a person talking to *Gott* is crazy, Deacon Miller?" She should have known he wouldn't tolerate her sarcasm. Looking down at her box then back to him, her eyes narrowed.

"This is a *gut* arrangement, and you are lucky Silas is willing to help you and Hazel. It is time to make yourself useful and stop being a foolish *maedel*. It is time you do the right thing and stop hopping around like a frog without a care." Thomas's words were cruel, just like his new temper. Neither looked good on him, and she squared her shoulders to remind him he did not intimidate her.

"I always do as I am asked. I hop from helping one

person to another with many cares. Judging others is a sin, ain't so?"

Thomas clutched her arm. "You will not speak to me this way. I am your elder, your deacon. You can tend to your belongings last. Now go help your *mudder*." He gave her a hard nudge towards the door. It was true obeying one's elders was expected, but respect should have to at least be earned.

"What is this?" Thomas growled out. Lydia turned to find him kneeled over her chest and pulling books out one by one.

"Those are mine. None of your concern." Lydia rushed over and attempted to retrieve them, but Thomas would have none of that, holding her wrist tightly to keep her at arm's length.

"No wonder," he said, his eyes like daggers boring into her. "I will tend to these, and you best hope I do not have a mind to speak to the bishop of this." His nails dug into her skin. Jerking away would only make matters worse.

His threat frightened her. What would the Bishop say to her hiding a few Amish romance novels?

Silas appeared in the doorway, a basket of folded linens in his arms. Unshed tears blurred her vision as she jerked from Thomas's hold and she quickly covered her arm as if hiding a secret. She didn't meet his eyes, not wanting to see the look she figured would be in them. Would he scold her for speaking to one's deacon so harshly? An eerie silence filled the room. When she dared to lift her gaze, Silas's eyes shifted from her to Thomas and settled on the three books in Thomas's hand.

"Libby is outside. I would like you and Hazel to come see the children. I think now is a *gut* time for that." His gaze pulled from her and quickly rested on Thomas. "*Danki*, Thomas, for helping today. I will see the rest of Hazel's household is tended to." Silas's words were measured, precise and unwavering, and sent goosebumps up her arms. The man had no qualms dealing with Thomas, and that earned him something akin to respect. She was thankful he intervened when he had, but she couldn't bring herself to thank him. She nodded before sweeping by him in the doorway and putting as much distance between her and her *onkel* as possible.

CHAPTER THREE

"Aiden is nine." *And a mirror of his father,* Lydia noticed more now that the two stood side by side. From the soldierly way in which they stood to the way their eyes roamed his surroundings undetected, Aiden's light brown eyes drifted between her and Hazel. He was plenty old enough to remember his mother, and that alone made her heart go out to him. Losing a parent, no matter the age, was life changing. She knew that all too well.

Even introducing his children, Silas held a firm countenance about him. "Gideon is a year younger. He has a habit of running off, but we are getting a handle on that. Aren't we, Gideon?" Silas squeezed his second child's shoulder, and the blond-headed boy peered up and smiled cunningly. Silas smiled in return, crooked and to the left, but a smile. Perhaps he had a soft spot hidden under all that cold and stern façade about him.

Gideon was the prankster of the Graber children, according to her best friend Hannah, who was their schoolteacher. Lydia often helped at the school but only to tend to the older girls and boys with lessons. She often brought treats to those of Aiden's and Gideon's ages. But she had noticed plenty that Gideon was one who always carried a smile with him everywhere as if holding a secret. Hannah said it was either for something he did or the thoughts tossing around in his head for what he planned to do that kept a smile permanently glued to his lips.

Lydia made a mental note to warn *Mudder* of *that one* later. Hannah had more warnings to hand out about Silas's second child. But she also had something to say about Lydia's need to work so much. It prevented best friends from seeing each other. Maybe once things settled, Lydia would invite her over for supper and an afternoon of catching up. *Maybe.* Spending time with close friends would require talking, and talking opened up emotions and remembering. None of which Lydia wanted to consider. Hannah would also want to address Lydia's new living arrangements. Lydia hadn't fully wrapped her own head around it herself so discussing it would be uncomfortable.

"And this is our Mary May," Silas said in a rather pleasing, softer, raspy tone. It was evident that the four-year-old little girl, like most little girls, held a place in her father's heart by the beam in Silas's eyes. It looked good on him, smiling. Maybe he wasn't such a stiff old widower after all. Had her *daed* ever looked that way introducing her or one of her sisters? She couldn't remember. There were so many things she had taken for granted about her father and now time was forcing her to forget them.

Mary May was the spitting image of Jana Graber from her blond ringlets to her tiny nose that wiggled and scrunched adorably. Lydia remembered holding her once, as a *boppli*, during Caleb and Tara Mast's wedding about four summers ago.

Everyone was consumed by the day's events, and Mary May had cried longer than Lydia could stand. Rebecca said the little girl would learn and no one disputed her tactics. Lydia disagreed any learning was taking place between the stern old spinster and the *boppli* begging to be held. Lydia swooped up Mary May and helped serve with only one free hand at the wedding table until the motherless child fell fast asleep in her arms. That was when she'd abandoned all hope Andy would return to her. That she would one day cradle her own *boppli* in her arms. She tossed out the stupid memory and studied the children more closely.

Mary May watched her brothers' every move and followed them just as close, like a faithful hound. Being the youngest herself, Lydia knew what it felt like being a shadow to siblings born before you.

"It's so nice to be here with you," Hazel said in a motherly tone. Mary May let loose her hold of Silas's leg and stepped forward, closing the distance to look at two more faces that would be filling her days. Blue eyes the color of a calm summer sky peeked upward. Something hard and cold in Lydia, melted. She leaned forward, reaching Mary May's eye level. *What a beautiful child.*

"I'm happy to be here with you, Mary May. *Danki* for inviting us to come." Lydia waited for something from her, but Mary May only stared at her with troubled eyes. Two more women in her life had to warrant a four-year-old's confusion. How Rebecca could just up and leave after being so present in these children's lives, Lydia couldn't fathom.

"Invite?" Aiden blurted out. "I thought you said—"

Silas shushed his son's following words with a grunt. Yep, communication here would be nothing she would get used to. And if they weren't invited, then what were they?

"If you young men would help me with a few sticks of wood, I will get supper started," Hazel said. All three of the children's eyes widened in anticipation. Without haste, Aiden tapped Gideon's arms, urging him to follow, and they stepped to the side of the house, where Lydia assumed the woodpile was.

Maybe tomorrow she could have the children show her around, so she could get her bearings of the Graber farm if they were even willing. By the look on Aiden's face, she was certain he wasn't. It would take some time for a routine, something of normalcy to be formed. That was if Lydia could muster up a sense of it for herself.

This was hard. Strange house, strange new life, her *mudder*'s strange and sudden joy still plastered on her thin lips. Who was really benefitting here, Silas or *Mudder*? Looking out over a farm equally singed by death as her own parcel had been, Lydia breathed in the scent of cold, wood smoke and rain. Silas did well to keep things in order here without a wife, but all she could see was gray metal, white fences, and a big white *haus* almost matching her own. Well, not her own anymore.

Something was missing here, despite the tidiness about. The dormant garden to the right made her shudder, as bare of life as she felt. The massive barn to the right was surrounded by gates and fencing and corrals. More lived-in than the house, it seemed. But that was the Amish rule: barn first, *haus* later.

Silas was most likely a firm and obedient follower of the rules. Color was uncommon in plain dressing as well as in a home's appearance. Here it showed that was faithfully followed. Not one color edged past plain, not one hue out of line. At least the grass in the pastures would reach emerald green soon, followed by polka dot yellow, once the dandelions bloomed. So there was that to look forward to, she hoped.

After a simple supper of ham slices, canned white beans, and cornbread, Lydia couldn't help but notice how the Graber boys devoured Hazel's attention, hers not so much. When she asked the children if they would like to play a game of checkers or draw, both Aiden and Gideon only hurried upstairs and into their rooms without so much as a glance her way.

They still needed baths and tucked into bed. She and *Mudder* had agreed Lydia could take on the task when they had planned out responsibilities. Knowing Silas would work his horses in the afternoons now that he had taken work outside of the farm, Lydia suspected she would spend nearly every evening caring for the children. But Silas bounded up the stairs behind them as she expected he did each night. It was the first night, she reminded herself again. Tomorrow would be better. Lydia couldn't blame the children for this arrangement. They were just victims of circumstance, and *Onkel* Thomas's bad idea.

Once the kitchen was tidy, Lydia slipped out the back door and into the attached structure she would now call home. The thing about miserable was that if you don't leave it behind you, it was still there like a layer of thin skin covering you from head to toe. How would she get comfortable in this strange place?

Silas tucked the children in and returned to his room for what he predicted would be the first of many long sleepless nights. It had been a long day, and his back was stiff from moving all the women's things. He preferred sleeping in the sitting room in that worn and deep place rooted out from years of sleeping and not sitting on the couch. But now the Miller women had come to live here, forcing him to swallow down that stubbornness to avoid his empty bed. It had been over four years now, and still sleeping alone was hard to muster.

At the nightstand, he began to wash his face, but that didn't help him feel cleaner. The varied expressions on Lydia Miller's face since he first arrived at her home, had left a thick layer of regret that washing hard with pure lye soap wouldn't even remove. Hazel had said the adjustment would be hard for her, said that her daughter would resist the change. Resist was a kind word for the hurt he'd seen in those angry, watery eyes. He never was good at handling tears. Hopefully, the old dresser and other pieces strewn about would help with any unsettled anxiety. Give her a small sense of home and the familiar again.

She was rather beautiful. Those blond hairs didn't agree with the confines of her prayer covering any more than her lips accepted being forced to smile. He had more than a few glances today into those deep blue eyes. Each time they appeared to hold back tears or hurt that he felt certain she'd forbidden to escape. Her life was changing drastically, and only a few years after Joseph's tragic death. Everyone knew that she had been there when her father was injured. Perhaps she was scarred, the wounds still fresh. Maybe she was haunted. Nightmares came in all shapes. He for one knew all about that.

He chided himself for not taking her feelings or her beauty into consideration when he'd agreed to this arrangement. A man didn't need more trouble to deal with when his life was already full of it. And he didn't need that kind of distraction in his life. Not this man, at least. He was just doing as the bishop suggested. Help another; get help in return. It sounded simple enough. Now, as the first day of this new way of life was bidden good night, nothing felt simple in it at all. In fact, he was certain the bishop had just complicated it.

He ran his fingers through his hair. *Things are moving fast.* Unless that was on the seat of a saddle, he didn't like it. The bishop had been forward that he needed to move on. Remarry and give his children a mother. It was expected and Silas often supported such unions, but he couldn't do that. He could not simply do such himself just because it was expected of him. There was only room in his heart for one love. If Rebecca hadn't come two years ago and agreed to help, he was certain the bishop would have done more than suggest it back then.

Once word of Rebecca's leaving rumored the grapevine of the community, he found Bishop Schwartz at his door once more. Joshua Schwartz was a good man, a respectable bishop, but Silas was not marrying again. Bringing Thomas Miller with him this time to speak of Silas's future was unexpected. Come to think of it, the way the two men spoke, it wouldn't be a surprise that the whole thing hadn't been Thomas's idea in the first place.

He and Thomas had grown up together, but they had little in common. Thomas always had an odd way about him that hadn't changed in his coming to manhood. Silas especially didn't like it now when he heard him raise his voice to Lydia today. Joseph Miller would have never allowed his youngest *bruder* to speak to his Lydia that way. Despite regretting making this agreement with Hazel Miller, now that the two women lived under his roof, he wouldn't allow for such behavior, either. He agreed to take on this responsibility and a man was nothing without his word.

He smiled, recalling the look on Thomas's face when he'd taken Lydia's books out of his hands. Thomas could toss threats and sharp orders all day to women, but he wasn't going to intimidate him. Silas knew what it took to see over a family and keep it on the straight and narrow.

He removed his shirt and sat on the side of his large empty bed. The scent of wood smoke and damp barn floors rose from his sheets. Laundry was not his most prized duty with being a single parent, and the evidence was overwhelming. Tomorrow he would go to work and trust that Hazel, who'd raised three *kinner* already, would have everything under control as she assured him she would. *Please help us make this work, Amen.*

CHAPTER FOUR

On a wide yawn, Silas stretched out his limbs to exceed his six-foot measure. He had fallen asleep, socked feet dangling off the side of the bed. Nonetheless, he felt rested, refreshed. It was a new feeling after years of the opposite. And he'd dreamed last night, as opposed to the gloomy nightmares that often visited him in the dark. Life here was disrupted, bringing the Miller women into his home, but he'd dreamed of Hazel's baking in the kitchen. Dreamed he was filling his belly while Lydia flew around like a blur. She was younger, and laughing, and always running away before he could tell her to stop. His children ran behind her, in the dream, unable to keep up. He rose to his feet, shrugged away the strange dream, and put on fresh clothes.

He didn't know Lydia all that well, having seen her only on occasion within the small community. Every time their paths crossed, she was on a mission, getting something done for someone. She was known for being one who quickly offered help as well as being rather easy to look at. After the man she courted moved away, many had attempted conversation with her, but she didn't seem to like the attention, he had noticed. Since Mary May was just a few months old and

Lydia had somehow ended up holding her during Caleb Mast's wedding dinner, he'd noticed the beauty that never slowed. Her energy was endless, like her father. Joseph was a man who got things done, without too many words, and behind the scenes most often. Lydia must have gotten that from him. Silas always believed Joseph a worthy example of a husband, a father, and his passing had been hard for Hazel and her daughter.

Hazel said coming to live with him would do them both well. Silas hadn't really considered what good it would do for a single *maedel* who buzzed around like one of those honeybees at her *aenti*'s homestead, but Lydia's energy could serve him well with Hazel working so often at the bakery. If only he could muster through seeing her and not Jana caring for his children. It was Hazel and her grandmotherly ways about her that he had put all his hope in, but Lydia appeared to be what he would get since the bakery was growing and getting busier by the day.

Rebecca had had no room for error, leaving the *kinner* bored and rambunctious in the afternoon. Children should be seen and not heard was not just an *Englisch* expression. Rebecca had proved that. Bedtime was a nightmare for children who were still full of energy. Mornings even worse. He knew Lydia's youth and energy was what was needed to tire them out proper at nightfall, but it would be difficult to witness.

He needed to trust God and himself for agreeing to this. He had three new horses to break and now working most days with John's construction crew he needed help, and the kind that didn't require a marriage to get it.

Freshly dressed, Silas quietly made his way to the kitchen. Suddenly he realized not one child had awoken in the night. Even they had slept well. He smiled and silently descended the stairs.

The warm scent of fresh-baked goods and coffee filled the house. It had been too long since his home smelled of homespun sweetness. If he was lucky, not all Hazel's goods were going with her to the bakery today. He missed having a *fraa* in some ways. Loose britches being one. There were only so many eggs a man could eat before it soured his will for nourishment, and Silas didn't know how to cook much else.

He stepped into the kitchen. Hazel stood motionless, a two-layer German chocolate cake cradled in both hands, staring out his kitchen window into a dark morning. The lamp reflected in the window glass as well as Hazel's un-flinching gaze. He paused to give her a moment. He, too, had done that a few times. Not with cake, but starring aim-lessly out that window, a cup of *kaffi* in one hand, pondering God's will in the other hand. He cleared his throat to keep from startling her and moved gently into the room.

"Sorry." Hazel snapped out of engrossing memories, turned, and put the cake in the center of his table. "I thought the *kinner* would like a dessert tonight so I made extra today. Did you sleep well?"

"Surprisingly well." He eyed the cake with greed. "You will have us spoiled, Mrs. Miller. I had hoped to do the milk-ing before you made it in this morning." Rebecca had always waited until morning chores were complete before starting her day. Silas looked forward to no more missed morning meals.

She threw up a hand to stop him. "Lydia is doing that now. She likes the chore rather well, and we have been with-out that blessing for some time now." Her smile didn't fade in the comment. Silas knew they had sold all their remaining livestock last year just to help with expenses.

"Let me get your *kaffi* and a plate. Breakfast will be done soon." Hazel opened the oven door—*cinnamon*. His mouth went wet in anticipation. Cinnamon rolls had been a favorite of his since he was Mary May's age. A long denied treat he had almost forgotten existed. Maybe this decision wasn't such a bad one after all. His stomach gurgled in delight.

After setting his cup before him, Hazel peered out the window once more, lingering into the dark of early April morning. Behind all that positive attitude and quick smiles, was she having difficulty with this change as well? She had expressed concerns with her daughter but never how she felt about leaving the home she and her husband had made.

"Does it get easier?" Silas asked as if able to read her mind.

Hazel Miller had lost a husband. He had lost a wife. She was wise, generous, and caring. None of the things he was, but Silas knew that with age came wisdom and at thirty-two he hadn't earned near as much as would serve him well. Surely Hazel knew the answer to his question. Would it get better? Could Hazel see a future that held peace in it for either of them? He was tired, mostly of the gloom suffocating his home and family, and ached for at least a thin ray of light in his world. Even if Hazel lied, he would be thankful for something positive said within these walls of heartache.

"*Jah.*" She turned to him again, soft grey eyes sending a warmth of comfort his way, her woes lifted from that little quiet place she kept them. "One day you will wake up, and it won't hurt anymore." She pressed a hand to her stomach. "Light will be brighter, and everything will smell new."

That was a positive he looked forward to.

"One day you will laugh and like how it feels. How it tickles the throat and makes you warm again. One day you will see *Gott*'s plan is bigger, better than holding on to what has passed from this world. Sometimes it takes longer to step forward. Sometimes all you need is a new window."

She waved an arm, pointing out his very window. He studied her in that strange awe of hope that framed her. It appeared that hope was there. Out there somewhere and delivered in words so perfectly placed he believed she had gotten them from a book. Maybe she'd read one of Lydia's Amish romances he had tucked in his sock drawer. Emma Graber, his mother, was one who knew what words a man needed to hear, and when. Hazel was much like her, in heart and hope. Still, his ray of light seemed crowded under some basket somewhere.

Silence settled between them for a moment. His shoulders sank from the weight of doing so much, worrying too much. He missed Jana. The love they'd had. The family they'd made. He'd assumed Hazel to be mourning her own loss, but she had appeared to have licked those wounds. *Licked them and found a new window to look out of.* Jealousy was a sin, but for the first time in Silas Graber's whole life, he felt it. Hazel missed what she had and smiled, heading into a new day. He wanted that. Wanted that resilience and reason to smile and look forward to the day. That kind of faith.

"One day perhaps," he said with a curt nod, trusting her wisdom. The door swung open and Lydia stepped in, a pail of fresh milk in one hand. She wore a battery-powered headlamp, keeping her hands free to work, its aim blinding him momentarily before shifting to Hazel. She was not the ray of light he was thinking, but she did look like sunshine that had long been shut out of his home. He quickly focused on his food.

"I smell cinnamon rolls." She grinned like a greedy child, strolled over to her mother, and kissed her cheek. He took a breath. Had she already gotten over her hurt and angry fit? The spring in her step and the smile on her face said as much. *Gut. No more evil looks.*

"Your favorite. Thought it was the least I could do for you this day." Hazel smiled, obviously trying to gain favor with her daughter. "Silas will be leaving soon for work. You can take the morning shift at the bakery. *Mammi* Rose said she could handle the rest of a Monday alone. The next four days, you will be needed here."

Silas paused, bringing his cup to his lips, and watched Lydia stiffen at the comment. Her hands slid slowly to her side, gathering the fabric of her pale blue, chore dress. She obviously didn't like her mother's plan, and that brightness she'd brought into the room drifted out just as quickly. Come to think of it, didn't she work at the bakery and at her *aenti*'s farm too?

As he pondered the thought, he remembered that she also filled in for Hannah at the school. It had taken a long time for Hannah to get over that lingering pneumonia that had hit her before Christmas. Aiden had mentioned her before in passing. Lydia often helped with math and science lessons with the upper grade children. And everyone knew she took more than her turn to see in on Benjamin Troyer. The elder was well into his eighties and had no family left to speak of. Many of the women in their community took turns seeing to his needs, and younger boys tending to wood and simple chores and upkeep on his small parcel.

Silas sipped the warm *kaffi* and glanced over his cup to study Lydia more intently. Rebecca had never helped at the school or with Benjamin Troyer. Her time was solely invested in seeing to his home and the *kinner* and that alone wore her out daily.

Suddenly reality hit, and Silas rubbed his head with his palms. He'd just made a commitment with two women who had sparse time to keep their commitment. Lydia glared his way, huffed, and turned on her heel. She readied the milk for straining, clenching her jaw again, he noticed.

"Hazel, I can put off going until next week. That will give you both time to better your schedules around—" He left off the *me and family* and stood. The sound of his chair scraping the floor caused Lydia's shoulders to jerk in a startle. Respectfully, he was careful putting the chair back, lifting it as opposed to scooting it back as he would have normally done.

"Nonsense. I work six days, but Rose and I will be getting help soon. She is already speaking to others about helping on Saturdays. I think I would much like a Saturday off. And Lydia here has stretched herself out so far across the community, it will be *gut* for her to let others step up and help, too. If you haven't noticed," Hazel chuckled, "my Lydia can be rather quick and hurried. Slowing would be *gut* for her."

Silas had noticed, just as he'd noticed the way she slapped the milk strainer on the glass container as her mother spoke. Anyone with an eye would notice how Lydia moved at the pace of a racehorse. Hazel didn't need to point out the obvious to him.

"She has been a great example to others. Now others should *kumm* forth and serve too. It is our way. I feel many have forgotten that within our community."

Hazel was right about that, but the awkwardness he felt between him and Lydia Miller was growing rapidly by the stone-set grimace on her delicate features.

"*Mudder.* I can keep my duties and do what is needed of me here. I do not need others to take my place."

Her tone took Silas by surprise, and he lifted a brow towards it. How was one woman going to do five jobs? She was being unreasonably ridiculous. He snorted, earning him another angry glare.

"We won't need you at the bakery so often. That is three more days you can be here. I know you are just there to help and do not have a real passion for it."

"I love the bakery," Lydia protested.

"*Jah*, but you would rather do other things. A *mudder* knows her *dochder*," Hazel said softly and playfully patted Lydia's cheek. "And now that Hannah is over her sick spell, you won't be needed at the school, either. There are so few days of school left anyhow. You will have time to find what makes *you* happy, not others for once."

Hazel cupped Lydia's cheeks with both hands with affection. "I want you to be happy."

It was sweet watching this exchange, but Silas felt he was intruding on something private.

"How am I supposed to make an income? I won't give up *Aenti* May and sitting with Ben. I just can't. They both need me."

She sounded like Gideon did when he threw a fit. "If this is about money," Silas interrupted, "I provided an income to Rebecca, and I told you, Hazel, I would do the same here." *It was about money.* He had little but, for his children, he would offer what he could.

"And your offer was generous, considering," Hazel said with a grateful smile and a touch of his sleeve.

Considering they sold their home and all their belongings. Lydia's gaze darted between Silas and Hazel. She wrung her hands in the fabric of her dress before slowly perching them firmly on the slight curves of her hips. And did she really just flare her nostrils?

"Did anyone think that maybe I like helping others? That maybe I don't care about money at all? There are those who depend on me."

Wrong again, Silas. He was glad she didn't desire such worldly things as money. It seemed passion to care for others was honest. But did she seriously think she could handle more duties?

"You have new commitments now. We have a responsibly here. *Gott's* will," Hazel said sternly, putting further argument to rest.

Silas could only stare at them feeling slightly responsible for the changes happening in their lives. "Lydia, I will be here as often as I can. I will also compensate what you made as well as help provide for any needs either of you two have." Caring for three kinner wasn't going to be easy for a *maedel* who never had *kinner* of her own. She obviously wasn't thinking clearly.

"My only needs were my commitments to others. Commitments I already made."

Icy defiance laced her voice, and her hands shifted to those hips again. If it wasn't that Hazel had sold her home and uprooted them for his benefit, he would end this whole agreement before it started, cinnamon rolls or not. It was obvious Lydia, who would help anyone who asked, didn't want to help him.

His gaze landed on her more intently. Those blue eyes were kind of pretty, boring daggers at him, but pretty. Like a deep blue sky with a flicker of lavender woven in.

Her lips tightened like Mary May's did right before a good pout. She was cute angry like that, but he kept his face blank of any expression. He shifted his gaze to Hazel, who was more focused on him than her defiant daughter. Silas cleared his throat. He best keep his airs in check. Last thing he needed was for the local matchmaker to get any strange ideas.

"Hazel, if you think this—"

Hazel interrupted. "It will work out fine if we all work together," she said convincingly. "We appreciate all you have done for us, and we will both do all we can in return for your kindness." The word 'both' held in the air.

"Kindness," Lydia said bitterly.

The woman is going to take a bit of getting used to.

"I should be going." He nodded a thank you to Hazel and retrieved his hat. Opening the door, he turned back. Lydia still stood there like a bruised *hund* contemplating whether to bite now or later. Her plump lips were almost in a full pout now. "The children know their duties." He put his hat on his head.

Lydia cocked a brow. Jana would have never looked at him with such contempt. "I reckon it is time you best ready them for the day." That order arrowed straight at her before the door closed. Now she knew hers.

Once at Miller's Bakery, Lydia took the morning to fill in her grandmother about all the recent changes happening so quickly in her life. *Mammi* at least would understand how she felt about living at the Grabers'.

"She doesn't understand, and the *kinner* don't even like me. They do chores and just sit around when they are done. Like they are afraid to move or something." Lydia pulled the money bag out from under the counter. "Aiden watches me out of the corner of his eye, waiting for me to do something to make that frown of his worthy of wearing."

She filled the cash register drawer with bills and coins from the cracked leather banking bag. "Gideon smiles at me, but I see the wheels turning in the head of that one. I will probably have toads in my bed by nightfall." She put away the bank bag, tied on a fresh apron, and walked to the front of Miller's Bakery to flip the closed sign on the front door to open. "*Mudder* did not ask me what I wanted at all. They need a *mudder*, not someone like me. She expects me to see to them nearly every day." Her voice rose an octave.

What did she know about being a caregiver to three children?

Her grandmother began setting cookies into the long trays of the glass case. Her slim, long frame was sturdy for a woman of sixty-six, but her pale flesh appeared ancient. A product of being a redhead who feared the sun and its cruel effects.

Rose Glick was a sharp older woman, both in wit and tongue. Traits Lydia often admired—unless aimed her way. She had patiently listened to Lydia's grumbling without a word all morning, but now that Lydia seemed to have stopped, she offered Lydia a piece of advice. She never lacked it and had certainly never seen that common sense required sweetening.

"Either find a nice young man and marry or get your head around it." Rose closed the glass case and faced her granddaughter. "Silas Graber cannot make a living training horses with three young *kinner* underfoot."

"Maybe he shouldn't be training horses," Lydia countered. "It seems the worst trade a man could ever have." She let out a weary breath. Of all the trades a man could possess, why did *mudder* insist they live under the roof a horse trainer?

"It is what he is meant to do. He no better planned for a life without a *mudder* for those *boppli* than you did without your *daed*," Rose said smartly. "Life ain't about our plans or being stuck in the past so far we can't see anything clearly."

She turned and reached for another tray. Peanut butter with chocolate chunks this time. "Your *mudder* works hard. This will be on you to see through. I expect better out of you." Rose stopped and pinned Lydia with a look. "For a woman who thinks she must spend her life helping others, you are being selfish on helping three *kinner* who need it."

Mammi Rose's words were like a cloud blocking out any sun, and Lydia's heart felt heavy to think of herself as selfish. "What about Ben and *Aenti* May?" Lydia asked.

"Ben would love to see *kinner* about and May would too. Take them along. It will set a good example seeing as Rebecca never took her turn at it. You aren't thinking straights dear. We are called to offer charity where charity is needed. Those *kinner* need what you have to offer."

Helping the elderly with a few chores was one thing. Helping three children who had lost their mother, was something entirely different. They didn't even like her. She was not the right person for this need and it turned her stomach to know that no one realized that but her. Some things a person just can't fix for others. Who was she to fix something so delicate as loss when she couldn't even accept the one she suffered either?

"They have lost so much. I cannot help them, *Mammi* Rose. I cannot fix this for them."

"It is not your place to fix anything. That is for *Gott* to do. You are responsible for helping them thrive and find their own path. Help them find faith and joy in the world *Gott* has provided them," Rose said.

Lydia couldn't be responsible for anyone's happiness let alone three small someone's. She didn't even have that. *So help them be happy.* Could she? Perhaps she had studied this from the wrong way. Nothing was going to bring her *daed* back or the home she was born in, but there was reason the Graber children should feel as she did. And three children, a home, and farm would keep her busy enough. If she tried, took on this new role as caregiver with an open heart, could she help those children find the peace and hope she never would?

CHAPTER FIVE

Two days later, Silas woke to the scent of pine from his bedding and a chill that had set into the house. Another night of restful sleep, he had neglected to add another log onto the fire somewhere in the night. He hurried downstairs to remedy the issue before Hazel made her way inside to start breakfast. Hazel and the children would appreciate the warmth upon rising and greeting a cold April morning.

Crouching down to the wood stove, he lit the kindling. Lydia would not need such warmth, he chuckled, oddly thinking of her so early in his day. Cold ran in those veins, warmed only by the rush that always carried her through each day. If she stopped, would she stiffen into stone? he mused. What made such a delicate creature treat everything like a race to be won? Did she even stick around long enough to see any good she'd done helping others?

He'd noticed her from the barn yesterday. That flash of white caught his eye as it wisped behind the house. He paused and waited for no other reason but curiosity's sake. She reappeared, feet moving as swiftly as always. He watched, waiting to see if her pale blue chore dress would get tangled up in her quick pace, but she was all forward

momentum and unwavering in strides. Her arms were filled
with kindling from the wood pile, stacked high, and blocking
her view.

She was much stronger than her thin frame suggested.
He'd feared she might walk right into the side of the porch
with so many sticks filling her smaller arms, but she'd managed. Many things about her were contradictory. She appeared stubborn, but with the children her patience was
absolute. She clearly didn't agree with Hazel's decision to
live here, but she tended to her mother's every need. Despite
her barks, she did Hazel's bidding without fail, even if her
lips carried a soured expression.

The house held a quiet at this early hour. He sat back and
watched a spark grow into a flame. If life was only that easy.
He had grown accustomed to the quiet, but it never felt
peaceful until right now.

Running his fingers through his hair, he pondered the before. Before Jana died and Mary May was born into a world
without a mother in it. Jana had liked the silence. Reveled in
it even. It was the one thing they'd never agreed on. Jana
often became overwhelmed when the boys cried at the same
time or visitors came unannounced. If she only knew how
many tears were shed and visitors had crowded these walls
the last few years, she would have certainly had a panic at-
tack or three. Being an only daughter had made her more
inclined to solitude. Whereas Silas grew up with the sounds
of a full house and missed the joys of it. Something told him
that all that quiet was about to change. He only hoped it
would be for the good.

After an uneventful breakfast, Silas rode toward town.
The job awaiting him was more pleasing to handle than
Lydia Miller's intense glares at the breakfast table. to speak
to him. Hopefully, his being away from home more would
give her time to adjust. Bound by his word and Hazel's assurances as far as his children were concerned, he would endure any coldness Lydia felt toward his uprooting her life.

She just needed some time and his patience. He was grown, with strong shoulders and back. He would endure. *Right?*

Morning light made a grand entrance over the horizon as he veered the buggy off the country road onto the state road leading to the town of Pleasants. Red lines mingled with gray, a sign that more bad weather would fill April.

"Sapphire or chicory?" he muttered to himself. He was still undecided if Lydia's eyes were deep like a sapphire or more wholesome like that of the chicory blooms that would brighten his pastures come summer.

She was nothing like Hazel. Heck, she was nothing like Joseph Miller either, apparently. Joseph had been a quiet man. A busy man, but one not prone to excessive chatter. Maybe a man with only daughters born to him had no choice, but he did. Where Hazel was reserved, Lydia moved around a room like she was on fire. Hazel was happily obedient like Jana had been. Lydia was all gumption and moody disposition, a trait often frowned upon.

Hopefully, they would all find a rhythm soon enough because it would take gumption on both their parts for that to happen.

He needed the women's help. No denying that. Rebecca had thought him too soft. Perhaps he was, overshadowing them as he did. Lydia had handled Mary May stuffing thread in her nose like a pro. When he suggested taking her to the emergency room, she'd actually had the gall to laugh at him. Then, when Gideon accidentally dropped butter in her seat last night, she'd only smiled and left the room to change and had returned looking all new with that cunning grin. Her murmurings were almost silent between the walls that divided their separate housings when she left to change her dress. Good thing, too. For a woman who wanted no reason to speak to him, she had a lot to say around him.

Silas dropped all notions of home and pulled the buggy up to the old warehouse where other horses and buggies rested in the shade. John Peachy, his brother-in-law, and

Toby Brown stood nearby, talking. John's hand flew up in a hello, and Silas waved back. After getting his horse, Jippy, settled, Silas grabbed his tool belt, took a deep breath, and went to greet them. It had been years since he'd worked outside of the farm. Breaking horses had profited well, but breaking horses with three small children underfoot was a dangerous job. Hard to keep one eye on a toddler and one on a defiant animal at the same time.

"Silas. Heard they had you framing walls the other day. Sorry we didn't tell the foreman of your purpose sooner. Had to handle the mess with building permits and regulations, but I am here now, and you won't be hammering all day," John said with a firm nod.

Relief washed over him. He didn't mind framing, but if he was going to be working on the job again, his hands needed to be doing what they were most familiar with.

"Toby, you remember my brother-in-law?"

The men shook hands. "I do indeed. You were the best stone layer we had when you were younger. That old bridge in Goddard never looked better. Hope you still have that skill." Toby turned, facing an area with pallets of brick and stone nearby. "The wall they started needs torn down, moved two feet over, and built the right way." Toby let out an exasperated breath. "These boys could topple a stack of Legos." He chuckled, and his whole body did, too. "I sure hope you can correct this."

Silas eyed the wall in question. Currently, it was about two feet in height and sixteen feet in length, and yes, it was a mess of stone and mortar and unleveled framing. He was good at what he did, and at taking things that looked rough on the outside and bringing out the best in it. Even the rowdiest horse had potential. "I can."

There was a different kind of joy that came with working with stone and brick. Building something with such natural, rustic beauty had always made his heart happy. It was a skill he had learned as a young man of sixteen, half a lifetime ago.

It was good a man knew how to do more than one thing in this world. Learning should be endless, but he had learned so many things like cooking and mending he ached for the familiar once more.

The three walked forward as Toby began explaining the plans for a wall aligning the walkway and the brick needed for the front of the building's soon-to-be entrance.

"I heard Hazel Miller and her daughter have moved onto your farm," Toby said. His baseball cap said Cincinnati Reds, but underneath Toby hadn't a hair on his head.

"*Jah*. They are tending to my children and settling fairly well." It was only a partial lie.

Hazel looked like life had sprung up and bitten her, but it was sadly not contagious one bit. The woman could bake and launder and clean and still hum throughout her day.

Lydia, on the other hand, could do all that and more, but there was no humming, no smile. Just busy, like a hired hand. Did she ever relax? Ever just sit on a porch swing and listen to the world around her buzz, instead of contributing to it? Did she ever take a walk and breathe in the day's freshness, or did she only find escape in foolish romance novels? He doubted her preferred reading would be acceptable under the Ordnung, but so much had changed for her, and been taken away. Even Jana had enjoyed reading and he saw no harm in it himself. He should stop letting his head be so consumed with Lydia Miller and focus more on what he was doing.

"Karen has been wanting to move from town for a long while. We were glad to run into Thomas when we did. I know your community takes care of its own, but that man would have sold the place to us right there on the spot for pennies if permitted."

Silas squinted. Had Thomas pushed the powers that be to pawn off his brother's family? *Typical Thomas*. He shrugged.

"Well, I am grateful for the help, and I am sure Karen

will like living there. Joseph Miller's home is one of the finest in the area."

Is that another reason why Lydia's so unhappy?

"I agree. Too big for my taste." Toby stretched and patted at his stomach. "But the wife likes it well enough. Women like having all that extra space just so they can clutter it all up." He chuckled. "They're still working on the electric, but we'll be settled soon." John returned with a few rolled-up scrolls. "Karen said she saw Lydia outside the other day. Just wandering around. I think she might not like us buying it. Then again, if I had seen my father go through what hers did, I wouldn't want to spend a minute on that farm."

Silas said nothing to this and unfolded the plans John presented for building a wall for the new office building. It would be best to focus on work and not what troubled the mind of Lydia Miller right now.

CHAPTER SIX

Lydia delivered baked goods for the bakery and stopped by her *Aenti* May's to check on the beehives. The cold April wind did little to nudge either colony from venturing out. Putting an ear to each hive, she listened to the low roaring hum within. It wouldn't be long now. As winter was ending its turn, she made a mental note to check on the hives more regularly.

While there, she made quick work to clean the flower beds encircling the bee boxes. After enjoying a cup of *kaffi* and a piece of *Aenti's* fresh bread smeared with a healthy dose of honey, Lydia climbed onto her bike and aimed for home, where more duties awaited her.

Home. But it wasn't her home. Her home was now Karen Brown's home. Her room was a guest room where handmade quilts hung on the walls like pictures and not on the bed she had slept her whole life in. That place near the fireplace where she played while listening to her father read in the evening now held a rug so bright it blinded you from the doorway. *Orange, not tangerine*, she scoffed. Karen had been sweet to let her in, sensing the difficulty Lydia was having with letting go. Her sorrowful expression all but said as much.

Gott, what are you trying to tell me? I've been listening, but you are so quiet.

God's plan was not always obvious, and she wasn't so naïve to think it was, but there had to be a reason she was where she was. She swallowed hard. The reason she was here was her doing, not God's at all, she settled.

Peddling along the blacktop leading to the far end of Miller's Creek, Lydia took in the ever-changing landscape. Homes and pastures that only weeks before were blanketed in snow, now looked ready to be born again. Cold air nipped at her neck, but the dandelion greens made her warm with anticipation that summer was already decorating along the roadway. It wouldn't be long now, just after the hummingbirds migrated, and *Aenti* May's honeybees would be darting from yellow flower to yellow flower, dancing their spring dance.

Would Silas allow for a hive or two on his farm?

His pastures and hillside would be covered in dandelions, clover, and wildflowers soon enough. Even the thicket of trees she'd noticed collecting wood from behind the house said there was plenty for bees to forage upon. She picked up her speed as her mind mulled over the Graber farm's potential. If she was going to wrap her head around living there, as *Mammi* suggested, she might as make it home-worthy.

She could plant lavender along the drive, sunflowers along the barn and garden, and yarrow and snapdragons would liven up the blandness around the house. Add color to the drab, add life to the forgotten. Was that not what *Mammi* Rose was telling her—breathe life back into the place, give the children something to smile about? It was a great idea and the perfect plan, making living there more tolerable.

Suddenly, her bike jolted. Lydia gripped the handlebars tightly and slid to a stop in the loosened gravel along the roadway. Luckily, she did not tumble and crash. Sliding off the seat, still a bit rattled from the emergency stop, she gave the bike a good look-over. The chain had slipped again. Lydia groaned as she muscled the bike upside down on the side of the road and went straight to correcting the issue.

"Stupid thing." She could always get the chain to slip back into place before, but now she struggled. If she only had a sturdy stick or a bar of steel. *That would be ideal right about now.* She looked about her for something useful. With nothing in sight, she tried again. Her fingers pulled to slip the chain into place again, but fresh oil made that harder than it looked. This was not going to be a quick fix on the side of the road like last time.

A blue car crept by. Lydia caught a glimpse of the man sitting behind the wheel, leaning to observe her current state. She adverted eye contact and made herself look busy fixing her problem, but the car came to a stop and began backing up. Lydia shook her head. The last thing she needed was someone noticing her struggle.

The older gentleman rolled down the passenger window with the push of a button.

"Troubles?"

"*Nee*, I can fix it. Happens a lot. *Danki*. I mean thank you for stopping, but I am *gut*." She didn't mind talking to strangers, even *Englisch* ones, considering she had so often at the bakery, but when the man opened his door and stepped out, something about the speed of his exit triggered her arm hairs to stand on end.

Lydia stiffened as he walked in front of his car and came to the edge of the roadway just a few feet shy of her. Any chill in the air disappeared, and a sheen of sweat broke out on her face. She had no need of the thin blue coat and black shawl she wore. "I assure you, sir, I am fine. Thank you for asking, but you can be on your way."

His dark eyes, the color of night with no sign of a pupil or emotion, eyed the bike, and then her. Like most *Englischers,* he was taking in the full look of her, from her black bonnet to her black shoes, and she hated it. He had gray hair mingled with brown and eyes that smiled when his lips did.

"What kind of man would I be if I left a damsel in distress?"

His jolly tone didn't hide pushy insistence, and he moved closer until only the upside-down bike stood between them. Lydia could smell the pungent scent of cologne, and her nostrils reacted. She sneezed not once, but three times. That was something she hadn't known was possible. The stranger chuckled at her, which only aroused her tempered side.

"As I said, I am not in distress." Her tone was sharper this time. She pulled a rose-embroidered hanky from her dress pocket, a twinge of concern pulling at her gut as she wiped at her running nose. In boldness, he placed both hands on her bike, picked it up, and moved toward his car. Lydia gasped. *Very insistent indeed.*

"I'll take you where you need to go, beautiful. You live around here?" He glanced around as he shoved her bike into the trunk of his car. He was odd and pushy and hard of hearing too.

"Sir. My bike. I am not going with you." Lydia reached out a hand as if the bike could simply be laid in it. A drop of rain fell, hitting her palm. She flinched but ignored it, hoping it didn't give the stranger another reason to insist on her accepting his invitation.

"Oh, don't be ridiculous. I have a car. More dependable than a bike." He winked, flashing overly white fangs masquerading as teeth. "And look, it's starting to rain."

A cold April rain shower was far less threatening than a pushy stranger. Lydia bristled as he pushed the bike further into the back of the trunk area of his cobalt blue car, the front wheel of the bike resisting a perfect fit. Like her bike, to fit his idea of damsel in distress.

Goosebumps raised on her arms when she grasped his persistence was no longer wavering on the line of simple chivalry. His manner became one shade lighter than demand. The evening sun fading to the west made her heart ache to be with it. If she hadn't insisted on a second cup of *kaffi* at her *aenti*'s, Lydia would have been home by now and not alone here on the side of the road with this man.

"I don't get into cars, sir." She tried to sound as sure of herself as she had this morning with Silas when he'd asked if she had laundered his bedding. Those sheets, as filthy as they had been, didn't compare to the scent of danger around her now. She couldn't disguise the tremble of fear in her tone, no more than she could when she refused to give Silas an opportunity to tell her she'd done something as simple as laundry wrong. Which he most certainly would have said if she'd admitted to doing the chore. However, holding her tongue right now would not help her one bit. Amish were to be passive, but at twenty-three, Lydia knew there were times when passive had to be put aside.

"Oh, come on, now. It's just a ride. I'm not asking you to marry me or anything." His smile widened, revealing a missing tooth on his left she hadn't noticed before. He stepped forward, offering an arm. She saw through the gesture and measured him for the wolf he was. She took a step back in reaction to his offered arm, and if her legs would stop trembling, she would run right about now. *Come on, limbs. I need you.*

"I said no." Her voice quivered.

"Now you are just being shy. Come on now darling. Let me see you home safe."

"I'll be seeing her home."

Where had Silas Graber come from? Lydia's heart jumped into her throat. She let out a muffled liberated sob. How did he pull up with a horse and buggy, step down, and come to her side without her knowing? *Your scared and pounding heart, that's how.*

"Silas." Lydia hurried to the side of his buggy.

"Is that your bike in this man's car?"

She couldn't answer but nodded it was.

"Just trying to help your woman here," the stranger said, pulling the bike out from the trunk. At least with the bike in there, there was no room for the stranger to stuff her inside. The thought made her shudder, and she bit her lip to contain it. Why was she overreacting? Or was she? The warnings, the alarm, were all there.

Silas's face was unseen from where she stood, but the stranger was in perfect view. He dropped her bike to the ground, gave her a sorrowful nod, then jumped into his car. Faster than she could wipe spilled milk from the kitchen table, he was gone.

"Are you okay?"

Silas stood protectively watching the car drive away and not turning to see her. She wasn't all right and was grateful his eyes remained fixed on the man's departure and not on her. Holding her breath so long, she feared she might have forgotten how to breathe. She forced herself to take a long inhale and crumpled forward. Maybe throwing up would help. It might as well because she was certain that was what she was about to do. The stranger had been pushy and unwilling to listen to her. She hadn't felt this vulnerable, this frightened since—she pushed thoughts of her *daed*, her only protector, out of her mind. That would only make matters worse.

The crunching of gravel signaled Silas's. He placed a large warm hand on her shoulder, and she jerked from being touched, her sensitivities already swollen beyond understanding. Forcing herself upright, she grabbed hold of another long inhale and looked to Silas. His brows creased toward one another as if angry, and she bent forward again. *Just go away.* Her mind screamed, but her lips wouldn't cooperate.

Still playing the whole scene in her head, Lydia couldn't find where she had gone wrong for the stranger to believe he could get her into his car. She'd said no. Said she was fine.

He was determined to not hear her. Her breath caught again, tears lingering on the edge of escape. Her eyes darted to the road, the pasture behind her.

She was not like those foolish girls who talked with strange *Englischers* for fun during their runaround years. Silas would probably tell Thomas what she'd done. This was all too much. She lowered to her knees, hovering over the ground and holding her middle as if willing her stomach not to embarrass her, holding its contents into place.

"Lydia," her name came on a sigh.

"My chain slipped. I was fixing it, and he stopped." Her hand movements helped the words escape. "I told him I was fine. I said no. He did not listen." She gasped. "I just need to get the chain on and get back before it gets dark. I never asked for his help. I did not need or want his help." The words came out fast and breathless. Tears were funny things. The longer you held them, the more determined they got, and regardless of her strength, a few made a run for it.

Silas kneeled and offered her a hand. "I know."

She met his eyes.

"You are safe now. Let's get you home." His deep gravelly voice softened.

He was trying to be nice, but she was not getting into his buggy any more than a stranger's car.

"No." She knuckled away any tears before standing on her own two feet again.

"Lydia. You cannot be out here at dark. You know this now." He stressed the *now*.

Rain began falling a bit harder. "I am not yours to tend to, and I'm not riding in that." *Lord, can this day get any worse?* Funny thing about asking God for something. Sometimes he delivered rather quickly. Rain plummeted in harder beads. Like a summer shower that made you want to jump in and play in it. April showers, on the other hand, had a way of adding to an already miserable, dark day. She shivered.

Silas shook his head. He clearly didn't understand. "You

think people will talk? I assure you, no one will. You have done nothing wrong. There is nothing wrong with you riding home with me. We share the same address."

In truth, two unmarried people riding around would stir gossip, but she could handle that. She just wanted to get out of the rain and into her mother's arms. The stranger had been menacing and had made her more upset than she'd believed she could get. It was a good thing Silas had arrived when he did. It was over now, and she was safe.

"No, that is not it. I am—well, not very comfortable with—" She pointed at Jippy, the old gelding.

"My horse? You will not get in the buggy because you do not like Jippy?"

She wasn't much fond of his snippety tone.

"Not your horse. Any horse." Droplets of rain trickled down her cheek, and she hoped he couldn't tell tears were mingling with them.

"Are you saying that you're afraid of horses?" His dark brows lifted in surprise.

She knew that being Amish and afraid of horses was like being *Englisch* and not learning how to drive, but she couldn't help trembling at the thought. "You don't understand," she said, marching towards her bike, sniffling.

"*Nee*, I don't. And you can tell me all about it later. Get in."

She remained steadfast on two trembling legs.

"You are in no shape to argue with me this time. Jippy is the best animal I ever raised. Mary May rides him by herself. She's four."

If he felt mocking her would get him any dryer quicker, he was wrong. "I cannot," she confessed, rain soaking them both.

Silas stared at her. "I'm not leaving you. What if that man returns? Get into the buggy, or we both get soaked sitting here all night."

Her teeth began to chatter. Gazing down the blacktop,

she considered her limited choices. Three miles of road stood between her and a warm fire and dry clothes.

He took advantage of her momentary pause and tossed the bike in the back. He pulled out a large umbrella from under the seat and forced her up into the buggy. Unsure why, she went through the motions, even when he opened the umbrella and handing it over to her. He carefully enclosed her cold shivering hands around the handle with his large, warm fingers.

"Hold on to it now." He stared at her.

She was so cold she found herself unable to argue. Silas let go and went around the buggy and climb onto the seat.

"Chicory," he said as Jippy pulled them onto the road.

"Chicory?" Her teeth clattered.

"Nothing of importance for now." Silas slapped the reins against the horse's rump.

CHAPTER SEVEN

"Why are we walking there?" Aiden's long legs kept in good timing with Lydia's. He rarely spoke, but when he did, it was only to remind her that she was not doing something like Jana or Rebecca would do.

Being plain does not mean plain boring. Aiden wasn't intentionally so questioning, Lydia concluded. Serious, but never mean. Behind those walnut brown eyes and stiff shoulders hid confusion. He was old enough to remember a mother lost to him and observant enough to see Lydia was nothing like the *aenti* that had spent the last few years raising him. Lydia had no mind to be anything like Rebecca nor any of the fine, gentler qualities of the mother lost to them.

"Because the three of you won't fit in my basket." She chuckled. "And I don't like horses." There was no sense in keeping it to herself any longer. She was sure Silas Graber had shared that with everyone he encountered after her meltdown on the road. An Amish woman afraid of a horse was not a common thing. Lydia sighed. Neither was getting your *daed* killed.

"And you all need a day away from the farm." She heard Aiden's surprised gasp, followed by Gideon's, then mimicked by Mary May, struggling to keep up behind her. "Now how about you put a spring in our step and pick up that pace." She smiled over one shoulder at Gideon. "We will be checking on the bees at my *aenti*'s, and maybe there will be *kichlin* afterward." What child wouldn't be more apt to help when cookies were involved? "The wind was pretty strong last night so it's important we see none of the hives were knocked over."

"Bees sting." Gideon blurted out the well-known fact. Lydia swooped up Mary May. By now her little chubby legs had to be tiring.

"*Jah*, but we wear special clothes to protect us." A sudden concern occurred to Lydia. She had never considered if the children had ever been stung before or if they had a reaction to it.

Hannah had told her about little Mirim Planck getting stung and having to be rushed to the hospital last year. Her worries calmed when she remembered her *Aenti* May always kept medicine in case anyone visiting had an issue. Benadryl in liquid and pill form and a couple tubes of hydrocortisone cream she insisted worked just as well as vinegar. Lydia made a mental note of their location in the medicine cabinet of the back room, just in case.

"Have any of you ever been stung by a bee before?"

"I have, but it wasn't so bad." Aiden shrugged. "I didn't even cry or anything."

"I got stung once, but I did cry." Lydia grinned. Of all the Graber children, Aiden would be the hardest to win over, but she was determined to do just that.

"Will we get to help?" Aiden asked.

Lydia peered over her shoulder, surprised by a question that had no vinegar in it. She was more than happy to answer. In the two weeks she'd been living here, Aiden had never asked to be part of anything. *Mudder* thought him to be a hard worker. Lydia couldn't disagree with that declaration. He did his chores without fail nor complaint, but when she looked at Aiden, she saw a nine-year-old who hadn't been a boy yet. He seemed wound tighter than *Onkel* Thomas sometimes. She wasn't sure he was capable of even laughing.

"Today Aiden will help. You can take turns each time we come until you all have learned to care for the bees and their homes." All three sets of eyes, from sky blue to walnut brown, gleamed. Had they never been set free before? Had they not explored outside of everyday chores and lessons?

"What kind of things did you all do with your *Aenti* Rebecca?"

"Chores." Gideon sounded disgusted.

Lydia snickered at his quick answer. Gideon always had one available. "Well, chores are important, but what else?"

"That's about it," Aiden added matter-of-factly. "She didn't have time to read at bedtime either."

His face tightened. Was that something Jana had done Aiden missed? Lydia stored the information away for now.

"I was thinking after we're done here, perhaps we would have a small picnic outside." Lydia shifted Mary May on her hip and flashed her a grin. Her little nose wrinkled. *Meaning good*, Lydia now recognized. Mary May crinkled that little nose so often it was hard to tell.

"Really?" Gideon's voice sounded shocked.

"Really."

The Graber children deserved a carefree day of childish play. Lydia remembered such days well enough. She could give them that, and maybe this was something that wouldn't earn her a frown from their father. She was starting to sense Silas might be a bit overprotective of his children and a lot untrusting of her abilities to care for them. Just because her methods were her own didn't make them any less useful. She straightened her shoulders. Proving him wrong would be easy.

God had a sense of humor, that was for sure and certain. After days settling into this new role and other than one picnic and a bucket with three crawdads from the neighbor's creek, Lydia was no better at it than day one. And here she felt that they were reaching milestones. The children had all smiled today. Mary May had even giggled, poking at the creatures darting backward in the small pail. But no sooner than one of the boys started to laugh, they tucked it back into their pockets for safekeeping. She would have to try a bit harder, it appeared.

Gideon had taken her bike and hidden it after they returned home. After a long search, Lydia found it in one of the horse stalls, pony included. He knew she was afraid.

"Not funny," she had scolded him. He was also making a habit of untying her shoes any moment she stood in one place too long. How she hadn't fallen on her face yet was beyond her. Mary May wouldn't let her move at her normal pace for clinging so often to her apron and skirts. She was certain this wasn't the kind of slowing down her *mudder* was referring to. But this afternoon the tables had turned. Aiden slowly submitted.

Lydia wasn't sure if it was her *Aenti* May's peanut butter oatmeal cookies or his getting to wear a bee jacket and veil that did it, but he had changed. Sort of. He had insisted she help him with spelling words for school so there was that at least. Never before had she needed to work so hard to gain approval. They were Silas's children all right.

Picnics, mud holes, and boys made a mess she hadn't considered when the idea of fun came to her. The consequences of trying to win over the affections of three children, she supposed. She laughed to herself. The floors in the house were in desperate need of a good scrubbing. Once Mary May was down for a nap, she sent the boys out to clean the chicken coop, and Lydia started the task.

A puff of cool air chilled her arms where her pushed-up sleeves bared flesh. "I need that bike." She tried to contemplate how she would get to the school tomorrow. She would have to rely on Mary Hicky, who carted the children back and forth to school each day to deliver the muffins she was making, but she hated asking more of her than she was already giving.

Pondering over bike rescues and smelly little boys, she went to her knees and began scrubbing the stubborn corners, neglected for years by the looks of things, and hummed. It felt good to unleash some energy and break a sweat. Back and forth she tackled it until her fingers and arms grew sore.

When the floor creaked ahead of her, Lydia raised her head. Silas stood in the doorway looking around the room until his gaze collided with hers from the far corner. He must have heard her humming. She would do well not to let that slip again.

"Sorry to interrupt." A hint of amusement ran through his words. It was one thing to know he didn't like her, wishing he had *Mudder* instead of her helping with his children, but she wasn't entertainment, either.

"It's your house." Her sharp words snapped through the air, and she resumed scrubbing the corner.

"Where are the children?"

Like I lost them. She rolled her eyes.

"Aiden and Gideon are cleaning out the coop. Mary May is down for her nap." She froze and waited for him to argue that late in the day was not a time for a four-year-old to nap, but Mary May had been so tired Lydia knew it was impossible to keep her awake at this point.

Silas said nothing, and after a long silence, she heard his retreating footsteps leave the room and climb the stairs to the upper bedrooms. A minute later, she heard him walk back down the stairs and out the kitchen door without comment. Strangers who shared the same world, and she hoped to keep it that way. He seemed as awkward to speak to her as she was to him after she had gotten herself into that mess with the stranger in the blue car.

He was a good enough man, she reckoned. No matter the time Silas came home from his construction job, he always checked on the children's whereabouts before heading out again. This time of day he would work the horses. The three massive beasts often lingered neared the fence come evening, anticipating his return. He had one young gelding, spotted with large white circles against black, that had done so well in the saddle the owners were anticipating coming to get him. The other two horses weren't as compliant. Silas warned all of them to not even pet them on the nose. Well, he wouldn't have to worry about that as far as she was concerned.

Why the man took chances with his life was beyond her. Did he not realize how quickly such a trade could change everything? He did have children to consider. Men thought they knew all, she concluded before finishing the floors.

Two hours later as supper cooked in the oven, Lydia helped all three of Silas's children do their part in helping make apple muffins. It was going well—until it wasn't.

The food fight was unintentional. The children's help was more a hindrance than useful, but *Mudder* always said one could learn a lot from even a mess. Lydia wasn't convinced by that, but the Graber children were learning something this evening.

Once Gideon laughed a second time at Aiden for spilling milk on the floor, she found Silas's eldest and mere shadow had a hidden temper too. Aiden turned the remaining milk left in the container over and onto Gideon's dirty blond head without a second thought. Lydia hadn't meant to chuckle, but when she did, it led to Mary May throwing an egg—at her.

Lydia jumped back, ready to scold the child for doing

such an impulsive thing, but before she could, Mary May's actions had furthered Gideon to consider adding butter to Aiden. Maybe because Aiden was the only clean one at this point. She could only presume what went on in that mind of his.

Now they were all a mess, a freshly-washed-clothes-covered-in-baking-ingredients kind of mess. Lydia started to raise her voice, scolding them good and fair but found herself unable to follow through. A stomp of her foot, and all bodies froze, all eyes drew at attention. They stared at her like she was some sort of crazy lunatic that was about to take them to the woodshed. Which probably wasn't such a bad idea at this point. If there was one thing Lydia had noticed in the Graber household was that discipline was seldom handed out.

Well, God wasn't the only one with a sense of humor. The laugh started in her belly and traveled to the length of her throat before spilling outward. Those sets of hungry eyes begged for life and yearned for laughter. When her eyes locked on Gideon's, Lydia reasoned that she did owe him one for putting butter in her chair that first night. He might fool his father with those kitten eyes, but Lydia knew it was no accident. Gideon's slow, creeping grin was all the momentum Lydia needed. So, on top of milk, butter, and batter, she added frosting to the chaos by way of spooning a dollop on the tip of each of their little noses.

"If you are going to do something, children, do it right. I won't have slackers in my kitchen." She grinned. Shock was what she expected she would earn from them. An all-out food fight was what she got.

Silas stepped onto the porch. Sore was not a word strong enough for how his body felt this evening. Working two jobs took a toll on a man, and yet he was now living with two women who managed even heavier loads than his own.

To his surprise, laughter burst out of the walls of his house, a joy seeping from an awakened void. How he had missed the sounds of his children's laughter. It was alive and breathing and reached straight to the deepest recesses of his being.

He heard her laugh above that of his children's. He blinked. So, Lydia could handle multiple jobs and still find the energy to laugh at the end of the day. He wished he knew her secret. Since Jana's passing, he hadn't had much reason to laugh.

He had let his guard down the other day when that stranger tried getting her into his car. When her blue eyes, full of fear, had glistened with tears, sentiment strong-armed him, and he'd forced himself to look closer at her. She was beautiful and fragile despite her unwillingness to expose it. She hadn't a clue just how vulnerable she appeared in that moment, or how it affected him. The sound of her voice from the house was touching something inside him he didn't want to recognize. Something he didn't want to be reminded of. He didn't like knowing it took so little of her to affect him.

He peered into the window just left of the door, and his jaw dropped. Squinting, certain he was imagining things, he strained to get a clear picture.

"What in the world has she done to my children?"

Just on the other side of the glass, Lydia was bathing his children in—butter, was it? Mary May was dripping in the stuff. Did she not realize how long it took Hazel to churn that on her only day off from the bakery? And there was Gideon, holding Aiden hostage with an egg. Lydia was on all fours, trying to get a hand on Gideon. It didn't look like it was to rescue Aiden but to deliver something gummy in her right hand. She got a hand on him, too, but Gideon appeared to be happy about that, surrendering to her sticky mercies.

Silas lifted a brow. Gideon was pretty quick to escape any other time. Lydia wrestled him to the ground, smeared something on his head, and pulled the egg from his hand. She offered the egg to Aiden, who quickly deposited it into his brother's—Lydia's captive's—shirt. Silas closed his mouth when he became conscious it had fallen slack watching the chaos unfold.

"Smash it, Mary May." Silas could hear his eldest encourage his sweet and innocent little Mary May to join them in spreading calamity.

What would the bishop and Thomas say to this? He scratched his head. Mary May's giggles overtook the room and reached his heart. As crazy as it all appeared from this side of the window, that side was full of something his home had lacked for far too long. His children were laughing, smiling, playing. Even if it was wasting food he worked hard to provide and staining clothes he assumed no soap could remedy.

Silas opened the kitchen door, filling its frame with his broad shoulders and perplexed frown. Lydia raised her head and her wide smile faded into a firm line. Under a mess of thick white clumps of something resembling pancake batter, her blonde hair hung in chaos. Her *kapp* was gone, as was Mary May's.

His gaze scanned the floor she'd spent so long scrubbing. The whole scene mimicked a telling his *onkel* once described when a coon had spent an entire weekend in his home while he was gone visiting family. Silas looked to each child, carefully examining them from head to toe. A thud hit the floor, breaking the silence. The bowl did one of those spinning motions for a few seconds before resting on its white flat bottom.

He turned to Lydia, the one responsible. He suspected there were many ways of teaching children to be useful in the kitchen. His *mudder* certainly had her own way about doing things. But destroying Jana's kitchen wasn't one of them. Teaching recklessness was not what he had hoped for when he agreed to this arrangement. Lydia had no idea what she was doing.

"My floors are dirty again," he said before stepping back out into the cool evening air where he wouldn't have to watch his children smiling from ear to ear. When he heard laughter rise again, Silas couldn't refrain from smiling as he headed back to the barn.

As soon as she finished bathing the children, she heard her mother's buggy pull up to the house. The front door below her leading into the *dawdi haus* opened and shut. She glanced out a nearby window. Silas was walking out to put away mother's horse and buggy as he always did.

Another late day at the bakery. *Mudder* would be tired, but Lydia had seen she had a plate waiting on her at their own small table. With the kitchen in such disarray, Silas and the children had to eat in the sitting room tonight. Now she would have two areas to tidy instead of one.

Lydia finished tucking the children in bed and hurried downstairs. She still had a mess in the kitchen to clean up before she could call it a night. She collected any remaining dishes left in the sitting room and aimed for the kitchen. She wondered why Silas hadn't said anything when he saw what she and the children had done. He said so little, but he made a lot of deep growls and grunts she had yet to decipher. Of course, he wasn't pleased. Perhaps it was reckless, but the spontaneity of the moment had made the children's eyes sparkle with joy. She would have to apologize for the mess. It was crossing a line, but she wouldn't apologize for making his children laugh. On that account, she stood firm.

When she slipped into the kitchen, Silas was already

scooping up the mixture of broken eggs and batter and pouring it into the trash can. "Let me clean it up." She pulled the dish clothe from his hands and dunked it into the sudsy sink water he must have prepared. A glance around the room, she winced noticing that even the cabinets had found themselves victim to the spontaneous fun.

She couldn't ignore the whiff of horseflesh that came from him. He smelled like Father after a long day, and it strangely warmed her, taking her back a time. A pleasant memory she had long been denied. "We were making muffins for Aiden to take to school. Hannah likes when I send things to help. I know I was to give that up, but the children like it when I deliver a treat every now and then. They like knowing they have contributed something too." He still said nothing, and she felt the need to fill in the quiet. "I paid for all the ingredients myself. Your food was not wasted." It wasn't an apology, but it was all she was offering.

Silas stopped cleaning and stared at her. He did that a lot. "You don't need to give up helping if you enjoy it, but I find it hard to believe Hazel Miller taught you to bake like this." His hands waved over the floor. His tone was unreadable as always.

Lydia waited for more, staring right back at him to unleash his disapproval over the food fight, but he appeared to be waiting for a better apology.

"Go on. I see you got a burr in those britches. Just spit it out."

His brows lifted in surprise, a hint of amusement in the corner of his mouth. The little dimple showing itself again. Did he find her amusing?

"Okay. What about any of this"—he motioned to the messy room again—"says teaching children how to behave? What lesson were you trying to give here?" His tone sounded upset but not overly harsh.

"Your children are craving fun," she lifted her chin and set her shoulders. "Did you not hear them laughing." She smiled recalling how sweet their laughs were.

"You felt wasting food and destroying Jana's kitchen would be fun? A worthy laugh?" The set of his shoulders shouted irritation.

"I—" She started to argue but fell speechless at the mention of his late wife's name. It was his house. It was Jana's kitchen she had spoiled. No wonder the man didn't like her. In all her own hurts and focus on the children, she forgot that he too suffered. He'd lost his wife and now two more women were filling her void. For all the changes she had encountered, his were harder. Still, he didn't seem to have the same coldness for her *mudder*. "You don't have to be such a grouch all the time. One of us had to bend rules for them to smile." It was stupid to say and yet all she could come up with on short notice.

"Is bending rules something you do often?"

She didn't respond.

"It is my house. Rules need not be bent for laughs. A good *fraa* keeps a clean home. Follows the rules. Does what is asked of her. A good *fraa* knows how to…"

"Well, there you have it." Lydia threw up an arm. He thought she was like every other woman in the community. A woman who spent all her younger years learning all the skills required to please a man and raise a family. Like she had time or a care for such nonsense. Lydia was the youngest of three and spent most of her youth shadowing her own *daed*. She knew when to plant and harvest and had seen her share of loading hay with no other menfolk around to help. She had responsibilities many did not. He had no idea who she was.

Stepping forward, she craned her neck to glare up at him. She shoved both hands on her hips. He was a bit taller than she had first noted. No matter, he would hear her plain enough. When he refused to budge and held his own ground, the near distance sent a sudden awareness over her. Silas's handsomeness washed through her. She ignored the surprising wave of attraction that rode over her senses.

"I am not a *fraa*, Silas Graber, and I have no interest in pretending to be something I am not, regardless of how you or Thomas or anyone thinks I should."

"It wonders me if you ever will be one."

His words sounding as perturbed as hers. "Well, let me assure you…"

"You two trying to wake the *kinner*?" Mother appeared out of nowhere, silencing both disagreeable parties. Despite her presence, neither one broke their glare.

Hazel looked around the kitchen before landing her grey eyes on Silas and Lydia, and then she grinned. "Well, this looks like the time Martha Sue tried learning how to make apple fritters." She chuckled.

Lydia shot Silas her best grin and crossed her arms over her chest. She knew this icing would top the deplorable tasting cake of his. Silas's focus shifted to Hazel.

"I had sugared glaze crusted to the chair rungs for days." Hazel laughed. "Messes teach lessons, *Mudder* always said, and now Martha Sue makes the best apple fritters in the whole county." Hazel rubbed both hands together. "So, I take it you were teaching baking today."

"She was teaching something," Silas said before walking away.

CHAPTER EIGHT

Lydia yawned as she wiped off the breakfast table. It had taken long into the night to finish putting the kitchen to rights again. This Saturday, the first of many she hoped, she at least would have the joys of spending with her *mudder*. Lydia couldn't remember the last time they shared a full Saturday together outside of the bakery. Filling the sink, she watched bubbly suds form under the spray of the faucet. It being a Saturday also meant Silas wouldn't be heading off to work in town. She let out an unladylike groan. He would be here...all day, training crazy horses. *Mudder* insisted she be more understanding of Silas's plight, more careful of his home, but even she chuckled when Lydia told her of the events that led up to the food fight. Proving him wrong, about her, was going to be harder than she first figured. And why did his dark glares and long looks make her feel all funny inside?

Scrapping plates before dunking them into the sudsy water, she frowned at the one plate heavy with wasted eggs. It was a common sight no matter how she cooked them. What kind of man didn't eat eggs? *A grouchy one.* She scrubbed harder, with the same force he bruised her feelings this morning when he grunted the minute she set his plate before him. So, he didn't only dislike her caregiving skills, but he hated her cooking, too. What had possessed her to spoil Jana's kitchen as he claimed?

It was the same as when *Onkel* Thomas came to take their best plow horses, and Lydia had all but accused him of stealing. It was childish, she knew that. But they were *Daed*'s horses, and it was three years before she let it go and forgave him. Then he became the new deacon.

Onkel Thomas had been right. The horses needed using, just like Jana's kitchen needed respecting. Perhaps she was a bit childish after all.

"Mary May, could you go fetch me that bowl?" Lydia pointed, and then Mary May bounced over to the table and returned with the bowl. Lydia pulled a chair up next to the sink. "Time you learn to do dishes."

Mary May eagerly climbed up onto the chair and preceded to push up her sleeves to match Lydia's. Her toothy smile and wrinkling nose were good indicators she was happy. It had come quick and easy. Mary May and those big blue eyes had wormed her way into Lydia's heart. Who couldn't fall in love with such a sweet child?

"I don't remember you being so eager the first time Gracie pulled up a chair for you to help." Hazel jested while pouring warm fudge into a buttered oven pan.

"Gracie wasn't exactly eager to teach." Lydia sported a grin.

The sharp sound of a knock at the door startled everyone in the room.

"I'll get it." Hazel wiped her hands on her apron front before going to open it. "Well, *gut morgen,* Jenny Schwartz." Hazel held the door for her, and Jenny stepped in.

Lydia gave her a curt nod from her place at the sink. Jenny's sky-blue eyes perused the kitchen with a suspicious gaze. There was no way she could have learned about her letting the children make a mess in the kitchen so fast.

Though just two years separated them, Lydia and Jenny had never been close. It was Jenny's sharp tongue most found offense with. Growing up the only female in a lot of boys surely contributed to her boldness.

Mary May climbed down from the chair, scooted it back a few inches, and squeezed her small body into the center of the formed triangle between Lydia, the chair, and the cabinet. Hiding in the flow of Lydia's navy-blue dress, she made herself invisible. Lydia stretched to reach the last few dirty dishes and pretended Mary May's sudden behavior wasn't strange at all. She was a shy child at times, but this wasn't her common behavior.

"I brought Silas and the *kinner* another casserole. I often do." Jenny smiled widely.

An unnecessary comment.

"I didn't expect him to have company today." Jenny marched past Hazel in long strides, passed Lydia at the sink, and plopped the casserole in the ice box a bit harder than necessary. A heavy dose of lavender filled the air.

The woman even smells good.

Jenny leaned against the counter, looking confident and comfortable in Silas's house. Had she ever cooked in this kitchen? And if so, did Silas eat her cooking? The sudden spark of jealousy made Lydia wince. Silas could eat all the casseroles he wanted. It was none of her concern but imagining Jenny with the *kinner* sent a chill up her spine. The way she spoke to her *bruders* often turned heads.

"That's very kind of you, Jenny. I'm sure we all will appreciate it." Lydia hid the smirk her mother's words caused and Jenny made no effort in hiding her frown.

They had lived here for more than two weeks. Jenny needn't pretend surprise.

"Would you like me to get you something, Hazel?" Jenny asked as if they had intruded on her day.

Lydia floated her *mudder* a long look. This must be one of the visitors to which Francis was speaking of. It made sense now that Lydia considered it. Silas was widowed, but with less than a handful of single men within the community of marriable age, it was clear Jenny hoped to make an impression. *Or stake a claim.* Lydia had suspected Mary Hicky also held an interest. Widowed herself with three *kinner*, she not only carted Silas's children to and from school, but she often came by at unexpected times with nothing particular in mind. Then there was Penny Lapp, who was years younger than Lydia, but they had always been dear friends. She had come by just yesterday with homemade noodles. Penny did have at least a talent for making noodles even if she didn't have one care about Silas's attention.

Everyone knew it was Penny's mother's doing, trying to marry off her only child.

It seemed none of them understood fully. Silas simply hadn't stopped mourning his wife. He obviously didn't want to consider a *fraa,* considering he'd agreed to this arrangement. She admired him that. Grief had no set limit of time. Each person mourned differently, did they not? Just because *Mudder* was accepting her new life didn't mean Silas had to. That same wisdom snagged Lydia's attention. Her own refusal to accept life as it was, holding on to her own grief.

"You are our guest, but you know that, ain't so? I will pour *us* some of my lemonade."

Lydia stifled a laugh. Hazel Miller was a rarity and capable of sarcasm, too. Jenny huffed and plopped into a seat at the table, chin up, poised, and still smelling like summer.

Dunking a cake pan into the dishwater, Lydia gathered it would take a better woman than even Jenny to bend the heart of Silas Graber. She felt her face warm just thinking how he'd looked down on her when they argued. It was silly—he was upset, she was upset, nothing romantic about it, but for one heightened moment she'd felt captured. How eyes could do that, she couldn't fathom. She shoved aside her silly thoughts.

Jenny took a sip of lemonade and eyed Mary May. "*Kumm*

see me, Mary May." She held out her hand.

Mary May tightened her pudgy little fingers around Lydia's leg, refusing to budge. Lydia and Hazel shared a look.

"So shy, she needs a *mudder* to help her out of the shell of hers. Rebecca did not do so well." Jenny looked her over with pity and disappointment. "I worry Silas spoils them too much."

Hazel nodded in agreement but continued cutting the cooled fudge. "*Kinner* need guidance as well as they need love."

"The two go hand in hand." Lydia gave Mary May a soft pat on the arm.

"I just love your fudge, Hazel. You will have to give me your recipe. You know how well my *bruders* think of your sweets." Jenny smiled.

Lydia felt Mary May's clench loosen around her leg. She looked down and gave the child a soft smile. Mary May returned the smile with a wrinkle of her little button nose. The little girl had taken to her, and Lydia found that she had taken to her, too. It was strange, this overwhelming protective urge that came over you where children were involved.

"No secret to it. I can show you sometime."

Lydia paused while rinsing out the sink. Did *Mudder* just invite Jenny to come make fudge with her? Here? She rolled her eyes.

"Lydia, I heard you stopped working at the bakery." Jenny pierced her with a look.

"Lydia has her hands very full now," Hazel said. "The *kinner* have taken to her rather well, as you can see. Aiden has already shown more interest in schoolwork. He will be right where he needs to be *kumm* fall and Gideon is becoming very *gut* with his numbers. I have very much enjoyed having little ones underfoot again."

"Silas must be glad of it. He's worried over the *kinner* so. It's good you're here to help Lydia." Jenny shifted to Lydia.

"You have so little experience with *kinner*."

If Jenny had one real true talent, it was stirring the pot. And if Silas was glad, Lydia was certain she wouldn't know of it. The man never appeared to be glad about a thing. Gone from sunup to sundown, he most likely hadn't noticed any changes in his children anyways.

"Silas seems pleased, as any widower would be under the circumstances/" Lydia lied but only to drop the subject.

"I could help too. If you have it in mind to continue at the bakery. I love *kinner*. I could be here daily if need be, and we both know I have had more practice at it." Neither woman responded, allowing an awkward silence to spill into the kitchen. "I heard Andy was back."

Lydia's breath caught in her throat. Everything froze as if the earth had stopped turning. Images of the boy she'd once loved flashed before her. Her cheeks warmed in the memory of the last words they'd spoken. She had hoped he would ask to marry her that day. Instead, they'd said their goodbyes, and he left her.

She'd written him four letters, but he never wrote her, only returned her penned heartfelts unopened. How careless she had been, wasting her youth on such a man as Andy Weaver. More so for pining for him for two years after he left. Time lost she could have spent with her *daed*. She collected her breath before answering.

"I hadn't heard," she managed to say. *Pining for Andy? Never.* Her sisters believed so, but that was water under the bridge. At the sound of her clearing her own throat, everything around her resumed its normalcy. Yep, the earth was moving again. Lydia hoped no one had noticed her disappearing into the past just then.

"My parents say he returned just last night and is staying with his *onkel* Gavin. A *maedel* should think about her future. Yours seems to have returned. I should think this is happy news."

Just another reason she'd never befriended Jenny

Schwartz. The woman had a way of crawling under her skin and leaving her itchy for weeks after she left.

Andy was not her future. He was a stain in her life that would forever mar her feelings on love. "You're older than I am, Jenny. Your future should be your first concern," Lydia said giving her a soft smile. Why did Jenny have to make simple conversation so hard?

"My future *is* my first concern. That is why I am here."

Lydia and Hazel both froze. Jenny's bold confession left both women speechless. And just because Silas wasn't ready to marry again didn't mean he never would. Looking down at Mary May still tangled in her dress, Lydia thought about how quickly life could change again. Jenny was here with one hope in mind and Lydia had never known her to not get anything she wanted. She would win Silas over, if not by love, then by persistence. What would that mean for her family, for their arrangement? She tensed. She would in no way live in the *dawdi haus* with Jenny living here. No, that punishment was too harsh.

Had *Mudder* even considered what would happen if Silas brought a woman into this *haus*, made her his *fraa*? Lydia met her mother's eyes, her concerns vivid enough that no words needed to be spoken.

Mary May clung to Lydia's dress firmer. Only four, but Lydia felt even she understood what Jenny was implying. Could someone like Jenny Schwartz be a mother to Mary May? The idea made Lydia cringe and brought about a wave of protectiveness she didn't know she had.

"Come, Mary May, let's see if Ruth and Esther left us any eggs today." Lydia pulled the little one up from the floor and settled her on one hip before hurrying out the kitchen door. Anything to put some distance between her and the woman claiming Silas's kitchen and possibly his heart.

Hurrying out the door with Mary May strapped to one hip, Lydia smacked into Silas just as he was entering. The impact was like bouncing off a solid stone wall. She let out a grunt on impact, tightening her hold on Mary May.

Two strong hands grabbed hold of her shoulders in an attempt to steady her. "Always in a hurry." She didn't appreciate the mocking in his voice.

He glanced over her head, noticing he once more had company, before looking down on her again. His strong jawline relaxed. Hazel eyes, bold hues of brown and green, fixed on her. Silas had impressive eyes. One could stare into them for hours and still not know them fully.

One bead of sweat had suspended on his forehead as if he'd dared it to move further until released. The dark curls on his head were dampened by his labors with the horses. Lydia loved the smell of *Mudder*'s fudge, but Silas's strong aroma of warm flesh and horse lather swayed her senses. Settling her gaze back on those eyes, she was captured for a moment in something she hadn't a name for. No wonder Jenny came by so regularly. A woman could get used to a man looking at her with those eyes, in that way. Lydia flinched. He *was* looking at her in that way.

One hand cradled Mary May, the other slid down and squeezed her dress. His eyes followed the movement as if he had anticipated it. His lips parted to say something, and Lydia found herself drawn to them, anticipating what clever thing was about to come from them. No matter if he was going to say something that might hurt, she had to hear it, watch it escape those lips.

Lord, what has come over me?

"You're here. I brought that chicken dish you like. I had no idea you had company, but the more the merrier *daed* always says. I'm sure there is plenty enough for all."

Jenny's voice pierced the air, rattling Lydia back to her common sense. She gave an odd snort and brushed by Silas as fast as her feet would take her.

What was he about to say to her? That thought was going to trouble her all the way to the chicken coop.

CHAPTER NINE

"Now Jenny Schwartz, you know we live here too," Hazel said in a sharp motherly tone.

Silas felt the headache that had been lingering for days, grow.

"*Jah*. Isn't Silas so kind, offering a place for you and Lydia after selling your home? And now that you have your finances in order, community funds can reach out to help another in need."

Jenny was being her normal self. Hazel nodded, but Silas could see the tension building there. He was glad Lydia hadn't heard the comment. Silas knew she wouldn't be as forgiving as her mother at Jenny's bold remarks.

"*Gott*'s will," Hazel replied in a mumble and offered Silas a glass of lemonade.

He had never seen Hazel shaky before. Silas took the glass and offered her a kindness, hoping to calm that nerve Jenny had a talent for reaching even in the strongest of others. "*Danki*, Hazel. You are a blessing to us."

She calmed, and Silas followed her back inside the house, Jenny shadowing behind. He wished her daughter had that ability. Or did she? When he caught her in the doorway, he'd wanted to tell her something important. Warn her about the skunks lingering out back the past few weeks. The last thing he needed was Gideon hoping for a new pet, or one of them being sprayed. But seeing Mary May snuggled on her frail shoulder and those violet-blue eyes locked on to his had rendered him speechless, an effect she'd had more than once on him.

Lydia was seldom brought to a halt or slowed in her comings and goings, but for one split second, he had found her as still as a post planted four feet deep. She loathed him. Blamed him for her current situation and a good many other things, he suspected. Except for those few seconds and the mammoth of emotions that peppered the room, the silence was explosive.

"Hannah might be coming by later today," Hazel said. "She wanted to visit with Lydia now that school is out and help with arranging the cellar."

Crates of canned food from the Millers' home still cluttered the cellar floor. It had taken three wagon loads to tote the last of Hazel's things.

"Those two used to be close as *schwesters*. It gut they are spending time together."

Silas nodded and gulped down his lemonade like a sponge in the Sahara. Hazel handed over her shoulder towel. He wiped his beard and lips clean and returned it to her.

"Let me pour you another."

"I am glad to know Hannah went back to teaching as she should be. Who knew a little bout of pneumonia could wear down someone as strong as her," Jenny said boldly.

Silas finished the second glass to keep his tongue from saying something hurtful. He had never liked Jenny's boldness any more than he liked knowing her reason for coming by so often. "Sorry. Thirstier than I thought."

"It's warm in here." She fanned herself, not one ounce of decency in it.

"A busy kitchen makes for plenty of warmth," Hazel said.

Silas couldn't help but grin.

"Here is another glass, take it on the porch."

Meaning *I'm not watching Jenny behave like a lovesick schoolgirl in my kitchen.* He happily retreated outside to escape the women inside.

Silas sat in a rocker, not the swing, in case Jenny decided to linger today as she so often did. He wasn't falling for that again. The screen door opened then closed. He muffled a groan and placed his straw hat back on his head.

"Weather looks to be warming." As predicted, Jenny settled in the rocker beside him.

"*Jah.*" Silas sipped on Hazel's wonderful lemonade contemplating just how long he would have to sit here and be polite when he needed to get back to the horses. He rarely had a full day to work with them.

"You need a trim. I can do that for you. I cut my *bruder*'s hair all the time."

He did need a trim, but she was the last person he wanted to give him one. When she reached out to touch his hair, possibly to consider its length or texture, and he shifted in the rocker just out of reach. She had been coming by unannounced for over a year, and still, he couldn't get her to understand he had no interest. She was a pretty woman on the outside, but Jana had found her a professional gossip, and Silas would have to agree.

Silas glanced over to her. Golden blond hair coiled under her *kapp*, not a loose strand daring to escape. Her rounded face like one of those porcelain dolls sold at the shop in town. Jenny's eyes were light blue like Mary May's and Gideon's. Like Jana's.

He averted his gaze. On the outside, Jenny was well put together. It was the rest of her that unsettled his stomach. He had tried, for her sake as much as his children's, but he couldn't feel something that simply wasn't there. She could never replace what he had lost, and he wasn't the kind of man who would settle simply because it was expected.

"Hazel will trim it this evening." Another lie. He was getting too comfortable with them. He caught sight of Lydia crossing the yard, his daughter on her heels. Lifting the glass with nothing more than a few drops of lemonade remaining to his lips, he concealed a sly smirk watching them.

"It must take youth to understand youth. Mary May seems to like her." Jenny's usual good spirits sounded rattled. She had tried winning over Mary May, but like him, Mary May found little she liked when dealing with Jenny.

"Like gum on a shoe. Or better yet, like butter on a babe." He chuckled. Jenny looked at him in complete puzzlement. Silas's grin fell back to a straight line.

"*Gut* she has something to do with herself," Jenny said with a hint of snippiness in her voice.

"Mary May is only a child."

"I meant Lydia. She spends too much time running here and there and never commits to any one thing. She barely sews, seldom bakes, and I have yet to see her finish a task. Martha Sue and Gracie were nothing like that. It wonders me if she has not disappointed Hazel with her childish ways."

Martha Sue and Gracie were Lydia's sisters. Silas had gone to school with them and agreed each of Hazel's daughters shared little in common. Gracie was a worrying sort, always fussing over something. Martha Sue was a sweet woman who loved everything and everyone. Jana and Martha Sue had been close friends. Lydia was—well, Silas wasn't sure yet what Lydia was. *Interesting.* He toyed with the concept. She was interesting.

Across the yard, Lydia and Mary May stepped out of the henhouse. His daughter cradled an egg in her new apron front, as Lydia cradled an egg or two in hers. Both smiled and laughed at something he had missed. He had missed a lot the last few days, truth be told. He felt Jenny's gaze set on him but refused to peel away from the simple scene in the yard. Hazel and Lydia were part of his life now, part of his children's lives. Maybe Jenny would get the wrong impression and go home. A sinful deception that would serve its purpose.

"I think it's *wunderbaar* to hear her old beau has returned."

Lydia has a beau? Had, he corrected his thinking. The community wasn't that large, and Silas remembered Andy Weaver in a vague way.

"I suspect he has returned for her. She has no other prospects to speak of anyhow. Either way, Lydia needs to focus on more important things, like starting her own family. It is *Gott's* will for us, is it not?" Jenny's arms crossed, jealousy marring her tone.

"She and Hazel have been through much these last few years. I don't think either is in a hurry for such things." Their lives had been flipped over and shaken and they needed something solid beneath them once more. At least that was how he felt for the moment.

"They have endured no more than you. She is very outspoken. I don't see how you two will ever get along." Jenny ran a long finger over her apron front. "And she cannot think to live under your roof forever. She must consider her future." Jenny turned her body to face him fully. "I can come by and help with the *kinner* so Lydia can return to the bakery. It would be best they had an experienced hand. I helped raise all my *bruders* as you know."

He did know. The Schwartz boys had a reputation for getting into more trouble than most. "Hazel will see to that. And Lydia and I get along just fine. Her bark isn't so bad." He scratched his chin. "She also knows she is free to come and go as she pleases." Watching Lydia and his daughter walking away from the henhouse he saw her as more than simply an angry woman burdened with grief, and more than a girl, as Jenny kept referring to.

"You have had loss and it doesn't make you snap at every little thing. Besides…" Jenny shifted. "A *gut fraa* should not bark at all. It is not *gut* for *kinner*. For family."

"A *gut fraa* does not speak ill of others, either." His gaze caught hers to remind her of her gossiping tongue.

The floor creaked behind him, but Silas didn't turn to address it. Had Hazel had been listening to their conversation? He placed the glass to his mouth, gulped his last drop, and came to his feet. "You may enjoy your visit with Hazel, but I have work to do. *Gut* day." He tipped his hat and walked away, leaving Jenny dumbfounded behind him. Not his best moment, that was for sure.

Silas was as tired as Cage by the time afternoon reached the farm. The air still breathed crisp, but it felt refreshing after working the stubborn animal so hard.

Blue, the roan mare, had already accepted bit and harness. She would do well for the Bontragers. Not Cage. That horse was as wound up as any wild animal could be.

Silas rubbed his side, wishing he hadn't taken on such an animal. Marvin Walker, an *Englischer*, wanted a broke horse, and Silas had promised he would have one. When he was a younger man, he'd accepted such challenges with a greedy smile, but he wasn't young any longer.

The midnight black steed bucked and kicked in victory before surrendering to his own exhaustion. Silas had tried to work him hard, but the animal proved to have impressive endurance. Strong will had decided the outcome of the day. He finished rubbing down the leather lines and hanging them in their proper place in the tack room, and then he made his way to the house.

He slowed his pace at the sounds of laughter sweetening the air and watched Lydia push his children on the swing in turns. Her visit with Hannah hadn't lasted long, but he couldn't help wonder if it had lifted her spirits some. Friends and community were important. He had forgotten how so these last few years.

The scent of Hazel's meatloaf wafted out the windows, and his mouth watered. Things were almost normal. Almost.

Removing his hat, he looked heavenward and stared into the sun so long his eyes were blinded. He wished it lasted longer. As much as he wanted normal, wanted life to feel real again, seeing his children smile and laugh with Lydia troubled him. Those smiles were meant for Jana.

CHAPTER TEN

Mondays were dreary enough without adding rain to it. Silas groaned as he stood on the porch, cup of *kaffi* in hand, watching Lydia and Mary May climb into Karen Brown's car and leave. If Hazel took a day off then Lydia saw it as an opportunity to wander off and help someone, somewhere. The busy bee simply couldn't linger any one place long. At least Mary May was happy to be going to play with other children. He couldn't deny her that or continue to deny how taken Mary May had become with Lydia. Rebecca hadn't shared the same closeness with her, even after four years. Lydia had only been here mere weeks and was already getting her fill of hugs and giggles.

Aiden and Gideon pounced out the door behind him, Gideon rubbing the sleep from his eyes. Silas dropped a palm on Aiden's shoulder and they both eyed the sky. He couldn't work with concrete and stone in the rain, but he could tackle a stubborn horse and a few forgotten chores.

Pushing his hat down firmer on his head, he grinned. Hazel had, in fact, heard his lie to Jenny Schwartz, and gave him that trim after all. He chuckled. It had been a long time since he had been reprimanded by his own mother. Hazel was a *gut* woman, and Silas was growing rather attached to her in his life. Not only did his house smell as fresh as a daisy, but his trousers were edging near a perfect fit.

"*Kumm,* you two." He motioned to his sons. "I will work Cage, and you can muck stalls and sweep the barn. I want it cleared for hay soon."

The three made a dash for the barn. Silas opened one side of the two huge barn doors. Both Aiden and Gideon rushed inside to escape getting soaked.

"I can put Penny out, and you two can start there." Silas opened the first stall door where Penny the cart pony was and paused. "That's not safe for Penny. Why is Lydia's bike in here?" he questioned the boys, but one look at their wide-eyed expression told him they had a hand in placing the bike there. Lydia had never once taken the liberty to go farther into the barn than the milking area.

That's why she has been riding with Karen so often. Drivers cost money, money she had little of, he figured since she was getting little time off the farm to work elsewhere. Silas first suspected that maybe the stranger that had tried to pick her up on the side of the road had been the reason for her depending on the *Englisch* driver so often. Had she even spoken to Hazel about the incident? He planned on speaking to Hazel himself. The idea of her walking did not settle well in him, nor paying a driver so often. He couldn't forget the way she looked at him that day. It was a scary thing when a woman could be hassled so by a man twice her size. He was glad he had been heading home at that exact time.

Both his sons' heads hung low. Silas crossed his arms over his chest. "Gideon." He knew where blame needed to be aimed.

Gideon took one lazy step forward. Both hands went behind his body, which was rocking back and forth, and he peered up with the same begging blue eyes as Jana. Silas swallowed hard against the image. He would always have the reminder of her each time he looked at his children. He crossed his arms tighter, awaiting Gideon's reply.

"He thought it was funny 'cause Lydi's afraid of horses." Aiden was never one to ignore an opportunity to squeal on his brother's antics. Gideon lowered his head, and his shoulders lifted, like a turtle attempting to sink inside its shell.

"You did, did you?" Silas leaned forward and raised his son's chin. Perhaps he had coddled the child for long enough. "That's not nice. Lydia plays with you, cooks for you, and reads to you at bedtime. If you knew she was afraid why would you do something to frighten her?"

Thoughts of Lydia walking to town or her *Aenti* May's farm and running into the man in the blue car again sent his pulse racing. Silas deepened his scowl to invoke his displeasure. Gideon could have put Lydia in danger. He had looked over his behavior out of pity, as he did all of his children, too long. He might have lost a wife, but they had lost their mother, the one person who had brought them into the world and was meant to love them unconditionally throughout their lives. So, he coddled them. But no excuse was good enough when it came to doing ill towards others.

"You knew we made the mess in the kitchen and you got mad at Lydi and not us."

Gideon pushed buttons beyond his years. Silas gasped, having his words thrown back at him like that.

Silas's gaze shot to Aiden. "You all did that?"

"Well, Gideon started it." Aiden stammered, like a trapped animal who set out one morning to simply do his regular thing but suddenly got caught and was now unsure what to do about it.

"Did not. You poured milk on my head first." Gideon's finger pointed to Aiden in defense.

Silas shifted his focus to Aiden. Gideon was always colliding with trouble, but he had expected more out of his eldest.

"Okay." Aiden exhaled. "That I did. But Lydia was mad. She really was. You should have seen her. I thought she was going to send me to my room or scream. Her face got all red and she stomped the floor really hard, but," his eyes widened, "then, she just started laughing." He lifted his hands and shrugged.

Gideon shook his head in rapid motions, agreeing that was just what happened. "I thought she was going to spank us," he said dramatically. "Truly I did *daed*."

Silas didn't imagine that was true, even if his children deserved it. Lydia didn't have it in her to spank no matter how red her face became.

"Laughing?" He remembered well the laughing and how it made him feel.

Gideon snickered. "She said if we were gonna do sump'tin, do it right, and rubbed food on our noses." He slapped his knees and bent forward in a full outburst of laughter, forgetting he was currently in trouble.

When Aiden started snickering, eyes dancing like fireflies let loose from a jar, lips pinching as tight as he could to hold it all in, Silas couldn't help it and laughed a little, too. Though Lydia beat to her own drum, she did bring forth a bit of joy in their lives that had been missing.

"Well, I guess that is *gut* advice. Except for boys in the kitchen. Now get the bike out and clean it up. You both *will* apologize to Lydia."

"We will," Aiden said humbly. "*Kumm.* You got me into this mess. You're helping." He grabbed Gideon's arm and dragged him towards the bike.

Silas shook his head as he watched the two push it out of the stall. The teenaged years ahead might just be the death of him yet with those two.

By evening, the rain ceased just in time for supper. It was a sloppy spring mess that always fouled his mood. Silas and his sons stepped from the barn and walked the length of the yard to the house. The smell of warm yeast bread and ham cooking set his belly in motion, growling loud enough to earn a snicker from his sons.

Hazel cooked the evening meal on Mondays, and though Lydia had proved a wonderful cook, something in Hazel's cooking noted a sprinkle of love and not dutifully made. Entering the house, Silas froze when he noted his mother-in-law, Francis Peachy, in *his* chair at the head of *his* table. He swallowed a groan.

"Francis." Silas greeted her in a low, unimpressed tone. He removed his hat and hung it on the hook nearest the door, both his sons matching his movements, removing hats then muck boots. They shadowed him to the table, where Hazel pulled out a chair opposite of Francis, and Silas took it. The boys settled into their own designated seats along the long cherry table his *daed* had gifted him on his wedding day.

Francis frequently visited to see how the children were, but Silas suspected she came around so little because the children served as a visual reminder of the daughter she had lost. She no longer was the kind, soft-spoken woman she once was, often cutting his words off short and leaving a sour feeling in his stomach. He'd learned to adapt to the flavor of it, much like Jenny's chicken dish that he really didn't like a bit. He peered across the table, seeing her stalking him with that sharp gaze of hers. He knew sooner than later she would come to approve or disapprove of what the Bishop believed a good arrangement for all.

"I was just telling Hazel here that Lydia has an *Englisch* driver." Francis' head cocked to one side as if waiting for him to answer a question not asked.

"Many make use of such. It is not forbidden." Even Francis had used a driver to travel to Ohio to see family on occasion.

"*Jah*, but not so regular like," Francis said. "It wonders me how she's caring for the *kinner* running around all the time?" Her voice was clipped.

Francis sipped from a glass, examining her surrounding with a pessimistic eye. Francis was a small woman, much like Jana had been, but those icy blue eyes were as cutting as her sharp tongue.

Silas peered over to Hazel. She looked weary, and for good reason. Even on her day off, she had much to do. As the head of the house, regardless of what kind of blended house it was, it was his duty to handle any questions concerning those in his care. Dealing with Thomas was easier, but he had an obligation considering he'd brought the women into his life.

"I have no complaints on her care of the *kinner*." Silas wouldn't dare mention that her fear of horses and a stolen bike was the reason for her use of a driver so much of late or how days ago the seat Francis sat in had been covered in milk and eggs, matching the walls and floors. She was good for the children, whether he wanted it or not. Her ways weren't Jana's ways, but slowly he could see the results in his children's eyes.

"Let us pray." All heads lowered.

God be with Lydia and Mary May as they travel and help me keep Francis from interfering and making life harder than it is already. Amen. He prayed the silent prayer and normally coughed or moved in his seat to indicate prayer was over. Not today. Before his head even lifted, Francis began talking.

"Where is my sweet Mary May? Why is she not at your table at this hour?" Francis barked before spooning a helping of baked beans into her mouth.

Hazel spoke up. "Lydia is at Rose's with my *dochdern* canning sausage today. Gracie and Michael butchered a hog over the weekend. Mary May is with her. It is *gut* she spends time with the women and has other *kinner* to play with. Not just a house full of boys."

Francis nodded starkly but couldn't disagree with Hazel's logic.

"But I do feel it important that family share their supper together. Of that you must agree," Francis said with a firm raised brow and filled her mouth.

They were like two strong forces on opposites sides

fighting for the same prize. Silas knew now why Lydia's father was such a quiet man. Thankfully he had only one *dochder*. Then again, the hope for more children, as he had always wanted, couldn't be ignored. Mary May deserved a sister to share secrets with and play her dolls with, just like the boys had each other. Well, that would never happen, and he should feel blessed that God had gifted him these three, no matter their pranks.

"I do," Hazel said. Silas knew she wanted to say more.

Both had the children's best interest at heart. Francis would have to find another means of showing her disapproval, which he was certain she would before her visit was over. He had endured years of her opinions of Rebecca, but what choice did he have when she'd arrived unannounced to help him in his time of need? Francis was too old to tend them herself, she claimed. And the thought of asking her to live here would have made the last four years even harder than they had been already.

As the children filled their mouths greedily, Silas picked up his fork and begin doing the same. It was a smart defense to avoid further conversation.

"It's getting late, and *Mudder* will wonder if something is wrong." Lydia turned to Gracie as her sister handed her the last large bowl to wash.

She glanced at the clock hanging on the wall behind her. *4:42*. The day had passed in a blur of busyness. Between her two sisters and her, they had managed to finish the entire canning job in one afternoon. Her arms felt like jelly from grinding meat all day, but she was already imagining sausage balls covered in her favorite barbeque sauce. She wondered if the children liked it, too.

"I know. We should go. Karen is supposed to meet me

in a few minutes to take us home." Lydia rinsed the pot and handed it back to her sister. In the next room, Mary May giggled and played with both her nieces. The variety of dolls her sister Gracie and her husband, Mike, had splurged on at a nearby yard sale had kept them fully content most of the day.

"Paid three dollars and those three are happier than I was with my first pony." Gracie laughed, a wisp of brown hair clinging to her neck.

Lydia remembered Sweet Pea, Gracie's stubborn pony. The high-spirited critter had overturned two pony carts, once with Lydia riding in it, and had a gift for jumping fences.

"She is a sweet child. Breaks my heart knowing she will grow up without her *mudder*." Gracie said in a soft voice. "How are things with the boys? Rumor is you're having a time with the middle one. Heard he unties your shoes and throws food all over the house. I'm not sure how you of all people can manage such a child." Gracie added with a pinched look.

Lydia chuckled, ignoring the unintentional jab. She should have never told Martha Sue about the food fight, but it was better than most of the chatter today. The whole day her sisters had seemed stuck on one topic: marrying her off.

"Gideon is a prankster for sure and for certain, but he doesn't throw food all over the house." She gave her sister a playful wink. "At least not alone." Lydia removed the soiled apron and went to gather her things.

"I don't even want to know what that means." Gracie removed her own apron and took both towards the laundry room door and gave them a toss. "I do recall having to explain to *Daed* why I had spaghetti in *mei* hair once."

Lydia remembered, too. Gracie had poured pepper all over her food on accident and tried forcing Lydia to eat it for lunch. When *Daed* walked in the door to check on them, Lydia had already taken a stand on what she felt Gracie should do with her peppered spaghetti.

"Well, I wasn't about to eat it."

"It was an accident. I thought I was just salting it, and we both had to scrub the floors for weeks over it when *Mudder* found out. I hope you're not teaching *that* to Silas Graber's *kinner.*" Gracie pinned her with a disapproving frown.

Lydia twisted the fabric of her dress with her fingers. It was no secret she had always been more rambunctious as a child. Rebellious, her *onkel* called her. Her sister probably considered her a terrible example for the Graber children. *Just like their father does.* "It just sort of happened." She didn't bother to go into details. That night in the kitchen had awakened something in Aiden—her too, for that matter—and since then, everything had only moved forward with her relationship with the children. It shouldn't matter what others thought.

"Well, I know you get tired of listening to us go on about you getting settled, but I don't think you should get too close to those *kinner.*"

"Why not? It is what I'm there for is it not?" Lydia wanted to say *too late* but thought better of it.

"It will only make it harder when you leave. No woman wants a ready-made family, Lydi," Gracie said. "And I can see you are getting attached to that one for sure." She motioned towards Mary May.

Lydia had, but she also felt connected with Aiden. He was much like Gracie, seeing after his younger siblings. And Gideon…well, that one made her feel young, alive, and adventurous. He reminded her of the child she had been, aside from pranks. Mary May brought out a softness in her Lydia hadn't known she had. They were so easy to love.

"She lost her *mudder,* and I don't think Rebecca even rocked her to sleep," Lydia said in a whispered tone as she stared at Mary May and her little nieces in the next room playing dolls. "How could I not give her the one thing she needs most?"

"She needs a *mudder,* and you are not her *mudder,*" Gracie said flatly, always the one to point out the obvious.

The back door opened, and Martha Sue walked in before Lydia could respond. Mary May needed the love of a woman and a safe place to snuggle. One didn't have to be a mother to offer such things, did they?

"I can't believe I am this tired, and now I need to go home and ready supper before Allen thinks I have forgotten him." Martha Sue blew on a dark strand of hair that found its way out from under her tightly pinned *kapp.*

"I would stay and help longer, but Karen is meeting us soon." Lydia went to fetch Mary May and kiss her nieces farewell.

"I stopped by the bakery yesterday, and *Mammi* Rose told me about the bike. Has Silas punished his *sohn* yet?" Martha Sue's lips pursed.

"Gideon didn't do it out of meanness." Lydia scooped up Mary May's dolls into her bag.

"I think this was a terrible idea. *Mudder* should have brought you both here to stay or at Martha Sue's. It makes no sense she would move over there, on the other side of the community, and take on another's family when she has one right here."

Lydia was aware of her sister's thoughts on the matter, but *Mudder* had assured her that helping Silas, who needed them, was what *Gott* had called her to do. Lydia might have weighed it a bad idea at first as well, but the closer she grew to the children, the more she understood how those words rang true.

"I admit I didn't see that coming at all." It was a puzzle, her mother selling the farm only to live with non-family when she had two married children with room for them both.

"You know what you should do?"

Lydia knew what Martha Sue *thought* she should do. Run and find Andy Weaver and beg for him to marry her. Well, that wasn't going to happen, and she wished her sister hadn't mentioned it so many times throughout the day.

"I should go. I'm going to be late for supper. As always, sisters, it has been nice spending time with you." Lydia lifted Mary May into her arms and went to the door.

"Don't leave angry. You know we love you and just want what is best for you," Grace called to her.

Lydia turned and nodded. "I know, but neither Andy nor Silas interests me in the way you two wish. And I have more important things to do than rush into marrying and having *kinner* of my own. There is plenty of time for that later. Please just let it go." She blew out an exasperated breath. "It's hard enough adjusting to living away from our home to also have you two always telling me what I should be doing."

Martha Sue stepped forward and embraced her in a hug. "You're right. We love you and only want to see you happy as we are. It is not to hurt you but to encourage."

"Well, next time can we just swap casserole recipes, or you tell me what a bad quilter I am." Lydia's lips twitched playfully. Her sisters meant well, but being the youngest meant free advice was handed out regularly.

"Funny. *Jah*, we can do that." Martha Sue smirked, showing off two deep and perfectly aligned dimples. "Give *Mudder* our love."

Snuggling Mary May into her neck, Lydia walked to the end of the lane to meet Karen. The little angel smelled of warm spices and an overly warm kitchen and was already growing heavy in Lydia's arms. It had been a long day for both of them.

Shooing a bee that was tempted by her honey-infused shampoo, she peered up the lane and back down. Karen was late and now so were they. *Mudder* would worry knowing how sometimes helping Martha Sue and Gracie took longer than it should, however, Silas no doubt would likely have something to say considering she had Mary May with her. She was surprised he'd let her take his daughter with her today as it was.

As Mary May drifted off to sleep, Lydia adjusted her *kapp* with her free hand and nuzzled her soft cheek. Would it feel this wonderful to have *kinner* of her very own some day? Maybe her sisters were right. Lydia was getting older, and many of her friends were already married or promised.

She smiled, thinking how easily each of the Graber children had sneaked into her heart. If only they weren't Silas Graber's it would be easier to pull them in even more. If she could stay part of their lives, she could easily afford to relinquish any ideas of marriage. One didn't need a husband to be happy, did they?

But reality told her that could never be. Eventually, Jenny would prevail and claim Silas, and that would be the day she would have to pack up and find a home of her own. No sense getting too attached. Gracie was right.

Stepping to the side of a large puddle, Lydia glanced up the road again. It would have made sense to have waited inside for Karen to arrive if not for her sisters' teasing. Martha Sue had even called her unapproachable by any young man available. Gracie claimed she was too old and stubborn to take her pick even if she could turn a man's head. Especially in her unwillingness to not attend singings like all the other single *maedels*. Well, unwilling since Andy left Miller's Creek.

"Just because my sisters married young doesn't make me an old spinster. I am not unapproachable. I am busy," she said, holding her head high now that no one was in earshot to hear her response.

The Lord knew what He was doing. *His timing, not ours.* Wasn't that what the bishop would say? And who was Martha Sue to remind her of Andy's return and that if she wasn't so pig-headed, she would have her own *bopplin* by now? He was the one that left, not her. Here Andy had been back in Miller's Creek for over a week, and she hadn't even caught a glimpse of him.

God's will. Gracie and Martha Sue had no idea what the

last four years had required of her. Here they were living in their own world with their new families, free from the burdens that plagued her.

The common clip-clop, clip-clop came up the road toward the east. Lydia shifted Mary May to the other shoulder and shielded the failing sun from her eyes. "You've got to be kidding me. You are just full of mischief now, aren't ya?" She aimed the question heavenward as Andy Weaver, wearing his biggest smile, approached.

Chapter Eleven

Lydia only agreed to accept a ride home from Andy, because Mary May was heavy, and her arms were spent.

"It is *gut* to see you again, Lydi." Andy gave her a sidelong grin. He had the same piercing dark eyes and heart-stopping grin she remembered. It would have been better that he hadn't.

He was no longer the scrawny, long-legged boy she once knew, but a grown man. A man she'd sat alongside in a courting buggy many years ago after singings and volleyball games. He had been *the one* and then he wasn't. She would do well to remember the latter. He left her and shortly after *Daed* had been hurt and later died. He hadn't even come to her most darkened hours.

From that moment on, life blurred into a streak of busy. She didn't even stop to blink during those hard times, doing her part to help soften *Mudder's* burdens. Filling every minute of her day was her best defense against thinking about the past and remembering the boy who promised her his heart and broke her own into pieces.

Andy Weaver had broken her heart right in two. Since then, she had learned a thing or two about hearts. They were impossible to mend and never beat right again.

The Lord worked in ways she could never understand.

"*Danki* for the ride. I was not looking forward to packing this little one all the way back to the far end of Miller's Creek. My *Englisch* driver is usually very dependable. I hope she didn't have troubles with her car." Realizing she was rambling, she pressed her lips shut and planned to do so for the next seven miles. She owed Andy no explanation. What had really brought him back to Miller's Creek? His family was in Ohio. His life and work for over four years was there.

"How did you end up with Silas Graber's *boppli*?"

She shot him a surprised look. He knew to whom Mary May belonged? A child he had never met before leaving Miller's Creek. Knowing he might have asked about her had her sitting up straighter in the buggy seat. She gave him a quick glance. His jaw clenched, the same way it used to when they were younger. Mary May stirred in her arms.

"Hello, Ms. Mary." Andy greeted her with a heart-stopping smile.

Lydia's heart thudded. He even knew her name. Oh, how she had missed his handsome smile. Andy floated her another boyish grin. The kind that used to make her palms go sweaty. She swallowed hard, but the lump remained there, stuck, with no sign of budging.

Stop it, Lydia. He left you.

"*Mudder* made an agreement with Silas to help him. They have been through so much, but things are getting better." She believed that now and caressed Mary May's chubby fingers with her own slender, longer ones.

Things were shifting for the children. Mary May's smile proved that. Maybe they were shifting for her too. She did stay busy enough she rarely reflected over *Daed*'s accident, and until Jenny revealed Andy's surprise return, Lydia had almost forgotten the man who left her. Now the man who had started her life's downward spiral was driving her home. What a strange turn of events a simple day brought.

"You will make a great *mudder*. I always thought it so."

If her sisters could only see her now.

"I heard about Jana. It must have been hard for them."

She positioned Mary May in the seat between them and focused on the passing landscape. It was hard. She had seen it in Silas's eyes more than once. The way he watched her with the children, lips pinched tightly, and the way he looked down at her in the messy kitchen after she destroyed it. All signs that pointed to how hard it was losing the woman you loved and watching others try to replace her presence.

"Death is hard on everyone." She didn't try hiding her sharp tone.

"I'm sorry about that, too, Lydia."

His eyes fixed forward, unwilling to look at her or give her an explanation for why he hadn't come or even sent condolences to her when *daed* passed away. Did he not know how badly she needed him during those dark days?

"What kind of arrangement is between you?" Andy sat chin up, jaws tight again.

His deep blue shirt showed off his strong arms. Arms that had once held her close when he confessed his love to her.

"That we would help with his *kinner* in exchange to live in the *dawdi haus*. *Mudder* sold our farm and *haus*." Fairly simple now that she said it aloud. I help you. You help me. That had taken her way too long enough to comprehend, to accept, and she chided herself for it now. Maybe she *was* a bit hotheaded like *Mammi* Rose said.

"So, there is no other arrangement involved with you and Silas?"

He shot her a glance, his dark eyes searching. It wasn't unexpected for widowers with children to marry soon after the death of a loved one, for the sake of family, for fulfilling God's plan.

But Lydia wasn't the kind of girl to marry a man she didn't love because of circumstance. Mary Hicky or Jenny

Schwartz would gladly fill any room in Silas's heart if he were willing to let them. The idea that he might one day marry bothered her once more, and not only because of the children. It was silly to think that those long, penetrating looks that passed between them held anything but contempt, but there were times Lydia felt as if they were something else. Loneliness did strange things to a person, but she couldn't help feeling the pull those eyes gifted her.

"*Ach.*" She shook her head. "If you mean... *Nee.* That is all."

His eyes brightened, and his lips morphed into another one of those gorgeous grins. She had fallen for that smile a time or two.

Guard your heart, she whispered the proverb for safety's sake. *He left, returned, and believed you were courting another.* "Andy, why have you returned to Miller's Creek?" It was a fair question, considering.

The buggy veered into the Graber drive. She noticed right away Silas helping Francis Peachy into her buggy. Francis had come to see her grandchildren and here Lydia had kept Mary May out past supper. Another strike against her.

"We will talk of this later. If you allow me that," Andy said as he pulled up toward the house.

So, he planned on a later. She nodded against her better judgment. She would get her answers. Then she turned and caught Francis Peachy's eyes, which were narrowing at their arrival.

Lydia took a deep breath. If sitting next to Andy after all these years wasn't rattling enough, seeing the woman who'd told her she would never marry was. Francis was known for her tight stitches and firm reminders of the rules. Her gray eyes had a way of appearing curious and gentle but were, in truth, sharper than a Cooper's hawk when it came to searching out things meant to be hidden. She could read what was inside a person without having to turn them inside out to do it. No mistake, Francis could turn a soul inside out if she felt it necessary and pleasing to God.

"Well, she leaves with the *Englisch* and returns with the wayward. The bishop would have something to say of this, Silas." Francis slapped the lines.

The horse surrendered to her, as Lydia suspected all living things did. If only the small woman's voice didn't carry so well. What did Francis mean by a wayward? Lydia turned to Andy to see his face stern, brows gathered, and a hint of red warming his cheeks. He was trying to appear confident, and it didn't look good on him, forced as it was. Francis had a knack for leaving you with such an expression, but today it wasn't Lydia wearing it.

"Did Karen forget you?" Hazel asked, standing on the top step to the porch, hand towel hanging over one shoulder. It didn't go unnoticed how surprised she was seeing her daughter sitting next to Andy Weaver in the buggy seat. How many tears had her mother help wiped away Lydia couldn't count.

"I think she did. I had planned on walking." She regretted the words the moment they slipped out. Had she just admitted to walking alone with his Mary May after what had happened? "But Mary May fell asleep in my arms. Thankfully, Andy showed up and gave us a ride. I would have never been so late if it weren't for Karen not showing up at five as we planned." She sounded as if she were making excuses.

Silas came to her side, and Lydia offered Mary May into his arms. His jaw clenched, and she cocked her head to check if his teeth were grinding. Why did he make her feel like she was always doing something wrong? She'd apologized, not something she easily did. Wasn't that something? Silas offered a stiff hand, and after shaking off the shock of his gesture, she took it. The ruggedness of his labored palm scraped at her fingers as he helped her from the buggy.

"Thought you didn't ride in buggies," he said in a near whisper as her feet hit the earth. She rode in buggies, with *Mudder* at least, but she knew exactly what he meant by that statement.

So that was what had him out of sorts. Not that she had not gotten Mary May home in time for supper or that she might have had to walk and risked being thrown into a trunk of a car, but that she'd ridden in a buggy after telling him no. Again, she felt a pinch in her gut she couldn't explain.

The moment Mary May reached his arms, the overwhelming scent of honey engulfed Silas's senses. His daughter now carried that same sweet smell that was becoming signature Lydia.

If she was trying to read his thoughts with that intent stare, Silas should have told her it was okay that she was late. That he was glad they didn't have to walk. Instead, all he could address was the fact Andy Weaver had brought them home.

"She has ridden in a buggy with me plenty," Andy said boldly.

Lydia's face flushed.

Silas ripped his gaze from her to Andy. It appeared the fella was hoping to make some statement by those words. The lad had moved away with his family, and from what Thomas said, had left broken hearts wherever he went. Jenny, for once, had been right about one thing. It seemed Andy had returned for Lydia. And here the children had been doing so well. How would they handle losing someone they just began caring for? How would he? His head started to hurt thinking too much.

Lydia had every right to find happiness, get married, and have children of her own. *Jah*, his head was hurting. Just the thought of not having her around, now that he was growing accustomed to her, dependent upon her, bothered him. He didn't like this new revelation overfilling him. He shouldn't care if she left—he had Hazel, after all—but he did. No fore-warning had announced it, but the feelings came unbidden. Silas was feeling again, things he wasn't ready to feel or ever thought he could feel again—protective, possessive, possibly even wanting. He didn't want to feel or care for another. He loved his wife, and yet, here he was feeling everything. The notion had him tripping over his own thoughts.

"Lydi!" Gideon's voice broke the tension growing in the front yard.

Silas watched his sons push Lydia's baby blue bike from the barn to the front yard where Lydia was *still* standing next to him. One side of his mouth lifted into a pleased smirk. The old bike shone like a new penny. Gideon had outdone himself scrubbing it.

Looking down to Lydia, whose eyes were softening into gratitude, he noted she understood quite well what the children had done for her. It was a simple acceptance, but one she obviously needed. What would his acceptance mean to her? Did he dare give it? There was a lot at stake if he crossed a line and let himself be tempted into getting to know her better.

With hands clasped over her heart, she gazed up at him in surprise. Not Andy who'd returned for her, or Hazel who'd given her life, but him. Lavender blue and stunning, those eyes. In them carried appreciation and disbelief. When she smiled, Silas's heart turned over in his chest. She knew he had a part in the boys retrieving her bike from the horse stalls. He smiled half-heartedly to her, not meaning to take the credit, but to think he could bring out the sunshine in her did wonders to his manhood. Lydia had lured him in by her strong will, softened him with her sun-flowery smile, and brought laughter back into his home. He would never tell her, but in that very moment, Lydia Miller took his breath away.

His eyes fixed on her as she strolled over to the boys. Aiden and Gideon had accepted her, done this for her, and he felt some of his concerns float away down that long stretch of lonesome that had filled his past four years. He had never considered a second chance, another love after having one so dedicated, but he was starting to.

"Oh, Gideon. *Danki. Danki* to you both."

She gave Gideon a hug and pulled Aiden into her arms, too. They both beamed Silas's way as they sank into her embrace.

Silas cleared his throat, knowing he was gawking, melting into this pivotal moment where his children were finding what they had longed for, and pulled his attention away from the uplifting scene. Hazel was watching him closely, a smirk she often gifted Gideon with for saying something smarter than his years plastered on her face. Her smile erased a few wrinkles around her mouth and deepened those around her eyes. He jerked his gaze from her attention, not liking being caught staring at her daughter any more than he liked knowing Hazel was pleased that he was.

"Now you won't have to ride in a car or with horses," Aiden said. He was clearly proud of himself.

"Yep. I cleaned all the horse mucks off myself. Aiden helped a bit." Gideon rolled his eyes, his thumb pointing to his *bruder*. Everyone began to chuckle. Everyone but Andy Weaver, who appeared none too happy at the moment.

Lydia's smile went to the man in the buggy. Silas wished she had forgotten he was there. He had.

"Is that not just so sweet?"

"You do deserve sweet." Andy grinned, gaze locking on to hers.

Silas grunted. He was not standing there another minute. He wanted to stay close, breathe in that sweet honey invasion a little longer, but why tease the senses and tempt the heart? "*Kumm.* Let's get you all in for the evening and get this one's belly full." He tickled Mary May's middle.

It was for the best, putting distance between him and one bad idea.

Come bedtime, Lydia climbed the stairs to the Graber house to tuck the children in for the night. She was beginning to enjoy this routine as much as they did. Telling a story, whispering prayers, and kissing their little heads goodnight. After one book, she pulled the blankets up to the boys' chins.

"One more story, Lydi," Gideon begged as she crossed the boys' room and picked up the lamp on the dresser.

"I am really tired tonight. Perhaps tomorrow I will tell you about Esther. She saved her people by *not* following the rules of man but of *Gott*." Maybe that wasn't a good way to entice Gideon, but Aiden obviously liked the sounds of it as he pulled the quilt up to his chin with a greedy smile. His dark hair was still damp from his bath and lay flat against his head.

"Aiden, one more before bed," she said, walking towards the door. "How do you spell blue?" She had chosen a simple word she knew he would know. It too had become their routine, practicing new words, just like making Gideon count so often throughout the day. She wasn't sure it was what mothers did with their children, but practice always made one better at a thing.

"B-L-U." He stopped.

"That's not correct. You forgot the E on the end." Lydia gave him a wry look.

"You asked how I spell it, not you." Aiden's laugh was followed by a deep, low chuckle from down the hallway.

Silas had overheard them and found Aiden's toying of her humorous. Lydia remembered to close her mouth before stepping out of the boys' room and into the hall. Silas had surprised her once today. No need in crashing into him in the hall and putting herself in another uncomfortable situation. Whatever had crossed over him this evening, she wasn't certain, but Lydia did recall the way she felt. Having

Silas Graber look at you with those handsome hazel eyes would make any woman go weak in the knees.

When she reached the hall, it was empty, his door closing just feet from where she stood. She couldn't help but make a loud huff, hoping he heard her response to his mocking. When she crawled under her own covers, Lydia didn't think of Andy Weaver or why he had returned. She didn't focus on the boy's acceptance. She closed her eyes and let her mind drift to a pair of hazel eyes and hoped to dream of an impossible future.

CHAPTER TWELVE

"Oh, Mary May, hold still," Lydia said. Morning light seeped through the bedroom, giving Lydia a better look at what she was dealing with. Where the child found a hard candy was beyond her. She had her suspicions—Martha Sue or Gracie maybe—but it didn't matter now. Lydia blamed herself for not checking the little girl's dress pockets, a mistake she wouldn't repeat in the future.

"Ouch."

Mary May whined as Lydia attempted to gently pull the sticky mess from her blond locks.

Peanut butter and lard obviously didn't work to remove hard candy from hair as well as it had gum when Lydia was a girl.

"Let's wash it with dish soap. That will work." Mary May sobbed uncontrollably as Lydia carried her to the sink. Lydia knew how the child felt. She wanted to cry, too. Nothing seemed to be working no matter how hard she tried.

Three washings and thirty minutes later, Mary May's hair was certainly clean, except for one thick strand still being held stubbornly onto by one small hard blue determined piece of candy.

There was only one solution she could see. With no other obvious choice, and after explaining her logic and receiving Mary May's approval, she picked up *Mudder*'s sewing scissors and snipped the strands. The ever-determined nuisance fell to the kitchen floor, a clump of blond hair with it. Lydia wanted to cry for her, but once freed, Mary May was all nose-wiggling and happy again.

Running the brush through Mary May's hair, Lydia measured what remained. It was roughly three inches on the side of her head, the size of her thumb. She studied the results, contemplating how to pin it under her little *kapp*, keeping it concealed. Mary May's hair would grow back by the end of summer. *Right?*

"There, *gut* as new," Lydia said with a smile, and Mary May hugged her like she wasn't someone who just cut her hair but one who saved the day.

How anyone could not just drink in these sweet children was beyond her. It wasn't hard. Love, that was. With that, she thought of Silas. He'd known love, had held it for a while, and lost it, but would he ever be capable of wanting it again? She pushed aside the fanciful thought. Just because he was stirring things inside her she couldn't explain didn't mean he felt what she felt.

The day flew by in a buzz. Laundry flapped in the breeze, filling the yard with a crisp, fresh smell. Spring daffodils sprang up in the back pastures in thick clusters of bold yellow on pedestals of forest green. Lydia begged more than once for Gideon to stop plucking them all. It was sweet he wanted to pick her flowers, but not all of them. His damp and dirty little fingers had handed over two handfuls already, his lips stretched into his biggest smile. He was eager to please, that one. No one had ever given her flowers before and she promised she would always remember that it was him that had. *Leave it to the prankster to be the first.*

However, letting the children help mix the sugary syrup for the hummingbird feeders had been the best part of the day. All three of the old glass feeders that once hung at her family home she had fetched from her family's old barn with Karen's approval.

"I have never seen hummingbirds before," Aiden admitted, surprising Lydia. "Hannah says she gets them every year. Some are green."

"*Jah*, they are many colors. I saw one with red on its top like a woodpecker once. They should start arriving any day now." She eyed the sky as if they were up there somewhere. "This will help feed them for their long journey as they migrate."

They went back into the house, and Lydia readied a meal of pork and cabbage and fresh yeast rolls. A buggy pulled up to the house. It was early for Silas to be home and work the horses. No rain today meant he would be building walls. Once, when Aiden had asked his father what he did at work, Silas had explained in detail. Lydia found his description fascinating, the way he spoke of using stones and concrete to build paths and foundations. Safer than training and breaking horses to her way of thinking.

It was too early for her *mudder* to be arriving home as well, considering that the bakery was staying open until five, and there was still cleanup to do.

After walking to the kitchen door, Lydia peered out. "*Ack*, Lord, help me," she muttered as Timothy, Tina, and Thomas Hicky spilled out of Mary's buggy and came running towards her and her freshly cleaned kitchen. Those three were as wild as the summer was long. Taking a deep breath, Lydia put on her best smile and stepped outside to meet the Hicky invasion.

"Mary. How are you today?"

"*Gut*. I thought the *kinner* would like to visit since we were close by today." Silas lived at least two miles from the nearest neighbor. Lydia had her suspicions as to why Mary had dropped by so late in the day. "Hope you don't mind. If you are busy, I can keep an eye on them as they play or help." Mary Hicky didn't look anything like the school-teacher she'd once been. Twelve years Lydia's senior she was only thirty-five. Too young to have more wrinkles than her own *mudder* at fifty-five.

"They can play out here. Let me get some things settled inside, and we will sit on the porch and visit." Lydia smiled and rushed back inside to stir the pot of pork and cabbage. She pulled open the oven door and noted the yeast rolls were done, a perfectly golden brown. She pulled out the hot pan to set aside and cool. A visit sounded nice. Lydia poured two glasses of water and headed for the porch. It was a great and beautiful day for company—the female kind that spoke in full sentences and didn't grumble or growl as a way of communicating.

"Here you go, Mary. Weather is sure starting to feel like a real spring. Hard to believe summer will be here in no time." Lydia took a seat in one of the rockers.

"It is at that. I feared we would be stuck in that cold forever." Mary tucked her dress underneath her to avoid the bottom of the rocker and sat next to her. "Are you and Hazel planning a garden here, or do you think you will be moving elsewhere soon?"

Lydia understood her forwardness. The woman needed a husband in the worst way. The few things Mary sewed for the store in town couldn't be enough to support three children. If Silas were to re-marry, Mary would be a better choice. And Mary would never question her nearness with the children. It was a thought.

"We will be planting soon. I don't like thinking ahead too far, but feel our situation here will last a bit, just not forever." Lydia hoped Mary understood she had no choice in the agreement made between her *mudder* and Silas but couldn't deny she was growing comfortable, too.

"Don't go near the horses, you two!" Lydia yelled when Aiden and Timothy aimed for the barn, sticks in hand. The boys slid to a stop and grumbled, but as soon as Timothy eyed a ball, they were off on another mission. Both Lydia and Mary chuckled.

"They are such a handful. I wish I had you and Hazel helping me."

Mary grinned but Lydia imagined she meant it. Three children were a lot for one woman trying to be both *Mudder* and *Daed*. A pang of pity went out to her, and Lydia wished there was something she could do to lessen Mary's burdens.

"I can imagine how hard it has been for you. I don't know if I could have managed as well as you, Mary. You are a strong woman." Compliments weren't common, tempting vanity and pride, but Mary deserved to know she was doing a good job. This made Mary smile, and she took a sip of her glass as her cheeks reddened. *Jah*, a compliment could go a long way.

"You are kind to say so, but *Gott* has seen we have what we need when we need it. I think if you had to endure what I have, you would do well yourself."

Lydia doubted that. She wasn't about to tell Mary that just this morning she'd cut over four inches of hair from Mary May's head. Or that she had spilled half of the morning milking down the sink when straining it because Gideon bumped into her running through the house after he, of course, had again untied her shoelaces.

"The *kinner* have taken to you," Mary said. "You will make a *gut mudder* one day."

Lydia's heart warmed in the sentiment. She thought of Andy, his words nearly the same as Mary's, and his desire to speak to her again. It was confusing, and Lydia wasn't sure how she felt about his return.

"I have taken to them, too. I did not plan on that." Lydia passed her a sideways grin.

"*Gott* sure has a way of changing our plans, *jah*?" Mary shrugged. "*Kinner* have a way about them. Pulling you in and making you love them."

That they did.

"I think it has been *gut* that you are here for them."

Mary had a kind heart and deserved a husband who would cherish that. Lydia shifted in the rocker and sipped a drink of water. "*Danki.* I'm not sure everyone would agree with you." Lydia set the glass aside and gazed out over the game of ball that was ensuing.

"You mean Jenny or Silas?"

Lydia turned, and Mary stared at her the same way *Mudder* would when she wanted the truth. "Both, I guess." What else could she say to such a question?

"Jenny is Jenny. Nothing new there." Mary waved off further comment. "But Silas. I know he is glad you are here for the *kinner*. He all but said so to me. Having Hazel here too is enough to make any man happy. She is an amazing baker."

"She is, but I think you are wrong about Silas. He thinks I am a *boppli* and cannot do anything right." Lydia knew she sounded wounded.

"Silas is healing. You being here has been a big change in more than just your and Hazel's life. He will come around. *Gott* is doing good things here. We all see it."

Lydia wished she would explain further but didn't dare ask.

"And if I am speaking honestly, I don't think Silas looks at you like you are a *boppli* at all." Mary snickered.

"What do you mean?"

The familiar sound of Jippy's neigh announced itself, as it did every evening the buggy turned into the drive. Lydia and Mary looked down the lane as Silas rode up, tall in the seat and looking nothing like a man who had already worked a full day.

Lydia admired his endurance as much as the new look on his face. He looked happy to be returning home. Perhaps he was happy to see they had company. Hopefully, he was in such good spirits he wouldn't even fuss that she had cut Mary May's hair. If he noticed, that was. Lydia wasn't about to tell him, but she would sure like to know which of them made Silas smile returning home today.

For the first time in weeks, Silas was glad to be home. He still had to work the horses, but after thinking about it all day, his mind was made up. Tonight, he would not allow for Lydia to serve them supper and leave to her own small kitchen table to eat alone. Or for her to wait to share the late meal with Hazel. She wasn't a servant, but a member of the community. It wasn't improper for them to share a meal together. There was nothing wrong in it. Tonight, he would ask her to stay. The children would like that.

After setting Jippy free and pushing the open buggy to the side of the barn, he made his way to the house where Lydia and Mary awaited. The two seemed to have been enjoying their visit. It was *gut*. Their friendship could serve them both equally. Mary had such a hard time of it, and there was only so much he could do to help lessen her burdens. Silas had already gifted her half of his flock of laying hens, spoken to Thomas on her behalf, and helped erase the only debt her husband David had left behind. Still, it had to be hard to be a woman alone. Some days it was hard to be a man alone, too.

"Ladies." Silas removed his hat as he greeted them. Both women looked comfortable sitting on the porch watching the day fade. Like two old friends catching up on life. Lydia sprang to her feet, a smile on her face. Was she happy to see him?

"What are these?" He gestured to the glass container hanging from the end of the porch.

"One of the hummingbird feeders. The children helped me ready and hang three of them today. Migration has started. I thought maybe they might like to watch them. It was something me and *Daed* did each year."

Silas glanced over the yard and spotted the other two feeders she mentioned. One hung from an old pole by an empty garden, the other staked in the center of Jana's flower bed where small purple crocuses added a bit of color to the wood chips he had laid last fall.

"Won't they attract yellowjackets, too?" He asked the innocent question but realized he shouldn't have said anything. Lydia had never spoken about her father until now. He watched her smile vanish at his comment.

"I will watch and move them if so. We've never had a problem before." Her tone lacked her normal snippiness. For Mary Hicky's sake, he assumed.

"You should take a seat. I'm sure you can take a break before heading over to tackle Cage."

He accepted the empty rocker. This was a side of Lydia he had never seen before—attentive—and he kind of liked it.

She went inside and returned with a glass of water for him. "I'll see to the children. You two visit." She offered him the glass and hurried away, leaving Silas alone with Mary.

His eyes followed her as she bounced down the steps and out where the children were tossing a volleyball back and forth. She was much like her father. Joseph was tall and lean and made from hard work. His gray hair had once been the same shade of sunshine as Lydia's. But she had a bit of Hazel about her too. Lydia was a fair hand in the kitchen and as far as he could tell so far, there wasn't much she couldn't do outside of her fear of horses.

"I've always been fond of all three of Hazel's *dochdern*," Mary said. "Lydia stands out a bit. She was always busier than a bee in a flower garden. I wish I had half of her blessed energy." Mary chuckled. "I think she could even wear out my *kinner* if she had a mind to."

"Lydia can wear anyone out." He gulped down half of his glass, hoping Mary didn't read too much into his words.

"I guess now that she is courting again, she might settle down. She deserves to be happy after, well, you know." Mary paused. "And Andy seems to be serious this time. I heard he had even visited with the bishop."

Silas swallowed hard, and the flavorless drink went down the wrong way, burning his throat before singeing his heart.

"So, he is going to join the church?" If memory served him correctly, Andy had refused to join with his family in Ohio just as he had as a younger man before leaving Miller's Creek. Lydia had been a member of the church since she was at least nineteen. If that changed, that meant—he didn't want to think what that meant.

"Guess so. Rumor has it that he took her golfing the other day. Everyone was talking about it."

Silas questioned when she'd found the time to go out and golf with an unbaptized man. It wasn't permitted for a baptized member to date an unbaptized one, though over the years such things occurred. Perhaps her baptism had been what led to Andy leaving when he did.

"That sounds lovely for a young couple," Mary continued. "David took me to the ocean once. It was the most amazing thing to stand next to *Gott*'s big wonder and hear the roar of the waves. Did you ever do such with Jana?"

Silas and Mary had always spoken openly over the years about their similar losses. As hard as it was for him to lose Jana, Mary's burdens were harder to carry alone. He also knew why she visited so often, but he could be honest with Mary, and he was. He had no interest in remarrying, but he had always been her friend.

"We went on picnics, long rides, like everyone else. But *nee*, never did we go see oceans or go golfing." His jaw tightened. When had Lydia ever found the time to leave and go golfing? She was either here, or helping her *aenti* May, or taking meals to Ben Troyer. And why now just as he was starting to see Lydia as the beautiful person she was on the inside as she was the out, did Andy Weaver have to return? Silas exhaled a long breath. He was nine years her senior, a widower with three children. What could he possibly have to offer that Andy Weaver could not?

"I should gather the *kinner*. It is getting time to get them home for supper," Mary said, coming to her feet.

"You are welcome to stay for supper."

"That isn't necessary. I have a roast warming in the oven, and it takes longer than it should to get those three bathed and in bed for the night."

Silas smiled and nodded his understanding.

"Thanks for stopping by. I think Lydia enjoyed the company." Silas followed her to the end of the porch.

"I did enjoy it. Lydia has always had a way about her to make others happy. I see it is working here too."

Silas hoped she didn't see everything.

"My own *kinner* even mind her." Mary laughed and stepped down from the porch. "May I say just this?"

Silas nodded.

"Be careful. Andy has plans for her and not everyone is pleased to hear it after he left her when he did."

Her warning was unexpected. He pretended to not care, but Mary saw through him. Fidgeting with his hat between his fingers, he tried to think how to respond.

"It's okay, Silas. I understand. Lydia is a special person. And she knows loss as well as we do. I have known her since she was young. She has a *gut* heart. It just hurts right now. She will soon get tired of running away from things that have hurt her and decide to run to what *Gott* has planned for her. And she deserves better than one who can't be trusted."

Mary touched his arm. "You are a good friend Mary Hicky." He couldn't finish what he knew she had hoped for between them. He didn't have to. It was written on her tired and understanding features.

"And you are a *gut* friend to me. *Danki* for listening to me spill my heart and my hurt. I am glad one of us can move forward. You best decide what you do want and go after it before it is too late. *Gott* doesn't give second chances for nothing."

She strolled away as if she had not just awakened a possibility within him. Mary knew him too well.

As both women begin wrangling and separating children, Mary's words shuffled around in his head like a scattered deck of cards, now collected in chaotic order in his hand. *Moving forward.* He surely didn't feel like he was moving anywhere.

Three-year-old Thomas yanked Lydia's *kapp* off as she lifted him into Mary's buggy. The child was always throwing or grabbing things not his own. Lydia spun on her heels, taking up a chase as it tumbled across the yard. The children all laughed at the display, but his heart grabbed when she finally took hold of it and turned to smile at her victory, *kapp* held high in the air, that smile of hers beaming. He would do well not to look at it for too long.

He placed his hat back on his head and aimed for the barn, where Cage would be waiting to remind him just what little control he had in this world. "Moving forward, huh?"

On the other side of the door, Silas stomped away the clinging muck and mud on his boots. Lydia would be setting the table for the late meal right now, and he peered in the kitchen door window before entering. *One never knew what he was about to walk into in his own home anymore.*

Inside, she was fluttering around the kitchen, Mary May shadowing her every step. His *dochder* was like a needy kitten begging for attention, taking any scraps of love thrown at her. Tucked under the supper table he spied Gideon. He knew that mischievous grin. Silas leaned in closer, wondering what warranted that grin, but nothing caught his eye to necessitate intervention. He hated scolding the children after what they had gone through, but it was becoming all too obvious that no good was coming from that way of thinking.

Aiden obediently began setting plates on the table. *Four*, Silas counted. She still had no plan to share the meal with them. As Lydia put down a large yellow bowl covered with cloth—rolls or biscuits—she wiggled her foot under the table. Gideon snickered behind his small hand. It was some sort of game between the two of them. Silas warmed at the scene playing out in front of him.

She stroked Mary May's head as she turned back to the stove. "Aiden, I think tonight we shall read about Samson."

She was good at this, balancing lives and duties in a delicate way that made his palms sweaty.

"The strong man with all the hair?" Aiden's face lit up.

"*Jah*. That is the one." Lydia grinned.

She addressed each child, individually, neglecting none. Something buzzed by his head and Silas turned, looking about in the dim sunset of day to find the culprit. His gaze shot towards the hummingbird feeder Lydia and the children had hung just today. The sugary concoction was a good quarter inch below the marked waterline in black Lydia had put on the side. She was already getting the hummingbirds she had hoped for.

As she stared at the glass container, Silas grasped it in his head. She was kind of like them—hummingbirds, that was, flying around so fast her feet blurred like fluttering wings. She could eat like them, too. He mused. He had never seen a woman always shoving something in her mouth no matter the time of day as he had Lydia Miller. Hazel being a baker sure encouraged her sweet tooth, too. Nourishment for all the buzzing around she did, perhaps.

Looking into his kitchen and seeing the contagious energy inside, he no longer felt worn out at all but ready to help an outnumbered chicory blue hummingbird all on her own.

Lydia set the food on the table, as Silas walked in front of the sink to wash his hands. She tossed him the towel and brushed past in a blur to help Mary May into her booster seat.

Silas pulled five glasses out of the cabinet and set them on the counter. Lydia returned to his side, reached for a pitcher of milk, and began filling glasses. She hesitated long enough to notice he had set down an extra glass tonight. Her face scrunched noticing there was one too many, but she said nothing. Lydia simply grabbed one glass, opened the cabinet, and started to place it back inside. Silas touched her arm, subduing her hurry. His fingers tingled in the innocent touch, and she froze, glass and hand suspended in the air.

"I was hoping to ask you something." *Spit it out*, he nagged himself, but when she glanced up to him, he was captivated. From the first time he'd laid eyes on her, he recognized Lydia to be an attractive woman. But she was much more than that. Everything about her was infectious. She was like sugar. The more you had, the more you wanted. Even further, she hadn't a clue she held such power. Innocence held its own kind of beauty. Silas admired both. He would ask her to stay, take a chance. There was no harm in seeing how she felt about sharing the family table with him tonight.

A knock came at the front door. If timing was everything, it was certainly off by at least two minutes, he figured. They lingered there, locked in each other's gazes, as if not hearing the knock at all. Was it possible she might feel just as confused as he was? The thought made him smirk and just as he opened his mouth, a second knock rattled her away from him. Lydia flinched and then set the glass back on the countertop.

"Hold that thought." Lydia held up a finger then flew away again.

Silas couldn't help but smile. She had felt that, too, that new and exciting surge of something freshly brewing. Hopefully, they could resume where they'd left off, and knowing he could steal away some of her attention for himself had him excited. He couldn't remember the last time he'd felt excited about anything.

He filled the remaining glasses and carried them to the table before fetching another plate. At the sound of Andy Weaver at the front door, his smile faded, and Silas's fingers slid the plate back on top of the stack and closed the cabinet door. Lydia would obviously not be joining his family at the table tonight after all. Dropping into his seat at the head of the table, he said, "Let us pray." Silas bowed his head and his children followed. Before he could signal the end of the silent prayer, the door shut in the next room, and all heads raised. Aiden's eyes said everything Silas was thinking. "Let us eat now."

CHAPTER THIRTEEN

Lydia agreed to a short stroll and followed Andy down the lane. The sky streaked a bright, autumn red and iris purple in front of them. She toyed with her *kapp* strings to keep her hands busy. Silas had been about to ask her to share a meal with them. She was sure of it. Why else were there five glasses and not four? Why else would he have stopped her from putting one of the glasses back? He had never done that before.

If Andy hadn't arrived when he did, what would he have said? The man was confusing. One minute Lydia felt like he disapproved of her being there, the next, he was looking at her like he was happy she was. Was Mary right? Did Silas see her and not the pain in the neck she believed he thought her to be? It was enough to rob a woman's good senses.

She inhaled a breath of cool night air and reveled in the notion that those hazel eyes had softened to her. Underneath all the growls and gruffness, Silas could be quite the charmer. She rubbed her arms, the place his fingers had impressed, and smiled. He was trying to stop her from putting that glass back. It had stopped her all right. Stopped her mind, her heart, even her feet. How could such a simple touch leave a *maedel* frozen?

"Are you cold?" Andy glanced at her as they walked side by side.

"I'm fine." She wasn't, confused as she was.

"You asked me a question. I would like to answer it now." Andy shoved both hands into his pockets.

Lydia recalled the last time they'd walked together like this. Frog songs had filled the evening that night, too. She had been so young, unknowing. She felt better equipped now to deal with someone who she had once opened her heart to.

"Go ahead then." She wasn't going to make this easy for him.

"I hoped to return and get to know you again. Court you."

"Court me?" Lydia stopped walking. He was serious. "You left Ohio to court me?" She should be flattered, but she felt more bruised than flattered. He left her and when she needed him most, he hadn't returned. "We did court, Andy Weaver, and you left, remember?" Pulling her shawl around her tighter, she walked on ahead again.

"I had no choice in leaving, Lydia. You know this. My family needed me." Andy caught up to her.

"You could have written me back. You could have at least told me to move on. Or did you prefer to have someone back here pining for ya?"

He smiled, stopping her in her tracks. He still had the power to do that to her. "Did you pine over me, Lydia?"

What a selfish question to ask. "I...no."

"I am only teasing." He touched her arm. "The truth is when I thought I would never see you again I didn't want you to pine over me, to wait for me. It wasn't fair. That's why I returned your letters. I couldn't read them. I wasn't ready to join the church and get married. I wasn't ready for the things you were." He was silent for a moment. "I thought you would find another man, settle down, and marry. When I heard you and your *mudder* sold the farm and moved in with a widower, I realized I still cared for you. I still love you, Lydia Rose. Always have." He caressed her cheek.

The soft warmth of his fingers sent a shiver of emotion up her spine. He loved her. Always had. Wanted the best for her. She stepped back, calculating every word, every emotion. Going ahead at full speed was what caused her to miss so much. It was time to pay attention and think before opening her mouth—or her heart. *Breathe. Think.*

"You returned because I live here now, but not when you believed me to be yours?" She cocked her head to one side, watching the way her words traveled over his confidence. "I lost so much, and you weren't here." She sniffed back any threats of emotion.

"I was a foolish boy." Andy's hand rubbed that place on the back of his neck where tension usually found respite. He moved closer and took both of her hands into his. "I am no longer that foolish boy. Please forgive me for this. Let us put this behind us. I will earn your forgiveness, Lydia, if you would just give me a chance. I will find work, a home worthy of you, and never leave you again." His eyes were wide, pleading, and promising.

She had once loved him with all her heart, but he had broken that heart. Could she trust what she heard now? A man's word was all he had, *Daed* had always told her. It spoke volumes about the kind of person he was.

"So, you committed to the church? You know, in Ohio?" Her question put a twinkle in his eyes, but all Lydia could think about was if she opened her heart to Andy again, it could lead to her one day leaving Miller's Creek. Change was one thing she knew enough about herself to admit she didn't like one bit. She could never leave Miller's Creek. It was home.

"*Nee.* I plan to be baptized here. I have already spoken with the Bishop. I'm ready now."

He sounded sincere.

"I want to make my life here in Miller's Creek with you."

Her heart stopped. No pounding or thumping—just stopped. Andy was here for her, for the life they could build together. Pick up where they had left off and live happily ever after.

"You mean it? You are serious about this?" But how could she be certain he meant what he said? She studied him closely, hoping to see the truth behind those dark eyes.

He nodded, grinning as if he knew her answer.

"If I agree to let you work hard for that forgiveness you seek, you have to be certain. I cannot simply forget how you hurt me, and I cannot just decide my future tonight without getting to know you again."

His jaw tightened, not happy with her hesitation in being what they once were, but, after a few seconds, he surrendered and wrapped her in a hug.

"*Danki,* Lydia. You will not be sorry. I will earn your trust again. Your love. I promise."

Silas leaned his elbows on the top boards of the fencing, resting his chin on his palms as the moon enhanced the budding oak and maples along his property line. Hazel had offered to make fresh coffee, but he declined. When she asked where her daughter was, Silas was surprised that she was as uneasy about Lydia wandering off with Andy Weaver as he was.

They had been gone nearly an hour. He listened for the sound of her laugh over the spring peepers that serenaded the evening's entrance. It was a beautiful sound when she let herself succumb to it, but he heard nothing but the chorus of croaks and chirps.

Any man would be fortunate to take a late-night walk

with her. Maybe steal a kiss. Would Lydia allow for that? The thought of Andy Weaver kissing her made his blood boil.

Cage bucked and kicked in the enclosure beside him. The animal wanted free, and Silas knew the feeling. He had felt trapped in his own darkness for so long, he was ready to step into the sun. Hazel said he only needed a new view, and Lydia had brought that with her. She radiated life. He saw it in his children, in the way the air carried their happy voices. He felt it in his veins when she was near, and God help him, he felt the emptiness when she wasn't.

He recalled his own mother's favorite verse from Proverbs. "A merry heart doeth good like medicine, but a broken spirit chillith the bones."

When Rebecca had been in charge of the home, she had filled it with unyielding order and a deeper melancholy than Jana's passing had delivered. His once happy home had converted into a hollow, mundane existence, and there had been no happiness.

Lydia was the energy, sunshine, that they had all been deprived of. Silas did trust the Lord and all his doings, and it was becoming clear that God had a hand in this arrangement in his life. The Miller women and their *gut* food and happy hearts were good medicine. There were different degrees of happiness, he was learning, and now it had sprouted around him, tempting him. And he wanted more of it.

"Didn't stay up just for us, now, did you?" Silas broke his stare over Cage and turned as Andy and Lydia strolled up behind him. Andy's tone was brazen for a lad who had yet to know the wares of a hard day's work.

"Working farm. Commitments. Means a man's work is never done. You should know that." Watching Lydia smile at Andy Weaver, a man known to wave away commitment, was disheartening.

Had Andy made promises, planned to take her away? If that's what she wanted, Silas would never let her know he had feelings. She deserved to be happy. He ran his hands

through his hair. Who was he kidding? He hoped Andy
Weaver didn't take Lydia anywhere. That would be hard for
his children to bear. That would change everything that was
coming alive here.

"*Gut nacht.*" He turned and forced himself back into the
house and the empty bed that awaited him.

The next morning, Lydia took all three of the children and
the remaining jars of last year's honey to the bakery. Mary
had told her of a shortcut through Silas's land which connected into that of Mr. Doyle's. From there one just took
the lake paths leading into town. It was a good four miles
shorter and no walking on the road with three children. The
children treasured the walking trail around Twin Fork Lake
as a great adventure. Lydia promised they could explore one
of the trails on the way home.

By the time they reached the old town drug store that had
been converted into Miller's Bakery, the children were a bit
worn. That was just what Lydia was hoping for. Gideon
would behave himself with no extra energy bouncing around
inside of him. "*Gut* behavior now. Agreed?"

All three nodded, but it was the middle child she gave an
extra stern look toward until he agreed verbally.

Moving inside the glass doors to the jingle of the over-
head bell, Lydia spotted Jenny Schwartz speaking with her
Mammi Rose at the counter. Jenny turned and eyed her entrance. The narrowing sharpness of her glare was almost
piercing as it ran over her and the children.

The bakery was full of customers today. Bishop
Schwartz's *fraa*, Edith, along with two others were eyeing the
jams and jellies to the right. In the far corner, a couple of
regulars Lydia had served many times were deciding over a
selection of cookbooks. Everyone noted her entering, three

kids in tow, before resuming with what had brought them here.

Lydia ignored any prickles Jenny's eyes posed on her. She repositioned Mary May on her hip and moved further into the room. Chin lifted, Lydia approached the counter a few feet from where Jenny stood.

"Morning, *Mammi*. I brought the last of *Aenti* May's honey before we harvest again. I will set them out for ya."

"*Danki*, sweet Lydi. I will be over to help you in a bit." Rose continued filling a box with an assortment of fudge and chocolate chip cookies for an *Englisch* woman carrying four bags from local stores.

Gideon slid underneath a table to play with Mary May while Lydia restocked a center aisle shelf of honey and fresh maple syrups from a local family. Aiden held the basket for Lydia as she pulled out each jar of honey and strategically displayed them in what she felt was an approachable display. It was all about presentation. Even the most ordinary thing, gazed over a hundred times, could be noticed if put in the right light or placing. *Mudder* often praised Lydia's good eye for presentation and often encouraged her to stock shelves and arrange the room on occasion.

"Did you walk all this way, Lydia?" Jenny asked, her tone laced with amusement carried throughout the store.

Lydia bristled. Jenny had that effect on people just as she had a talent for drawing attention. "Walking is *gut* for the body and the soul, ain't so?" She peppered her words with sarcasm.

"Any sensible person would take a buggy." Jenny smirked.

Lydia's breath held. Had Silas told Jenny about her fear?

"I think walking does both mind and body *gut*. And *kinner* are no exception," Edith said.

Lydia had never expected the bishop's wife to come to her aid but was glad for it and the flinch of surprise it put on Jenny's well-placed features. The small, rounded woman was often quiet and reserved, as any bishop's wife was expected to be. Jenny silenced as Edith smiled over the full bakery.

"She is afraid of horses," Rose blurted out as she wrapped freshly sliced cheese in white paper for Jenny. Hazel shot her mother a glare for outing Lydia. A glare that would have no real effect now that the words were out there.

"Afraid?" Jenny's voice hitched.

Lydia's stomach rolled and inverted if that was a possible thing. *How could she? And in front of Jenny Schwartz at that.* The heat was not the only indicator that her face was beet red now. Nothing was more embarrassing than having your worst fear announced publicly.

"It is not our Lydia's way. I agree with Edith. Walking is *gut* and did not hurt us as *kinner*," *Mammi* added once she noted Lydia's surprised expression.

"We walked the lake and picked out a tree for a picnic," Aiden said.

This took Lydia by surprise. The boy who had once treated her as if she had no idea what she was doing now sensed she needed his help. If she could, she would have cried right then and not from embarrassment at all. Silas would be proud of the young man his son was becoming.

With trembling fingers, Lydia placed the last jar on the shelf. She stepped around the center table, ready to leave as quick as her feet would take her when suddenly she was stumbling. Helpless to stop the inevitable, she smacked into the bakery floor. Hard. There was no limitation on humiliation. In the matter of a few seconds, Lydia had been scolded for being careless with children, outed as a coward, and now she could add inept at walking to her lists of lacking.

"Gideon Michael Graber, your *daed* will have you in the woodshed by supper! I have told you that is not funny."

Lydia heard her *mudder* scolding along with a few feminine gasps. That's when she realized that Gideon must have untied her shoes again. She should have known better than to turn her attention away from him long, but Jenny's remarks had shaken her good sense just long enough to let her guard down. She rose to her knees as *Mammi* Rose came to her side and placed an arm over her.

"Oh help." *Mammi* Rose spurted out. "Are you okay, my *lieb*?"

"Bad, bad timing, *bruder*," Aiden whispered to his brother.

Lydia's chin and elbow had made first contact, but it was her pride she knew had suffered the most.

"Gideon, *kumm*. We need to take a walk," Jenny said in a voice that would make a schoolmaster proud.

Lydia ground her back teeth together. Jenny spoke as if she had some right to even think to discipline Silas Graber's son.

"I think it is time someone with more experience handles this before it gets further out of hand."

Gideon's flesh went pale, his eyes as big as saucers. Lydia sprang to her feet so fast everything blurred, but she managed to keep from tumbling again thanks to *Mammi* Rose's hands holding on to her. She would certainly be feeling this misstep for a day or two. Her chin was throbbing as it was.

"That will not be necessary," Lydia said. She pulled Gideon close to her, tucking him into her hip. The look on his face said he was sorry. Either way, he had been told more than once, and a trip to the woodshed might be the only way to put an end to his defiance. Only that would be for his father to decide, not Jenny Schwartz.

Jenny chuckled, shaking her head. "Lydia, my sweet girl, I think it is obvious to everyone here that the *kinner* need..."

Lydia interrupted. "They need what Silas decides is best for them. What he has provided them: two women who care for them very much and will do everything they can to help them thrive within our community." She bent forward and made quick work of lacing her shoe. Looking dignified at this point, no longer mattered. "Women who put *Gott* first. They need to learn by a loving hand, not one with an *agenta*."

Where did that come from?

"Silas is spoiling them, and I know how to handle mischievous *buwe*. You cannot even handle yourself," Jenny said, and that perfectly lined brow lifted to punctuate her point.

"That is why out of three *bruders* you helped raise, three smoke cigarettes during the singings, smash mailboxes for fun, and have yet to commit to the church. I think not. My boys are *gut* boys and will one day be *gut* men." Lydia turned on her heel and headed for the door, all three Graber children following her without a word.

CHAPTER FOURTEEN

When it rained, it poured. At least that's how Lydia felt at the moment. The long walk home did little to soften her wounded pride which was a hard swallow if one didn't chew on it for a while first.

Jenny would make matters worse after the way she'd reacted today. Lydia should have held her tongue and not gotten under the woman's skin. If *Mammi* hadn't outed her fear of horses, she could have left unscathed. Rubbing her scuffed chin, she felt the embarrassment wash all over her again along with the sting. There was no coming back from the teasing that would ensue from this day on. What a mess she had made once again while trying to do the right thing.

She glanced at Gideon. He did deserve a good trip to the woodshed, just as *Mudder* had suggested, but his sorrowful, tear-filled eyes and absent smile told her he knew his actions had been wrong.

No one in that place had the right to handle him.

Just because his *mudder* was gone on to glory didn't mean these children didn't have—*Oh no!* Lydia had called them her boys and in public. In front of, well, everyone. Now her head and heart felt the sting, too. Silas would have a few harsh words to deliver once he found out, and for once, Lydia deserved every one of them. She should have never been so bold, and in front of the Bishop's wife too. What had she been thinking to call them her own?

"Lydi."

Gideon's soft wounded voice broke her rambling worries as they reached the Grabers' fence.

"*Jah*." Lydia glanced down at the little straw hat and soft voice just under it. He peeked upward, tears pooling in his dark blue eyes.

"I sorry. I did not mean for you to get hurt."

"Oh, Gideon." She kneeled before him, placing a hand on both small shoulders. "I know you did not want me to get hurt. But you must know that the things you do have consequences. Everything we do has consequences. Tricks and pranks may seem fun and innocent, but they can change lives. All that we do, we should do in love for others." She couldn't remember the verse word for word, but it held the same meaning.

"I know." Gideon sniffled, fighting back a full blow-out.

Mary May leaned her head on Lydia's shoulder. This was their first important, real life lesson. *Best make it a good one.*

"I remember once when I was your age how a bunch of boys went around playing tricks on others. They didn't mean for it to hurt anyone either, but one time they put one of those firecrackers in a friend's mailbox. That trick hurt her family's life forever."

"A firecracker? How?"

Now Aiden was listening. Lydia sat down on the grass and urged the children to join her.

"Well, you see, the people who lived in the house had an older *bruder*. He had left home long ago. They missed him so much." She held Mary May close to her side. "But one day *Gott* spoke to his heart, and he wrote his family a letter. He wanted to *kumm* home. He was ready to join the church, ask for forgiveness for his sinful ways. The family was overjoyed, and they wrote the *sohn* back how happy this made them. They offered to pay his way home and promised to be there to pick him up when he was ready. Their lost sheep meant everything to them."

She looked down at Gideon with her best serious expression. "Only he never got that letter. Receiving no word, he thought his family had rejected his return, that they simply didn't want him. He believed his family had abandoned him and did not care for his change of heart. That young man died shortly after, of a broken heart."

Gott would forgive the near lie, she hoped. Lydia didn't have the heart to tell the children the man had taken his own life for fear he was not wanted by his family any longer. The story had been one of woe, a lesson her *daed* used to remind her and her sisters what meddling into the lives of others could do.

Lydia often thought about the man with no name, no face. Nothing was sadder than to think how close life could have changed for him and his family, if not for some foolish prank.

"The firecracker ruined the letter, right?" Aiden asked with a solemn understanding.

"*Jah*." She cupped Gideon's cheek in both hands, punctuating her point. "You see, everything we do must be for the better of others. No trick or prank worth a laugh is worth hurting someone else." She ruffled Gideon's sweaty, blond hair and placed his straw hat back on his head. "Let's get on home now."

Not another word was mentioned of firecrackers, untied shoes, or to whom they each belonged as they walked the rest of the way home.

"You two boys get you a drink and do your evening chores. Me and Mary May will tend to supper before *ya daed* gets home."

The boys followed her orders without a word. Lydia pulled the meatloaf she prepared earlier this morning from the ice box. No sooner had she gotten the pan in the oven and potatoes boiling on the stove than she heard a terrible scream from outside.

"Gideon!"

What had the boy gotten into now?

"Now don't touch it." Lydia tenderly placed a vinegar-soaked washcloth on Gideon's hand. "I told you not to play around the feeders." Ever since Lydia had told the children about her *daed* catching a hummingbird, the boy had lurked under the feeders in hopes to do the same. What had she been thinking? *Consequences.* Silas was right; those sugary feeders attracted more than hummingbirds. It might not have been a yellowjacket that got ahold of Gideon—a wasp maybe—but he had been stung. Lydia cradled him in her arms as he did his best not to cry. "You are so brave. Is he not, Mary May?"

Mary May nodded her head as she nursed her thumb. Gideon swiped away any visible tears that might make him not look so tough after all.

Silas pulled up to the barn and unhitched Jippy. Lydia held her breath. He would have something to say about this. She wasn't sure she could handle further scolding today, but what choice did she have? The way he lumbered across the yard told Lydia he was worn. Today, she knew the feeling.

"What has happened here?" he asked as he took in the solemn faces.

"Gideon got bit," Mary May said before Lydia could stop her. "Lydia got hurt and broke Jenny's *agenta.*"

Lydia gave herself a mental slap to the forehead. Why had she accused Jenny of having an *agenta*?

"Mary May." Lydia hushed her. *Of all the stuff*, she wanted to add. "He was stung, but he is good now. Nothing to fret over." Silas eyed his son then her. Yep, he was not just going to let it go. She let out a long huff. Who cared who was watching at this point?

"Children, inside." They all froze, refusing to move, eyes darting from their *daed* to Lydia. She set Gideon off her lap and got to her feet. With a heavy heart and a nervous stomach, she opened the door. Without so much as a single word, one by one the children entered the house. Silas walked in behind them, and Lydia followed, though she wasn't sure why. It was safer on the porch, the way she figured it.

"I warned you this could happen." Silas's tone was stern. He gave Gideon's hand a close inspection. "I told you they would attract more than hummingbirds. What if he was allergic? Help is miles away, Lydia. Why didn't you think…" he paused, not finishing the remark. Tossing his hat to the floor, he picked up Gideon and set his little body on the counter.

Silas studied the huge red welt on the small hand. Lydia watched his scowl soften. Had Jana never made a mistake, ever?

Either it was the horrible day she had or the way Silas had made her feel, but every part of her insides quivered. He didn't find her capable of tending to his children. His words were rougher than old, weathered barn wood, and she scraped up her feelings and stomped towards the pantry. *Andy would never speak to me like that*—would he?

"Bee stings happen. Things happen," she said. "And I always think. Faster than you even." She stomped to the pantry, opened the door, and pulled out a crinkled-up paper bag.

"You are not a parent. You do not understand how foolish it was hanging those things everywhere."

He couldn't even look at her.

"Maybe if you spent less time golfing and more doing what you were brought here to do—"

Lydia halted, dumbfounded by his choice of words.

When had she been golfing? Heck, when did she have time to do anything but take care of *his* children?

"At least I am present," she said, despite his being right. He'd told her of the dangers, and she hadn't heeded his warning. She was no *mudder*, not much a caregiver either, and it was obvious Silas would not allow her to pretend being one much longer. She tossed the paper bag onto the table. "Supper is in the oven. Prepared by a childless spinster. Hope it serves you well enough." Her tears held as she stormed out of the kitchen and into the evening air before letting loose in a hurtful flood. Any chance at making an impact here and adding color to their lives stormed out with her.

Silas dabbed the rag Lydia had soaked in vinegar over Gideon's hand.

"It not hurt no more, *Daed*. Don't be mad at Lydi. She told me not to. I just wanted to catch one of the hummingbirds so I can be *gut* too."

"What?" Silas barely heard the words over the pounding in his own head. *Silly woman never listens.*

"He messed up big time today," Aiden said. "Thought he could fix it. Lydi's *daed* caught a hummingbird once. *Mammi* Hazel said a man who could catch a hummingbird was a *gut* man. A godly man of patience. Lydi did warn him not to be messing with the feeders. He never listens."

Aiden crossed his arms, looking more perturbed than Silas figured the boy could. It seemed Gideon wasn't the only one who needed more patience.

"*Mammi* Hazel?"

Aiden shrugged and grinned. The children were calling Hazel Grandmother now.

Silas picked up the paper bag, unfolded it, and poured the

contents onto the table. A tube of hydrocortisone cream, a small box of liquid Benadryl, and a pink bottle of calamine rolled out.

"What that for?" Mary May asked, an oddly short strand of hair poking at her eye.

Silas's eyes darted between the box and his daughter's hair to both sons. It seemed he was the only one who doubted Lydia's abilities. He had been cruel, and Silas was never cruel. He let his bruised feeling about her and Andy cloud his judgments.

And why was Lydia's little chin all bloody and blue? And what was Jenny's *agenta*? Silas ran his hand down the length of his face, the warm aroma of meatloaf filling the room.

"This is medicine...for bee stings." He admitted. "It's Lydia's way of thinking ahead to making certain nothing bad ever happens to any of you." The children didn't even question this, which made him feel even worse if that was possible. "Go wash up. I will ready supper."

Well, it wasn't like she had anything to lose at this point. With two carrots from her own dainty little kitchen, Lydia walked toward Cage's corral. The large black beast snorted and ran straight to the gate. Lydia closed her eyes and waited; breath held. If God wanted her trampled on any further today, then so be it. *His will*, right? It was only fair, considering she never could do a thing right. In the stillness that followed, musky, alfalfa-infused breath hit her face. She opened one eye, then another. Cage stared at her as if wondering why she was standing there like an idiot who was afraid of horses. If she had a breath in her, she couldn't find it. Decades passed in that sudden moment, and neither flinched in that gaze held between them. Lydia took in the much-needed air around her and spoke.

"I cannot believe I am saying this, but after the day I have had, even you do not scare me." It was a lie, but if she pretended, maybe he wouldn't stomp her to death. There was no way a few gates would hold a beast this size who was determined.

As she brought forth one of the carrots, Cage sniffed and nibbled but wouldn't accept her gift. Jenny was right. Silas was right, and now even Cage found her unworthy. The tears came in a flood and didn't stop. "I bet you have no idea how hard it is to be a constant failure." He took the carrot and chewed slowly as if waiting to hear more. That earned him a weak grin. It didn't feel silly at all talking to Cage, a horse of all things. He finished the carrot, and Lydia produced the second. Those eyes were easy to talk to.

"I did try to help, you know. It isn't easy helping children who lost so much. It's not all my fault they are a handful." Her shoe kicked a clump of hard mud over the ground. "They can break your heart one way or another. Did you know Andy came back and wants to court me?" Cage snorted in response, pulling a faint chuckle out of her. "Almost five years since our first buggy ride, and he thinks he can pick up where he left off. I say he will have to work for that forgiveness, don't you?" She snickered and ran a sleeve along her damp face.

Cage nudged closer. Animals must have an extra sense about them. They were close enough, and touching would be a new whole other level of insanity. He nipped at her *kapp,* and she pulled it from him just as quickly. "Don't take what doesn't belong to you." Cage's long black neck leaned over the gate again. She stilled.

He wanted her to touch him. "Just like a man. Always wanting more than one can give." She took a step back and slowly raised her hand. "If I do this, you can never tell a soul, deal?" Cage nickered and shook his head. "Silly horse."

Closing her eyes once more, Lydia extended her arm. Sensing her fear, Cage seemed to decide to not use it against her and leaned closer. A tickle of his hairs startled her at first until her palm rested flat between those two large, earthy eyes. The shudder that ran through her brought tears again. Regrets and pains carried longer than she should have allowed.

"I have made many mistakes. I hurt when I only want to help. I cannot help him, no more than I could my *daed*." Cage seemed to understand her dilemma if that was possible. "Please don't kill him. Do not leave those sweet children without both parents," she whispered in begging breaths. "This will be our secret." She winked and headed for her room.

CHAPTER FIFTEEN

"Nonsense. You have all that baking to do for the local fundraiser. I will help with the *kinner* today," Jenny insisted as she continued taking up space in Hazel's kitchen. After the incident at the bakery, Hazel wondered why Jenny even thought to come over at all. If ever a woman was born more persistent Hazel hadn't met her yet.

Hazel poured the dough out on the floured surface and studied the woman briefly before giving the yeasty mixture a good jab in the center. "It wonders me that your *mudder* can spare you today."

"*Mudder* encourages each of us to be of use to the community around us."

"*Jah*, she is a wise woman, but I assure you that Lydia and I need no help taking care of sweet *kinner*," Hazel said.

"After the scene at the bakery, I disagree," Jenny said.

Where the young *maedel* got such a disrespectful attitude was beyond Hazel. Her parents were upstanding members of the community.

Hazel turned and shoved both fists on her hips. "Jenny Schwartz, it was not kind the way you spoke to Lydia and you know I have raised one family already and need no help tending to this one."

Jenny fetched a glass from the cabinet. "Of course not." She filled the glass with water under the faucet and turned to Hazel. "But you have the bakery and Rose see after." Jenny turned to Mary May. "*Kumm,* Mary, let us take this to your *daed.*"

Hazel watched as they exited the kitchen side door. Desperation on an aging *maedel* was an ugly thing. Maybe Hazel was focusing too much on Silas and Lydia. What she needed to be doing was finding a strong-willed man capable of handling troublesome *maedels. Jah*, that's what she should do. Finding a match for Jenny would be no easy task, but when doing the Lord's bidding, one had to put in the extra effort.

Putting all cares of Jenny aside and resuming to hum, she started kneading the dough. Bishop Schwartz had been right when he first approached her. Silas needed saving, just as her Lydia did. Both seemed to be stuck in their grief, and a person couldn't go anywhere when they were stuck now could they? It wasn't right that two people should miss their chance at happiness.

The whole plan had been perfect, help two hearts heal and become one. That was until Andy and Jenny derailed their good intentions. Her Lydia was building a life for herself she hadn't even thought of before.

She forced another fist into the dough and folded it twice before punching it again. She'd witnessed weeks as quarrels turned into understanding, and acceptance grew into appreciation. Love was the only reasonable next blessing. Her Lydi deserved love just as Gracie and Martha had. It didn't seem she was going to find it on her own, so Hazel had meddled, as she was prone to do. Her youngest was special in many ways, and it would take a special man to love her the way she deserved to be loved. And Hazel believed with all her heart that Silas Graber was just that man.

Silas finished helping Mr. Bontrager load Blue into the trailer. The men shook hands and Silas accepted the check for making the mare ready for a teenager to trail ride on. She was a good horse, smart, and learned quickly. Silas glanced towards the house, noticing the old mare tied out front, and let out a sigh knowing Jenny had made another unexpected visit.

"I have a friend who shows racking horses. Have you ever worked with them before?" the wiry-figured man asked.

Silas pulled his gaze from the house and glanced down at the man's boots, the kind that fit the part, but nothing more, and nodded. "*Jah*. But I don't have the weights required for their legs no longer. Sold most of the tacking and gear off a few years ago. If he has the proper equipment, I can handle the rest." Silas could always use the extra income.

They exchanged the proper numbers and Silas watched the truck and trailer lumber down the gravel drive and turn onto the main road. He dared another glance towards the house. He was thirsty, but the pump would do fine for now. Then he realized Jenny Schwartz was stomping his way across the yard with a glass in her hand and Mary May miles behind her. *Not today.* He shrugged.

Mary May wore no smile, just as she had when Rebecca had lived here. A man could learn a lot about people by the way a small child viewed upon them first.

Jenny's mouth began speaking long before she had reached him. "Hazel says she needs no help, but she has so much to do, and at her age—" She took a winded breath. "I am certain it is more than she can handle. I would like to help. Perhaps look after the *kinner* today."

"Hazel can outwork both of us. She needs no help. Besides, the children have chores to do."

"Surely I can see over Mary May." Jenny smiled down at

Mary May.

"That won't be necessary. I'm sure your *mudder* would appreciate you at home. Doesn't she also help with the fundraiser?" Silas removed his hat and brushed it on his britches leg.

"I just thought with Lydia running off all the time and courting and all, I could get to know the *kinner* better."

Silas refrained from reacting to her abrupt comment, which he suspected was her reasoning for it in the first place. "You know them as well as any in our community," he said.

"You know what I mean." Jenny smiled, her dress swaying as if she were nineteen again.

Silas was never in favor of women who liked to play coy. "Lydia tends to the children. Hazel too when she gets a day off." His tone was solid, leaving no room for misunderstanding.

"She cut Mary May's hair, you know. Tried to hide it from you, but we all seen it. You know she will leave. She will take on this little charity like she does all the others and wisp away like she always does. I know what is necessary to see a thing through. I would never do such a foolish thing without your consent, of course."

"I am aware of Mary May's hair, and I don't need what you consider necessary. *Danki*, but today is not a *gut* day for company. I have things to do and suspect you do too. Mary May will be helping me." His daughter's eyes beamed in sparkling blue. Leaning over, Silas swept her up and into his arms and strolled away from Jenny Schwartz and her need to intrude on the lives of others.

"So, my little one," Silas said, twirling a finger around a short, thick curl of hair, "how did this happen?"

Lydia brushed out her damp, long hair, fifty strokes just as

Mudder had taught her as a child. She hoped she had not made a mistake agreeing to see Andy again.

The children were all tucked in for the night, and not dreaming of Jenny Schwartz being their *mudder*. Lydia hoped. She shuddered to think of it, but there was nothing she could do to change that. Mary May had all but told her how Jenny wanted to take her to a quilting bee tomorrow. A quilting bee Lydia was certain not to attend now.

She coiled her hair carefully and secured it before placing the prayer covering over her head. The deep blue of her dress matched her eyes. It had been her favorite to wear for church Sunday. Lydia slipped out of her room towards the door of the little *dawdi haus*.

"He is not replacing you. The *kinner* love you." Her *mudder*'s voice called out from the nearby bedroom. Lydia stepped into the doorway, both hands grasping the other. Hazel was propped up in her bed, Bible on her lap. The flicker of lamplight illuminated a few silver strands blended with her natural brown color. "I know my *dochder*. Just because I told you about Jenny's visit today shouldn't make you want to do something foolish. Silas would never want you to leave here. You are meeting Andy tonight, *jah?*" Her mother grinned.

"You cannot know what Silas wants. I don't think he even knows, but if he were to marry her, we will have no cause to be here any longer. I must consider *our* future. Your future as well." Could *Mudder* not see her future was insecure here?

Hazel chuckled. "I am blessed to have a child who worries over me so." Hazel waved a finger at her. "And you are thinking ahead too far, following one path because you think it the right one. Let *Gott* show you the one He wants for you."

God was leading her, Lydia wanted to say. Why else would Andy be here?

A light caught her eyes out her *mudder*'s window, and she

realized it must be Andy waiting for her. "I must go." Turning, she paused. "Could you pour the feeders out tomorrow? They should be tossed away. It was stupid to hang them here anyways." Before her mother could reply, Lydia ran out into the night.

In the backdrop of a fiery sunset, Andy veered the horse onto the county road. She glanced over and took in the full look of him. He wore dark trousers and a crisp blue shirt. She preferred suspenders on a man. He also smelled of musk, the kind the *Englisch* driver wore. The one many turned to when Karen wasn't available.

"I thought after ice cream we could take a drive over by the lake just like we used to." She had agreed to spend some time with him, but the idea of a late-night drive around Twin Fork Lake with Andy made her uncomfortable.

"I think ice cream would be nice, but if you don't mind, I would like to return early tonight. I have much to do *kumm* morning." She had children to tend to, laundry and mending, and seeds to sow. There would be color on that farm if it were the last thing she did. *For the children.*

"I'll take any time you will give me." Andy floated her a smile. At eighteen, she imagined a life with him. Now, she needed to know if she could trust him to stick around.

At the ice cream diner, Andy jumped out of the buggy to fetch them both a treat and returned, presenting her with a chocolate mint cone. Not her preferred flavor, but if she could eat Lily Peachy's chicken and tomato casserole at gatherings, Lydia could manage to eat one small ice cream cone.

"I remembered your favorite," Andy boasted and offered a flirty smile. They had shared ice cream at the diner three times years ago, and each time she had eaten butter pecan. She wouldn't begrudge his forgetting after four years.

"Rumor is Jenny Schwartz and Silas are courting. You think they may have a Christmas wedding?"

She was mid-bite when the question came. She choked on the hard swallow it forced upon her. When did Silas find time to court?

"Are you okay?"

"*Jah*," she spit the bite out and quickly brought a napkin to her mouth.

"You always did like ice cream." Andy used his napkin to reach over and swipe her chin.

They sat eating ice cream and watching locals mill about, but Lydia could only think of the children. Silas was a grown man. He could court and marry and do whatever he saw fit.

But the children.

She shivered. Would seeing them at church and gatherings be enough? And who would tuck them in at night, read them stories?

"Do you think we could go now? I really am tired this evening." All the way home, Andy talked of his sister's new *boppli*, of his work in his *onkel*'s buggy shop, and of his willingness to start taking Bishop Schwartz's baptismal classes. Andy never tired of talking. Moonlight had brightened everything in sight and made the night look beautiful. She wanted to enjoy the ride, this time alone with him after all this time. Instead, she found his talk of their time apart hurtful. He had lived a whole life without her, and while he was doing so, she suffered heartbreak after heartbreak.

When they pulled into the drive, Andy stopped just a few feet beyond the mailbox. "Let me help you down." Andy came to her side of the buggy and lifted Lydia to the ground. His hands remained holding her waist as he paused, looking down into her eyes. It was a look of wanting coated in confidence.

For a moment she considered that long-awaited kiss. She had dreamed about it so many nights. Then she remembered the promise she had made to herself when he left. She took a step to the side, and his hands fell away from touching her. Twenty-three and she had never been kissed. Hannah had teased her more than once about that. What was wrong with her? Here *Gott* was laying opportunity at her feet, and she was wasting precious time. It was just a kiss.

"I should go," she said.

"At least let me walk you all the way to the house." He offered her a hand.

She stared at his outstretched hand with a mingle of emotions. She loved him once and yet, nothing about tonight felt familiar. There were no butterflies or nerves, only unease. Andy was trying, she could see that. He said he had changed. Perhaps he wasn't the only one.

Andy nodded, sensing her hesitation. "It's okay Lydi. Take all the time you need."

"*Danki* for the ice cream."

He tipped his straw hat curtly and climbed back into his buggy.

"*Gut nacht,* Lydi."

Watching Andy drive away, she hoped she hadn't just let her only chance ride away.

She took her time strolling down the drive. Fresh air did wonders for a cluttered mind her mother always said. Frogs sang in the distance. Cage nickered in his corral. She lifted her head, spied the stars, and felt so small.

She took a second glance at the main house. A light flickered over barren walls in the top bedroom window in the distance. At ten at night, the children surely wouldn't still be awake. She picked up her pace, hoping no one had fallen ill in her absence. *Once I wrap my head around this, accept Andy as my future, how will I tell the children goodbye? Gott* remained silent to her question.

Gravel crushed under her shoes, and she suddenly recognized it was Silas's window that held the light. He was up. She stared at the window for longer than she should have, wondering what troubled his thoughts tonight. The man was

a mystery wrapped up in warm hazel eyes, lips that were to-
tally kissable, and rough hands that touched tenderly. The
lantern faded away until it was out. Had he waited for her
return? Just the thought that he had waited up for her, awakened every nerve in her body. She placed a hand to her chest,
but it did nothing to slow her racing heart.

He didn't need light to maneuver around the house, but at
the sound of Mary May's whimpering seeping into his room,
he grabbed up the lamp and hurried down the hall to her.
He stepped toward her little twin-sized bed, noting she was
in fact asleep. Something had disrupted her innocent dreams
tonight. He had his ideas but pushed them away as he
brushed the hair from her face with his fingertips. He lingered on the shortened curl.

She snuggled deeper into the quilt, and he tucked it
around her. Standing, he saw a light out the window bouncing down the drive, telling him that Lydia had returned.

He remembered courting, sometimes not returning
home to sneak back into bed before daybreak. This was a
good sign.

He crept back into his room and dimmed the lantern until the light was extinguished. Moonlight revealed the shadows and he leaned on the window frame to take in the slim
shadowy figure strolling down the drive.

When she glanced up, Silas held still. She probably
couldn't see him, but he waited until she continued around
the house before slipping back under the covers.

He didn't want to think of Andy Weaver kissing her good
night, tainting those fragile lips. Andy had probably kissed
those lips plenty. He shouldn't care. If he was what made
her happy, he shouldn't care, but he did. He knew by heart
the ruddy lines of her mouth. He had memorized the

contours and changes. When she was angry, they grew taunt into a firm line, when frustrated, they separated to expel a hard breath. He would be lying if he said he hadn't been thinking what kissing her would be like. It would be in his best interest to assume she tasted bitter, soured by what life had thrown at her. He should do more thinking like that. Maybe it would help him rid his mind of her.

CHAPTER SIXTEEN

"Shh. He will eat when he wakes," Lydia whispered to the children as she readied a plate for Silas. She made sure there were no eggs and covered his plate with a hand towel. *Mudder* had left right after the morning meal to visit with Ben Troyer today. It had been months since she had taken a turn with the elderly man.

Off Sunday, a Sunday without church would have given Silas a full day with his children. Considering he was still in his room sleeping at this hour, Lydia would be happy to spend the time with them. If what Andy said was true, Lydia wanted to enjoy every moment she could with them.

"You all finish your chores, and I will pack a picnic." Three sets of eyes beamed at the idea.

"Can we go to the pond today? Fish a little too?" Aiden whispered. He had shed his quiet nature, and she warmed each time he let the child in himself emerge.

"That is a *gut* idea, Aiden. *Jah*. We will go fishing." She lifted a pail of milk onto the counter from this morning's milking and stifled a laugh when his smile widened. "Be sure to catch a few worms after you feed the animals." She couldn't remember the last time she had gone fishing. "I'll strain all the milk and find a blanket and a basket. Get going. You got me all excited to go fishing now." Lydia urged them to get a move on, shooing them forward with her hands. Aiden scooped up his straw hat and headed out the door, with Gideon shadowing.

There were moments Aiden resembled his father in so many ways she could almost imagine a young Silas.

Some girl is going to be blessed one day.

Lydia just hoped she was worthy.

Silas opened one eye, then the other. The sun peeked through his south-facing window. Warm streams of light crossed the room. He lifted his arms out from under the thin quilt, stretched, and smiled. When was the last time he simply slept?

The house was quiet. Months ago, it wouldn't have felt strange. Nowadays, it didn't feel normal. He rolled out of the bed and slipped into fresh clothes.

Downstairs was as quiet as upstairs had been. There was no sign of Hazel, Lydia, or his children. At his seat at the head of the table was a tattered blue dishcloth with a folded paper on top. He plucked the paper up between thumb and finger and then lifted the cloth to find a full plate of sausage, potatoes, and a biscuit. He unfolded the paper.

Gone Fishing, sleep well.
L.

"Fishing huh?" Silas grinned, scratching his bristly jawline. Fishing sounded perfect. A lot better than golfing. He hurried and wolfed down a piece of sausage and a few forkfuls of potatoes. Then he quickly smothered Hazel's raspberry jelly on a biscuit before heading to the barn. He hoped they had taken working fishing poles and not the ones he had neglected to fix.

Silas crossed the pasture at the lower end of the property, two newly strung fishing poles in one hand, a cup of worms in the other. He slowed to the sounds of Lydia and the children singing a familiar hymn. Within the walls of an open house or barn, the words were woeful, reminders of what their people had once endured. Today in the open air where red-winged blackbirds clustered in cedars and emerald-green painted the landscape, the words sounded hopeful. He shook his head. *Funny how that works.*

The beautiful blend of Lydia and his children's voices lured him closer just as he suspected it would any wild thing within earshot. It was Aiden's voice that surprised him the most. Strong and loud, so unlike the boy. Silas listened to each word carry over a lazy May wind. When they came to the end, he moved forward.

"*Daed!*" Of course, Aiden saw him approach first. His son had a talent for noticing things even he missed. "We were going to fish but only one fishing pole works. Lydi tried fixing it, but we agreed to share." Silas held up the two extra poles and smiled.

"*Daed* saves the day," Lydia said. Her cheery voice was a balm to his heart.

"Now let us get a worm on these and see if we can catch a bit of supper." Silas bent to one knee and readied each of the poles.

"Where did you find such fat worms? Ours are skinny," Aiden said, poking around into the tin can he brought.

"It is a secret." Silas grinned. "You catch a big one, and I will tell you."

"I will."

Gideon puffed out his chest, ready to be the one to get the secret and a fish, first. Silas guided Mary May to a hollowed-out area so there was less chance of her tumbling into the cold water. He could feel Lydia's eyes on him, but he kept his focus on the children. It was only fair she took in the full measure of him, considering how many times he had done the same of her.

With the children settled nearby, Silas turned and strolled over to where Lydia sat on a tattered quilt that must belong to her. Jana had never been one who liked flowery patterns.

"May I?" He pointed next to her, and Lydia nodded for him to sit down. Removing his straw hat and setting it aside, he sat. He took the liberty to glance her way. The sun shimmered off the blond hairs peeking out from under her *kapp*. He had never noticed her small, perfectly placed ears before.

He turned back to the children, willing his senses to get ahold of themselves. Other than the day at the sink when he'd wanted to ask her to join them for supper, this was as close as he had been to her. It was more than attraction, this thing pulling and tugging at his heart. It was more than a man who knew the benefits of marriage and missed them. It was her. She was home, a crisp fire on a winter's night, a warm quilt made for curling into. She was laughter and energy and a million other things he couldn't lay a name to.

"They are happy. I know how you have worried, but you shouldn't."

He studied each of them and smiled. He couldn't agree more. "You and Hazel had a hand in that." It was a small compliment that earned him a bashful smile. Running his fingers over the tight stitches holding the quilt intact, he thought about each of the children and how losing Jana had affected them.

"Aiden remembers her. Gideon tries but has a hard time. Mary May has no memory of a *mudder*, except for Rebecca." They both made a sour expression at the same time.

"Well, at least she was here for them. I am sure she did her best," Lydia said. She was being kind to assume such.

Rebecca did as little as she had to. Unlike Hazel and Lydia, who had taken on this position as if lives depended on it. "Jah, it is important to have love around you when you have lost someone." Their gazes held. He tried to think back to that time before he suffered his own loss when she felt the world crashing down on her.

"You miss Jana, don't you?"

Taken back by her question, Silas stiffened. Honesty was always the best way to handle all matters in life. "At first, every day."

"And now?" Her gaze lingered on the children, not him.

He wished he could read her, understand what encouraged her to be sitting here and talking with him as if they were dear friends instead of…whatever they were.

"Hazel has been a great example of how one can move forward."

"*Mudder* understands a lot."

She looked down at her hands and he noted the blade of dry grass rolling between her fingers.

"So, are you moving forward?"

Her curiosity made him smile. Crossing his legs at the ankle, Silas leaned back on his elbows. A light wind carried Lydia's scent closer. Honey and something he couldn't put a finger on. He drank it deep into his lungs. "As you are it would seem."

Her fingers stopped fidgeting with grass, and she began that little habit of hers of twisting her dress like a nervous child.

"I'm not sure if forward is the right direction for me, but I think Mary Hicky is a very kind woman."

Lydia now fingered the quilt threads for distraction. This was sweet, watching her toy in thoughts.

"Have you ever considered Mary as someone you could…care for?"

He shot her a grimace. "Mary and I are friends. You should leave the matchmaking to your *mudder*. It doesn't suit you." That playful shrug of her shoulders and half-smile had him thinking about kissing again.

How had no young man ever gotten ahold of her? 'Cause, she is never still, that's why.

Then again, here she sat, like a hummingbird perched on

a branch, next to him.

"I do feel that forward might be the direction I want to go." He waited for her response.

"*Ach*, Jenny. Guess I already knew that." Her voice clipped.

"Why would you think that?" Had he not shown all the signs of a man uninterested in Jenny Schwartz?

"She is always present for one." Lydia snorted. "It's no secret that she likes you, and she is very pretty."

Silas recognized the familiar sharpness in her tone.

"She helped raise her *bruders*. Obviously knows how to care for *kinner*."

Yeah, Silas knew all about the Schwartz boys and their menacing, from shattered mailboxes to snakes in the Hilty barn before a church Sunday.

He snickered. "What about you and Andy?"

"What about him?" Her lips flattened as she glared at him.

"Never mind. You have every right to speak with anyone you choose."

"As do you. And if you have plans for your future, it would be *gut* to know, for *Mudder*'s sake."

"I have no plans, and you and Hazel need not make any." He didn't want her running off before he could explore this thing between them. "The children are happy with how things are. In fact," he ran a hand along his beard hoping his next words would be welcomed. "I would like…"

"*Daed*. I got one," Gideon yelled, stealing the moment.

Silas looked up as Gideon dragged his pole, fish attached, toward him. Silas unhooked the bluegill from the hook. "Not big enough for supper." Silas tossed it back into the water.

"Lydi," Mary May said, coming to her with open arms.

"Someone is sleepy." Lydia pulled her into her lap.

He watched his daughter curl into Lydia's arms. He cast the fishing line for Gideon and returned to the quilt. He would have to thank his daughter later for keeping Lydia still. For a few moments, they sat in silence, watching the boys on the pond bank. When he glanced over at the woman, her delicate fingers were tucking Mary May's short strands into her prayer covering.

A few moments slipped by when Lydia shifted beside him.

"I should leave," Lydia said, sliding a sleeping Mary May toward him.

"You cannot remain still for more than a minute, can you?"

Her nose flared at the question and she got to her feet. Silas also stood.

"I'm sorry." He blew out a breath. "About the other day. I should have never spoken to you that way."

"Well, you were right."

Her neck leaned back as she gazed up to him, and he couldn't help but take in the slenderness of it.

"I am no *mudder*, nor have I helped raise siblings, but I was prepared. I picked up the medicines after the first day I took them to *Aenti* May's farm, just in case. I would have never put them in danger."

"I don't think little of you. Quite the opposite, actually." He studied her. Could she not see she was filling his every minute, stealing his rest? As she searched his eyes for truth, he searched hers for hope.

The rise and fall of her chest as they stood just feet apart, had him thinking about kissing again. Those lips needed kissing. The thought sent a warm surge through his veins.

"I...I should leave you to spend a day with your *kinner*." She took a step back.

"Don't."

"They are the reason I'm here, after all." With a quick pivot, she turned and ran away.

He almost had her and she flew off again. He could only watch her leave—a habit he was no longer enjoying.

"Ouch," Gideon yelled.

"What did you do?" Silas inspected the hand Gideon held high towards him.

"The grass cut me like knives. It burns." He whined, but no tears were present. "I need honey."

"Honey?"

"*Jah*, because honey cures everything," Aiden said with a hint of humor in his voice. "They put it on my scratches when I slid down the steps at school, and look"—he raised a pant leg—"not a mark left."

If only all life's troubles could be fixed with a bit of honey.

"Lydia and Hazel are wise. I'm sure they know a lot of ways to mend a thing torn."

"Lydia tells us all kinds of things you know. In case she has to move away if you ever decide you don't want her anymore."

That made Silas's heart drop, a few degrees shy of broken. He couldn't imagine not wanting her and was she saying these things to his children because she was planning to leave?

"I think that's why she likes to read to us so much."

"Makes sense. What kind of things does she like to talk about?"

"You know, stuff. Like how we should never tell lies or run off without telling her where we are going." Aiden gave his brother a pinned look.

"She says that sweets aren't good for breakfast, but she puts sugar in my oatmeal," Gideon said.

"She said there are things we should do and enjoy while we are young. Things not permitted after we join the church." Aiden fingered his fishing pole.

"Not sure I like the sounds of that."

"She says there are bad things, like smoking and using firecrackers in mailboxes that we should never do no matter how tempting. That what we do has…" Aiden blinked and glanced away.

"Consequences." Gideon rolled his eyes. "But dancing is not so bad." He shrugged.

"Dancing?" Silas cocked his head.

"Well, she said dancing was the one thing she wished she did. It was not a terrible thing, and Jesus even talked about it."

Ecclesiastes, if memory served him right.

"But she said that a *gut* Amish man follows the rules even if he can break them. That's what makes him a man who serves *Gott*."

He stared at his eldest son. Silas had certainly underestimated the hummingbird. There were no words for how he felt right now.

"Lydia says we should try it. It's not just for girls." Gideon seemed doubtful.

"She said we *could* try it once before joining the church. That it should be our only bad thing to ever do, ever," Aiden said.

Silas could think of worse advice. Lord knew too well how he'd tested dirty waters in his runaround years.

"She said all of that, did she?" Silas scratched his beard. *To everything, there is a season.* "What other things does Lydia say?"

CHAPTER SEVENTEEN

Monday morning Silas walked into the kitchen to find Hazel readying breakfast.

"Heard you moving about," she said offering him a plate. "Lydia says you prefer potatoes with your breakfast."

"I do," he said and then bowed his head in prayer.

He was in no rush to hitch Jippy and leave for work, so he took his time eating, devouring every delicious bite. The kitchen window was lifted a bit, letting in a cool whiff of morning air. It was amazing what a full night's sleep did to a man's mood.

He had dreamed again. This time he and Lydia were fishing. She wasn't a child, nor giggling, but just as plain in his dream as she had been on the blanket beside him at the pond. She didn't fly away. Instead, she stayed, and they talked about children, about honey and horses. They talked about dancing and how the Lord healed broken hearts.

"Where's your little hummingbird today?" The nickname was fitting, but he hadn't intended on using it aloud.

"You finished your eggs. How nice," Hazel said, scraping grease from an iron skillet into a jar.

"Was I not supposed to?" The way Hazel said it, Silas

wasn't certain.

"You rarely do is all."

If Silas didn't know any better, something was eating at Hazel this morning.

"I only cooked eggs before you came. Never was one for cooking. Guess I got a bit soured by them." That caused her to perk up.

"I know a *hummingbird* who would be glad to know that's the reason."

Now he was confused.

"It would be *gut* for Lydia to know you appreciate her cooking." Hazel lifted a sharp brow. "All want to feel appreciated."

Silas hadn't paid attention, but now some of the glares that passed in his direction during the past weeks made perfect sense. He had never considered telling her he was tired of eggs. No wonder breakfast earned him so many sharp looks. "I will make sure to tell her," he said and readied to leave.

"Ben Troyer's," Hazel said as she began washing the dishes, her back to him.

"Huh?"

"She went to see Ben and take him breakfast early. I agreed to stay home today now that we have more help at the bakery. My Lydia has a long day planned. Always busy that one."

"I've noticed."

"I don't expect to see her until supper." He wondered what plans she had, but he didn't dare ask. Walking to the door, he pulled his straw hat from the hook, put it on his head, and turned the knob.

"Hazel, if it is not much trouble—" He turned to face her. "Hang those feeders back up. I kind of like all this buzzing about." With a smirk, Silas walked out into the warming May morning feeling he had a few duties to tend to himself.

Silas hummed all through his day and before he knew it,

he had finished one whole brick border wall for the new office building. Around the site, suited men in hardhats milled about. Their eyes searched while their hands held clipboards. He figured a job as big as a five-story building might warrant for inspections and paid no mind to them. For the first time in a while, he looked forward to the end of his day, returning home to his family. To her. Only when he got there, Silas grasped Hazel had been right. Lydia had still not come home.

Once he put Jippy out to pasture, Silas checked on the children before heading to the barn. All three were playing volleyball while Hazel removed laundry from the line.

A shimmery green hummingbird darted across his path and he tipped his hat. He'd seen this one already before the feeders were taken down. "Glad to see you back." Now if only his hummingbird would return.

If Lydia had taught him one thing, time was best used in being busy. He couldn't shake the concern that she was away from the farm, not knowing if she was company to an eighty-year-old man needing a friend or a young man needing a *fraa*. Andy Weaver was an obstacle. One that shared a history with her that Silas didn't. But Silas took the liberty to ask around and found out the fella hadn't no job and was living off the goodness of his *onkel*. Gaven Weaver was not one to tolerate slackers.

Silas stepped into the barn to retrieve a saddle. It was time. *Time to take chances.* One mean old horse might as well be first in line.

An hour and a few bruises to his pride later, Silas unsaddled Cage and limped back towards the barn. When a buggy approach, Silas's heart kicked up a notch. Either Lydia had an escort home this evening—he sighed at the possibility—or Jenny was making another uninvited visit. Did she not realize that some men like to pursue and not be pursued? That if a man was interested, he welcomed the chase. Whatever happened to doing things the proper way?

Dropping the saddle and blanket to the barn floor, he leaned against the ladder to the loft, deciding whether to step out or remain inside the barn. His luck, trouble came either way. Silas had managed to get into the saddle today. Not much more than get in it before Cage bucked him off, but he did make it that far. Whatever awaited him on the other side of the barn door, he could handle too.

He stepped out, closed the large door, and turned to find Andy watching his exit with a discerning brow. Lydia must have gone inside. Had they spent the whole day together? His heart sank a little deeper in his chest.

"I see you brought Lydia home safe again." Silas stared up at Andy sitting high in the buggy seat.

"Lydia is not with me. I thought maybe she was with you." Andy's tone was no friendlier than Silas's had been. *Gut, no golfing, but not here.*

"*Nee.* Hazel will know of her whereabouts." He crossed both arms over his chest. "If you must know." He eyed Andy with distaste.

"I must. I don't like this arrangement Hazel and the Bishop has forced Lydia into." Andy tried to appear confident, stiffening his shoulders.

Silas chuckled. "If you knew Lydia, you should know she is not easily forced into anything."

"I plan to marry her," Andy said.

Silas at least appreciated that of him. "*Jah.* Well, plans are nice to have. All the best intentions start that way." They locked glares, neither willing to say what troubled each of their thoughts.

"You should know. In case you were thinking otherwise," Andy said, his knuckles turning white as he gripped the reins.

Silas remained steadfast, saying nothing to them otherwise. "I assume you have found work and possibly a home to offer then? Are you joining the church as well?"

Andy's face tightened, as did his firm grip around the

leather reins of his *onkel's* horse. The man didn't even have his own horse. It was good the children were with Hazel right now.

"I'm working on it," Andy said between clenched teeth.

That's when Silas realized he had a bit of an advantage after all. He had work, a home, and had joined the same church as Lydia and all her family had. But was he the kind of man who would use the advantage? Was it not their way to accept Gott's will in all matters?

Both men turned when they heard crunching gravel. Lydia, on her robin egg blue bike with her azure blue dress and sunflower smile, came bouncing down the lane, unaware of the two men at the barn both gawking in her direction.

Silas narrowed in on his target. She was a contrary woman, all stubborn, wild, and defiant most of the time. Yet she was all Lydia, beautiful, kind, and captivating. Andy's head turned to meet Silas's gaze once more and Silas presented him with a challenging grin. Like Cage, a restless creature needing something four walls couldn't provide alone, Lydia wanted to be free. From what Silas hadn't put a finger on yet, but he would. The horse had been the kind of challenge Silas had never encountered, but he was softening. He inhaled deep and turned to focus on Lydia coming their way.

It was such a bad idea, a terrible idea, and yet he walked away from the young man who had once broken Lydia's heart with a smile that said, *Challenge welcomed.*

"You want to walk right now?" Lydia asked Andy again. She wondered what he and Silas had been talking about when she rode up but thought it best not to ask. Things were shifting with Silas. And though she knew nothing would come of it, it didn't change how he made her feel.

Andy gawked at her as if she had forgotten her promise.

"I have to help *Mudder* with supper and bathe the children. I have been gone all day." She was weary to the bone, that's what she was.

"I see. Where have you been all day?" He crossed his arms over his chest.

Leaning her bike just inside the barn door, Lydia took a slow breath. Somewhere in the back of the barn, she could hear Silas moving about.

"Everywhere," she said and moved out into the sun. "I cleaned Ben Troyer's *haus* and restocked his pantries. I delivered cookies for *Mammi* Rose to the bank for customer appreciation day, twice"—she held up two fingers—"and helped *Aenti* May pack for a trip to Indiana after helping her hoe her garden."

"You agreed we can spend some time together today."

She didn't want to walk another inch. What she wanted right now were a hot bath and a soft pillow. "I have responsibilities."

"Lydia, I am trying here. Can't you try too? I don't want to share you with the widower Graber and his *kinner*."

She gasped. "Share me?"

"I want you. Want you for my own. This is our chance. We could have a family of our own."

She wanted that, a family. She wanted what her sisters had, what she watched her parents have. And here it stood, waiting for her to take hold. She hesitated. Not sure what she wanted to say. She focused on her feet, one hand clenching the side of her dress.

"Forgive me." He was begging, in his own way.

"I do." Because holding on to the hurt was harder, more distracting, than letting it go. When she glanced up again, Andy caressed her cheek and planted a kiss on it.

"*Danki,* Lydia. That means a lot. I'll leave you now to tend to the *kinner* and get some rest, but I will return tomorrow and every day after if that's what it takes."

Lydia watched Andy ride away. Touching her cheek, she

wondered if this was what God wanted for her. She cared for Andy, and maybe they could have a good life together, but where was the spark her sisters spoke of? That spark she felt…when hazel eyes looked down on her?

After supper, *Mudder* sat at the table with the children for a game of Blitz. Face cards were forbidden among the Amish. A game where four players picked one stack of cards. They could choose from a plow, bucket, pump, or buggy. Gideon always chose the buggy stack. Everyone then laid out three single cards in front of them, face up, and a pile of ten with only the top card's face showing. This was the Blitz pile. The rest of the stack you held in your hand, which Mary May often struggled with.

Lydia poured herself a cup of *kaffi* and waited for the signal—"Go!" Once they started going through their stack by threes, searching for a matching color for their selected card, Lydia slipped out the door. The game of quick hand and eye usually came down to Aiden shouting *Blitz!* first.

Days were getting longer, nights shorter. Lydia found a seat at the end of the porch and settled. Her mind ran amuck with thoughts of Andy. He was trying, she'd give him that. Once upon a time, his promises had filled her with hope. Now she wasn't sure what she felt.

She thought about the kiss on her cheek, the lack of spark. Even when he helped her into the buggy, she hadn't felt it when their hands touched. His hands were soft and warm like a new quilt.

Maybe she didn't deserve love. After all, she had been the sole cause of her *mudder*'s loss of it. She shoved that guilt aside.

"Stop thinking so much." She took a deep breath of warm evening air. It smelled of him, after a long day working the horses. She gripped her cup a bit tighter and looked up as the moon and sun shared the same sky. Soon the moon would win over, and she hoped to wait and watch the exchange in full.

Silas's deep voice drew her, and she scooted her chair to the end of the porch to watch him work Cage this evening. The man had a voice that was capable of intimidating or assuring, but right now intimidation was getting the upper hand as he tried willing a beast ten times his size into submission. She doubted either worked on that ornery horse. It was late for Silas to be out saddling Cage. She would never understand this trade he preferred over the safety of building walls.

Horses were unpredictable creatures and seldom obeyed if given the mind to. Despite the scene, the way her heart kicked up its pace watching the children's father put his life at unnecessary risk, Lydia couldn't pull her eyes away either.

Cage ran in circles around Silas, a thin line of leather connecting them. The saddle bounced in sync with Cage's rebellion of it. His massive body of horseflesh was lathered and as determined as the man working him who also wore dampened lines of sweat along his strong back. It was kind of mesmerizing, the way the western horizon laid her red and purple hues down on them.

Neither wanted to submit, both holding on to what control they presumed they had. They both needed to blow off some steam and wear down what ate at them. Lydia understood that part of it. A hard day's work did wonders for troubles. Man and beast stilled for a moment, catching their breaths.

Silas reached over the horse, adjusting something, she wasn't sure what. This presented a pleasant rear view clad in blue. Lydia cocked her head, biting the inside of her cheek. He was a well-made man. Not just handsome and hardworking, but also tender.

In an unexpected and powerful move, Silas tossed his hat out of the corral and jumped onto Cage's back. Lydia jolted upright. She watched wide-eyed, her breath racing as Cage made every attempt to relieve himself of the man on his back. Silas was just as stubborn, holding firm, neither willing to concede. A gasp escaped her when Silas's leg banged against the metal gates forming the arena. She could hear both Cage's deep pants and Silas's firm grunts as they reared and came down hard.

"Please Lord, keep him safe." She muttered the prayer and clapped a hand over her heart. God would not be so cruel as have her witness such a tragedy twice in one lifetime. At least that was Lydia's hope because she couldn't turn away.

The ripple of the horse's mane danced like a purposeful wave framed in the deep sounds of Silas urging the beast to comply. His own dark hair swayed in unpredicted waves. Sleeves rolled to his elbows, tanned forearms strong, he was strong, his muscles without exaggeration. She hoped strong enough to endure what her heart wasn't sure it could right now. The longer she watched, the more she learned. Silas Graber didn't give up, held on no matter how Cage tried to rid himself of him. *He holds on.*

Fear and captivation lured her towards the top of the porch steps. Cage whirled around a third time, bringing Silas into view again. She froze, dumbfounded about what to make of it all. Silas was smiling. It took her a moment, but soon she understood it was that male need, that surge of power taming a wild animal. That feeling of letting go that she had yet to find herself.

She hadn't remembered coming to her feet, but when her legs became unsteady, she leaned on a post for support. Cage bucked and bounced, gaining a second wind, but Silas held steady, rocking with him. She forgot to breathe as the two separate beasts fought for power. The raw determination dancing inside the small corral was intoxicating.

What would it be like to be that brave? So unwilling to fail? The air wasn't that warm, and yet she could feel beads of moisture trickle down her spine. Any other day she would refuse to watch Silas working with the horses, protecting herself and the children from ever seeing the things she'd once seen and couldn't forget. Tonight, she couldn't avert her gaze, even if she should.

She was starting to like Cage. However, it was the man she hoped to witness become victor. A man who was equally stubborn to hold on to something until it bent to his will.

CHAPTER EIGHTEEN

Every family took their turn at hosting the bi-weekly church service. This week, Silas walked into the Zook's barn with two pies in his hands and five shadows trailing behind him. It felt different than before. He could enjoy this again.

All throughout the three-hour service, he did well to pay attention to the message and not the woman sitting directly across the room. Mary May's wrinkling nose and clinging arms validated her own affections.

After the final prayer ended, Silas rose to his feet and walked to his family, taking Mary May from Lydia's arms. She had to be tired of holding her this long.

"If she has to go, you know, just bring her back. I don't mind taking her," Lydia said and hurried away to help the women ready the fellowship meal.

"Hello, Silas." Thomas walked up to join him as he stepped outside. "*Gut* Lord's day, *jah*."

"It is a beautiful day, *jah*." Walking out into the open air, Silas put Mary May down, but she continued to cling to his leg.

"I have been meaning to speak to you of a few important matters."

"Which are?"

"Rumors of Andy Weaver's intentions have reached the grapevine."

Silas had firsthand knowledge of these such rumors. If Thomas's intentions were to inquire of Lydia, he would give him nothing if it meant Thomas thrashing Lydia with his newfound temper.

"If the bishop says he is taking classes, then maybe he is ready to submit, but I hope you will let the bishop know if she is dating an unbaptized man," Thomas said. "If she is setting a bad example for the *kinner* of this community, I should know so that it is dealt with swiftly."

"I know the rules," Silas said.

"*Gut.*" Thomas puffed out his chest mimicking a banty rooster ready to impress. "Not sure I trust that fella to not take her and just run off. He said he was ready once before you know." Thomas Miller's red beard glistened in the sunlight the same as the hairs on his head when he removed his hat to wipe his sweaty brow.

Silas whipped to face him. "Lydia would not do that. She could never leave Hazel or her community." *Or my children.* The way she poured over them, he knew she couldn't just leave. If only she felt the same of him.

"Not sure I agree. She has always been…different, more rebellious."

Silas fended off a laugh. Lydia was different, but not in the ways Thomas was implying.

"Hate to see her do something stupid and get herself shunned. I think that fella is just buying time."

"What do you mean?"

"Andy caused quite a stir in Ohio from what his *onkel* tells. I stand by my words that he won't commit to nothing here very long. He will break her heart, like the ones broken there, or he will take her away. I cannot tell you how this concerns me. As deacon now, I have many responsibilities. Tending to Joseph's widow has been a challenge but part of it I guess." Thomas sighed again. "If Lydia marries that man, who has no home, no means to provide for her, and that wandering eye of his, it won't be long before I will have to take them all into my *haus*. Libby cannot handle no more with her sister and *boppli* already underfoot."

This was about Thomas's fears of doing what was rightfully his job to do. Silas did well to control his growing temper and remember Thomas was chosen by lot. He too was doing his best and nothing more than a mere man.

"I welcomed them into my *haus* and have every intention to honor that responsibility. You needn't worry. Hazel and Lydia will be provided for."

Thomas slapped him on the back. "I had a feeling I could count on you, Silas Graber," he said and walked away in a hurry.

Indeed. Silas watched as the deacon strolled away. Yes, bringing these women into his life had been a desperate plan made by a few, all having a different goal. Thomas's goal was delegating his obligation to his brother.

Silas stood alone on the grassy field brooding over his talk with Thomas Miller. The man's intentions had been to pawn off his *bruder*'s family, and still, Silas had accepted the invitation. If he took the time to consider everything, he would have still accepted.

The Miller women had become the family he no longer had, and he adored them. A little more than he should in fact. The idea of Lydia leaving his home, his children, him, sent a long ache through his body that no remedy could soften.

"You look to have a pain in your side."

John's words reached Silas as he watched Lydia help the children start a game of volleyball. "About a hundred-pound pain."

John laughed as his eyes lingered towards Lydia. "She doesn't look to be capable of too much trouble."

Arms crossed, Silas added, "You have no idea."

John chuckled louder. "*Kinner* don't seem to mind. But you do look like a man in pain. What did Thomas want?"

That was John. Getting right to the root of a thing. A few inches shorter and wider, John was not only his brother-in-law but his dearest and closest friend since their scholar years.

"To make sure I would tend to Lydia and her *mudder* so he wouldn't have to," Silas said.

"Figured as much. He has a talent for delegating duties. A natural-born leader, some might say."

Both men chuckled.

Lydia left the game to help ready the meal. As she flew across the yard, chin up, searching, he watched her noting everything that needed to be done. Mary May had been shadowing behind her, a clutch of spoons gripped in both her tiny hands. Lydia came to stop, turned around, and scooped Mary May up onto her hip. After dropping the spoons on the table with the others, they buzzed off again. Jana would be happy to know their daughter had a woman in her life. He hoped she would be just as happy that it was Lydia as he was. Someone she knew and had always thought well of.

"Maybe." Silas shifted, keeping an eye on his boys playing ball and Lydia at the same time. John shifted with him. Squinting against the sun, they watched the women fill the long tables with chicken, beans, potatoes, and other desirable side dishes. Mary May let go and ran toward the house. Silas watched her search Lydia out and smiled.

Lydia flew from table to table. Plates stacked at one end with utensils next to them. She lifted a box and began placing small jars filled with fresh daffodils in the center of each table. When finished, she stood back and took a quick look at her work. Her eyes lifted to meet the bishop's, who was staring in her direction. Silas watched a silent dance pass between them.

Joshua Schwartz's eyes scanned the tables, and then he

nodded, turned, and picked back up the conversation he was having with a group of men. Lydia grinned and scurried away, no doubt feeling a bit victorious right now. It took so little to please her, he had come to learn.

Fellowship and faith flowed like a wide river. Laughter filled the air as the community found the day as perfect as he had. Removing his hat, Silas eyed the pastel-blue sky streaked with white and took in a long breath of a true spring mingled with the aromas of barbequed chicken, baked beans, and happiness. Beside him, John and Michael Schwartz chatted about work and family and eagerness to plant spring gardens. Silas listened, his focus rested on a hummingbird in the distance.

Lydia took a bowl from Rose Glick and received a loving pat from her grandmother before she was gone once again. He chuckled out loud. Did she ever tire?

Then Lydia helped Justa Plank, a small girl, with tying her shoes. Minutes had passed and yet Silas couldn't turn away, as if seeing her for the first time. She disappeared again and reappeared with a little boy on her hip and a pie, a little heavy in meringue, balanced in her palm. She was a hummingbird after all.

Then his hummingbird jerked to a halt when Jenny stepped in line behind her. Without turning, Lydia stopped, pie suspended in mid-air, along with her nose. Her pretty smile sank into a straight, tight line. Like Cage, she had sensed unease, or maybe it was that suffocating lavender scent Jenny cloaked herself in. Silas had always enjoyed the scent of lavender. Jana had often added sprigs from the garden to her oils and shampoo, but Jenny reeked of it to a point of offense.

Lydia was all honey and sunshine, good-hearted, and going out of her way to help others. She did so with such a passion it made one wonder if he was doing good all wrong. He understood now why Hazel insisted that Lydia spend most of her time with the children. Allow her to taste the sweetness of just an ordinary day.

He watched in curiousness, feet apart and arms crossed, at the interaction between the women. Lydia snapped out of whatever had stilled her and slid the pie onto the table with the others, and even though Jenny's mouth was moving, Lydia turned and walked away as if hearing nothing. Silas snorted, and John, whom he had forgotten was near, did too.

"She handles her own too, I see," John said and walked away.

That she does. Silas grinned.

"You look happy." Lydia turned and there stood Hannah, her auburn hair shimmering in the light of Zook's kitchen doorway. Hannah had served as the local teacher this past year, but her family owned a large apple orchard and summers gave her no relief. Hannah had always preferred the outdoors and it had surprised Lydia when she accepted the teaching position last year.

"If we all didn't know better, we would think you've claimed those *kinner* as your own."

Lydia took a sharp intake of breath and glanced about to see if anyone might have heard. "You shouldn't say such things." Hannah was never one to speak softly or do anything with a light touch. In fact, few could outrun, outplay, or outwork Hannah Troyer, and that included most grown men.

The Zook kitchen was spacious, but with forty women bustling about, surely ears had caught the comment.

"Don't get all flushed and bothered," Hannah teased and came to her side. "It's not like we all don't see it."

"You are doing a *wunderbaar* job helping with them Lydia…Hannah is right to say such," Bethany Plank said, stirring a pitcher of fresh tea.

Lydia appreciated the kind words but hoped no one was getting the wrong idea. When she glanced around the room, her eyes locked with Francis. She must miss her daughter, and seeing another woman caring for her granddaughter had to be difficult. Francis picked up a tray with brownie squares stacked high, and with a huff, she scurried out of the kitchen. *Mudder* said she shouldn't let what others think trouble her, but she was a duck out of water. There was no right or wrong way when it came to such delicate matters.

Emma Byler, an older woman who lived just next door, gave Mary May's head a pat as she wisped by. "I think you're *gut* for more than just the *kinner* there," she said, but not low enough.

Lydia's face went crimson as heat flashed to the top of her head.

"Emma," Lydia said shocked by the comment. Was everyone out to embarrass her today? She didn't dare tell her best friend that she had imagined it. What it would be like tending to the children and the man who made her knees tremble every time his eyes caught hers. But Andy had told her about Silas and Jenny courting, so try as she might, she had been keeping her imagination reined in these days.

Lydia closed her eyes. *Lord, please let this day fly before I die of embarrassment*, she prayed before addressing the room of women.

"I am only doing what any of you would have done if you were in my position." Lydia didn't mean to sound defensive.

"Oh, Lydi, relax." Hannah gave her a hug. "No one is trying to embarrass you. We are just saying you are doing a *gut* thing here." She knelt to Mary May's level and tapped her little nose. "Your Lydi is a special woman, and you are lucky to have her."

"*Ach*, Hannah," Lydia warmed at the sentiment despite her dearest friend making a spectacle. "I appreciate all the kind words, but I assure you all, I have no idea what I'm doing most days."

"None of us did at first," Betty Schwartz said as she pulled a large pan of chicken from the oven. "I have five *kinner* and helped raise a nephew. I still rarely get it right." Betty laughed.

"Well, did you know Gideon had a lizard in his pocket today? In church?" Lydia shook her head. "I'm not doing *gut* at all." At least he hadn't untied any shoes lately.

"I saw Aiden at the woodpile before we left and he shoved something into his *bruder*'s pocket," Hazel said with a clipped tone. "Should have known it." She lifted a large plate of chicken and headed for the door. "It's the quiet ones who are always the instigators. I think we have been keeping our eyes on the wrong one."

A few women laughed.

Lydia was stunned. Aiden had never revealed to her he was a trickster. How had she missed that?

When more laughter grew, Lydia gave up trying to look like she was doing her best. She had spent years in similar kitchens, doing her part to help with the fellowship meal, but this was the first time she had felt like one of the women.

"You all remember when Zeb and Maria Schwartz's boys were *kinner*," Mary Hicky said. "I taught all of them as scholars and still would have never suspected them capable."

"Now, Mary, *mei buwe* learned their lesson that day. All was forgiven," Marie said.

"It must have taken those three all night to collect that many apples. I can still see the look on Francis' and Edith's faces now when they opened that outhouse door." Betty, Marie's sister-in-law, guffawed.

Lydia couldn't believe the women were all laughing at such behavior, but she did remember the Schwartz boys and the apple incident when she was twelve. Worse, she remembered the yellowjackets that came to feast on the apples that had somehow managed to fill the outhouse to the brim. No one was perfect, and no children were either. In fact, Lydia bent an ear to hear more.

"And those were my apples," Hannah's mother said, causing more eruptions of laughter.

Lydia's worries about her abilities ebbed, and joy filled her heart. She was in a room with the women of her life, laughing about motherhood. She made a mental note to never forget this moment, right here and now, and that no matter what Silas decided for his own future, she wanted to always be part of the Graber children's lives.

Today had given her a glimpse, an acceptance, and she admitted to herself, she still wanted things she hadn't believed she deserved after her father's death.

And she couldn't see Andy being part of that future. Deep down, she knew she could never trust him, not after breaking her heart as he did. He hadn't even come to church once since his return. Where was he all the time if he was committed to proving his love for her?

"Here, let me take her and go check on the *kinner*," Mary Hicky said as she swooped Mary May up into her arms. "Between *mei kinner* and yours, I figure we should take turns keeping a close eye on them in lots."

Lydia couldn't ignore the comment. Mary had just called Silas's children Lydia's own. It wasn't right to claim another woman's family, and yet Lydia felt a love for each of them as if they were her own.

"I suspect you should help serve the men and see that some handsome widower has plenty of lemonade." Mary winked and stepped out of the kitchen.

The kitchen temperature rose a few degrees higher. Lydia found herself blushing, again.

Hannah leaned closer. "I have missed too much helping *Daed* with the orchard. You best be telling me what that was about."

Lydia shrugged her off. "Maybe after the fellowship meal we can talk." Lydia hoped they had the chance. She wanted to share everything with Hannah.

"For sure and certain we will. If my best friend is falling

in love, I should be the first to know." Hannah picked up two pitchers of tea. "Grab the lemonade." She smiled. "If it matters any, I think he is handsome and more trustworthy than…the one who isn't even here."

CHAPTER NINETEEN

For three days all Silas could think about the way Lydia smiled at him Sunday at the Zooks. Something had changed in her, and he for one welcomed it. He never imagined he could care for someone again, not like he had Jana, but God has a way of showing us what little we know.

The week had been so busy he and Lydia had barely crossed paths, but today it would be impossible for his busy hummingbird to avoid him. May twenty-first and Aiden's tenth birthday.

Most birthdays were small, private with only immediate family, but Silas knew the moment wheels began turning in Hazel Miller's head, this would not be the case for Aiden this year. Hazel called it a milestone, but Silas figured it an excuse to turn his house into a large gathering. How long had it been since the community graced his home? Too long, he recalled.

The Graber farm buzzed with activity. A few family and friends had already arrived. Silas caught sight of Thomas and Libby with a buggy full of white *kapps* and straw hats pulling up and figured Hazel must have invited them too. He let out a ragged breath as he finished setting up the last folding table.

"I will man the grill," John said, poking Silas in the ribs.

An unnecessary stab. Silas hadn't forgotten the last time they'd grilled out or what happened when a man forgot to use foil on the grill. Grease fires were quite the spectacle and earned you a few years of ribbing. Silas hadn't used the grill since.

"*Gut.* I had no plan to step near that grill anyhow." Silas laughed at his brother-in-law.

"Silas, it is time to start the grill," Hazel hollered from the porch.

He arrowed a finger towards John, indicating who would be heating a few hot dogs, Silas laughed again. Hazel was right. He did like the way it tickled his throat and uplifted his mood.

When the screen door burst open, Lydia came out of the house like a woman on fire, one arm holding tablecloths, the other dangling bags of assorted chips. He hurried to assist her.

"Let me help you," he said, pulling the bag loops off her arm.

"You have to run the grill. The children are getting hungry. I think I forgot to buy mustard." She tapped her chin with a slender finger and gave the table a careful glance. "Should we make more lemonade?"

She was rambling and he didn't mean to laugh. Somebody would think he'd lost his mind with all this laughing. He lowered it to a chuckle.

"What's so funny now?" Lydia asked, spreading out the first tablecloth.

"You. Just slow down for once and enjoy the day Lydia Miller." She paused, looking up at him with those lavender-blue eyes that had the power to stop a man's heart. "John is manning the grill, the children are having fun, and mustard is not that important." He made a face indicating he didn't prefer it anyhow. She eyed him for a moment and then proceeded to unfold a second tablecloth. At least he'd had her attention for thirty seconds.

"Someone is having a *gut* mood," she said, a hint of a smile teasing out of her.

"You have that effect on me, it seems," he said and strolled away, giving her time to comprehend his compliment. He wasn't sure how it was done, not having it done it before himself, but slow and steady seemed the best method to take when one was trying to catch a hummingbird.

By afternoon Silas had to admit he was tired. He swatted at a cluster of gnats and plopped down into one of the three rockers on the porch. He had the perfect view up here. Children were swinging in the front yard, a basketball game going down by the barn, and a couple families on spread-out quilts under the large maples. A man could get used to this.

He was blessed. After years of melancholy, darkness, and limbo, Silas could sit back and count his blessings. He had three beautiful children, a home, and wonderful friends and family. Jana would be smiling on such a day. It was the first time he'd thought of her without guilt or longing. In his heart, he knew she would want her children happy, him happy, and today, he was.

"May I?" Jenny motioned to the empty rocker and sat down before Silas could respond. "Hazel did a *gut* job. Aiden looks happy."

Silas nodded, and his relaxed muscles began to stiffen. "They both did well to see him enjoy his day," he said.

Lydia stepped onto the porch in a hurry, arms full of leftover potato salad and beans. She hesitated at the sight of him and Jenny together, sitting in the two rockers. Catching his gaze for only an instant, she took in a deep breath, let it out, and went on into the house.

"She is always running. No wonder Andy is having such a hard time catching her." Jenny snorted a snobbish laugh.

"Maybe she does not want to be caught." *Until I am ready to do the catching.*

"Oh, don't be ridiculous. She loves that boy. Pined over him for years. What do you care if she does or doesn't? She isn't your concern."

Silas ran his hand through his hair, one ear listening to Jenny, the other listening to Lydia's bare feet patter across his kitchen floor. Yep, he'd asked for it. The second he'd rescued Lydia Miller from a stranger on the road, she had become his concern.

"She lives here." *And I think I'm falling in love with her.*

"For now." Jenny snapped her jaws together just as Andy Weaver pulled up in his buggy.

Hazel had surely not invited him. Silas knew Hazel wasn't fond of him and would have never gone out of her way to invite him. Did that mean Lydia had? His perfect day started dwindling faster than Hazel's three-layer chocolate birthday cake.

Andy came to the porch, tossed Silas a glare, and removed his hat.

"Silas. Jenny."

His eyes caught Jenny's, and something passed between them unsaid.

"Lydia inside?"

"*Jah.* You can find her there. I'm sure she will love to take a break and maybe walk with you," Jenny said.

Silas felt his blood warm as Andy stepped inside his kitchen.

A few minutes later, Lydia and Andy stepped back onto the porch and strolled off. Silas sank into the rocker. *Stop making excuses. Time is running out.*

"Don't they make a *gut* match?" Jenny said.

Silas narrowed his gaze as they walked out towards the side pasture. His heart skipped at the sight of Andy reaching for Lydia's hand.

"Told you she pined for him. I bet they marry by Christmas," Jenny said, looking at the same scene as he was.

If Silas were a betting man, he would wager Jenny was

the cause for his unexpected guest today.

When Lydia pulled from Andy's hand and held her own in front of her, Silas couldn't mask his grin. "Maybe not."

"I heard about her taking food to that family over by Benjamin Troyer's," Jenny said. "Thomas seemed quite angered about it."

"What family?" Silas sat up straighter.

"*Englisch* one. *Daed* will not work, and the *mudder* ran off and left him three *kinner*."

He raised a curious brow. "Our deacon, responsible for helping with the needs of others, is angry that Lydia is helping a family in need?" The narrowmindedness of some amazed him.

"She is likely taking food from your *kinners'* own mouths. We tend to our own. We are to be separate from their world, ain't so? She is always stepping out of line like that." Jenny snorted before folding her arms over her chest.

Silas held on to what remaining patience he had while Jenny continued rambling on next about Mary Hicky's unruly children.

Less than twenty minutes later, Lydia and Andy merged back into the crowd. Her new cobalt-blue dress clung to her frame, but she lacked that smile she had been carrying for days.

Everything about her, even mere thoughts of her held him captive, a prisoner to his own devices. Had he even fallen this fast, this hard, for Jana? Those finer qualities, even as Lydia hurried about, held him. A breeze blew, swaying her *kapp* strings. Her fingers brushed the tickle away from her slender neck as Hannah Troyer whispered into her ear.

Yep, it was without a doubt that Silas Graber had been smacked upside the head, and heart, by Lydia Miller and all her so-called qualities. He was no young man who needed to beat around a bush, nor was he willing to sit by much longer wondering if she had feelings for him too. A man could be patient and quick at the same time he figured. It was time to toss his hat into the ring, help her face whatever held her back from moving forward, and then catch her with both hands.

Jenny snickered and nudged him, breaking him out of this trance. He had forgotten she was still there. Silas scanned out across the way to see Mary Hicky stepping out of the blue-boxed porta-potty provided for the slew of guests, thanks to Lydia, a white trail of toilet paper clinging to her black-soled shoe. She was unaware, as Mary often was.

"She is a *blamieren*."

What was embarrassing was sitting next to a woman like Jenny Schwartz, who made fun of others. In all his days on earth, Silas had never heard an Amish woman speak with such disregard.

With Mary's youngest, Thomas, on one hip, and Mary May on the other, Lydia rushed up behind Mary Hicky and launched one leg forward, stomping the white trail following her friend and freeing her from any further embarrassment. Lydia did so without any cause for praise or gratitude. She did it because it was the right thing for one to do, for a friend.

Silas chuckled and got to his feet. "*Gut* day, Jenny. I have to see a beautiful woman about a horse."

Chapter Twenty

Hazel and Hannah helped Lydia clean Silas's kitchen down to the last dish. Lydia had never known tired before and after three cups of *kaffi*, she realized the effect worked in reverse. Jenny still hadn't left, holding down the front porch rocker like it might disappear, and she hadn't offered to help either. For a woman trying to convince Silas she was marrying material, Lydia, the amateur, was certain she was going about it all wrong.

"Did Andy leave?" Hannah asked, and Lydia nodded, not willing to talk about how upset he'd become when she'd refused his hand. He had answered none of her questions. Where he had been recently and had he found work? Gracie would insist she was being picky, wasting her only chance, but it didn't feel that way. Wasted was what she had felt she had done all these years leading up to right now.

"*Mudder*, how did you know *Daed* was the one?"

Hazel tossed a dishtowel over her shoulder, her signature as she worked, and floated Lydia a warm smile. "He was the first person I wanted to share my day with. I fell hard for that man."

Hazel blushed, and Hannah made a face to Lydia.

"Your *daed* was kind, patient, and never hurried into a thing without thinking it out. It was an admirable trait. Too many young men now want to hurry into things." Hazel's face pruned in disapproval.

Like Andy.

"I know what you're thinking, and don't," Hannah said.

"What?" Lydia gave her a hard look. No way anyone could know what she had been thinking. Lydia did well to guard her thoughts.

"You are thinking Andy is back, claiming his love for you and making promises all over again." Hannah put both hands on her shoulders. "Lydi, you can forgive, but are you really considering this?"

"We can't live here forever, and Andy has said he wants to try again." Lydia placed a pitcher of tea and one of lemonade on the counter.

"You have been letting your *schwesters* into your head again. I can see it," *Mudder* said in a sharp tone. "*Kumm*, take a seat."

Lydia did as she was asked.

"We can stay here for as long as we need to. This is our home, Lydia Rose. You should pray about this thing between you and Andy, and what I see growing between you and Silas."

Lydia inhaled a breath.

"I am your *mudder*; I am not blind."

There was no sense in hiding it now, Lydia realized, looking about to see if anyone else was within earshot. "Fine." She put a hand on her hip and sighed. "What do you think I should do?"

"It is not for me to say. Ask *Gott*. Listen to your heart. The two hold the answers to anything you have to ask."

Hazel moved toward her, placing a hand on Lydia's shoulder.

"I only ask that you promise me one thing."

Lydia nodded.

"Don't hurry into anything. Don't make a decision because of me or what you think someone else wants."

Hannah agreed.

Gracie stepped into the kitchen, and Lydia floated a look to her mother and best friend to drop the conversation about Silas. Gracie would think she was crazy. Silas was nine years older than her, and Gracie always liked Andy.

"We are about to head out. I hope Aiden liked the book we got him." Gracie studied the faces and lifted a dark brow. "What have you all been chatting about in here?" She tucked her hair under her *kapp* and leaned against the door frame.

"Apples," Hannah said in a rush. "I'm going to be up to my eyeballs in them this year. I think *Daed* would trade three *dochdern* for boys any day."

Lydia bit back a laugh. "Your *daed*'s orchard has been blessed, and I know he wouldn't trade you three for all the boys in Miller's Creek." Lydia stood and searched out a peanut butter cookie from the leftovers.

Gracie smiled and turned to Lydia. "Oh, before I go, I have to know, did you enjoy golfing? I've never been and have been meaning to ask."

"Golfing?"

Hannah and Hazel passed a look at one another like they had just solved some great mystery. Lydia even heard the subtle "*Ach*" in Hannah's voice.

"I have never been golfing before." Hadn't Silas even made a harsh remark about her golfing?

"*Ach*," Gracie said in a regretful tone.

"Since when would I find the time or the want to go golfing?" The room grew silent, knowing gazes crossing paths with one another. "What is going on here? I don't like surprises. You all are waving around a secret, but not sharing it."

"Lydia, you are my closest friend, but you hurry about so fast you miss things that others don't."

Was Hannah insulting her? Her soft green eyes didn't say

her naivety was in question.

"Sit back down, Lydia. We must talk." Hannah pulled out a chair and Lydia fell into it as if her world were about to change once again.

"Of all the stuff," Gracie said, waving her hands. "I just made matters worse."

Mudder shushed her.

"There have been rumors," Hannah said. "Things Jenny Schwartz mentioned during the quilting bee last week. She told everyone about Mary May's hair."

Hannah continued from Gideon's bee sting to Lydia going for ice cream with Andy. And not once had Lydia ever refused to bathe the children out of laziness.

"Gossip is a sin. You know me, Hannah. Do you believe these things about me? I cut it as a last resort. Of course, I tried everything," Lydia said. Reality hit her, and she lowered her head to the table with a thump. "It wasn't me golfing. You are all trying to tell me something more. This is about Andy, ain't so?"

"Jenny said Andy took you golfing. She isn't the only one who has mentioned such," Gracie said, sounding for the first time in a while sympathetic to Lydia's life. "Others have claimed to have seen you two courting. Since he isn't baptized, it has caused some concerns."

"I have only been on two walks and one buggy ride with Andy. All three of you were aware of me leaving." She stared up at her *mudder*, a tear streaking her cheek. "I have not left the house late ever. Is Gaven Weaver certain of his leaving so often?"

Hazel nodded, and Lydia lowered her head to the table again. She had been right not to trust Andy. Now saving that kiss felt validated.

"Is Jenny trying to have me shunned for going out for ice cream?" Lydia asked, a tear slipping down her cheek.

"*Nee*," Hazel said. "All know Jenny is just stirring trouble here because she wants something she can't have."

"Wait, what else am I missing here?" Gracie asked but was ignored.

Lydia wasn't about to share her growing feelings for Silas after Gracie's comment about how no woman wanted a ready-made family.

"There are other rumors, Lydia. I tell you because you are my friend and I love you, not to gossip."

Hannah held her hand and brushed away a tear. Hannah she could trust with her heart. Her friend had no ability in her to tell a lie. Hannah Troyer was the truest person Lydia had ever known.

"What kind of rumors?" Lydia said, her voice frail.

"About Ohio and possibly a *maedel* or two waiting there."

More shame than heartbreak was the cause of her tears right now. God had been making her hesitant, even when she believed Andy was her only chance for a family and a future for her *mudder*, and now Lydia knew why.

Long after *Mudder* had fallen asleep, Lydia pulled the tub into her room and readied for a bath. She could take a shower in the main house, as always, but feared waking the children when the pipes did their little sing-song jingle.

The day stuck to her like a hard sticky candy drop, and no scissors were going to erase its persistent hold. Andy making a fool of her, Jenny Schwartz's sitting next to Silas on the porch all afternoon. It all covered her like a thick layer of grime.

Her future was dark, darker than the clouds building outside her bedroom window. Thankfully, the storm had held off until now and hadn't ruined the day for Aiden. That's what mattered today, and he'd had the most wonderful day. She would do well to focus more on that.

Walking back to the kitchen to retrieve a pan of water on

the stove, she spotted them. On the flowered quilt pulled snuggly over her bed lay her three books. Books she'd thought Thomas had destroyed back in April.

Silas had walked in on her being scolded that day. It was he who had taken her books. It was him that had seen she got them back. Like the dresser in the corner and the hummingbird feeders that *mudder* said he wanted to be hung back up, Silas had been making an effort since the beginning. How had she missed that?

He was a man adjusting to a life he never wanted just as she had been coerced into a life she hadn't planned for.

Pouring the second pot of hot water into the tub, Lydia checked the temperature by her fingers' touch. *Daed* had always said, "If too many thoughts consume you, pick one and start there." She picked one.

Thunder clapped outside, a few streaks of lightning brightening up the room. Silas had barely spared a word to her all day, but he'd watched her. She'd felt his eyes follow her even when she went walking with Andy. Once she'd even felt he had been seeking her out. She had been talking with Penny Lapp and noted him walking their way, but Gideon aiming towards the chicken coop with Mary Hicky's boys had sent him veering off.

She pulled the pins from her dress and let it slip to the floor. She removed all her undergarments and eased into the tub. The warmth engulfed her sore muscles, and she moaned in relief. Unpinning her long hair, the blond locks escaped and fell to the floor behind the metal tub's rail as she leaned back.

"*Gott,* what will you have me do? *Mudder* is my responsibility. I owe her more than I can ever repay. I thought marrying Andy would mean a real home for her, and, well, you know what I heard today," she said. Picking up a washrag, she began scrubbing. "At least I convinced Amos Mast into speaking with Penny Lapp and kept Gideon from fingering his *bruder*'s cake before we could serve it." She teased a smile heavenward.

"Do you really want Jenny with these children? Do you know if Silas's heart has room for a second love in it?" She exhaled a long breath. "I think I love him, but I cannot do anything about it. Maybe some divine intervention would be a *gut* idea right about now. But that is just me, confused and scared Lydia talking." As usual, the Lord didn't reply.

Lydia leaned back and tried to relax. *Silas will marry Jenny.* He no longer looked like a man determined to be alone. It was plain to see that Jenny was the best choice. How could he not want a woman like that beside him? She was beautiful, with hair the color of honey and eyes as bright as the sky. Like the bright multicolored hummingbird that frequented the feeder at the flower bed, Jenny had it all. Lydia was plain and simple, and nine years younger. But try as she might Lydia couldn't imagine a life beyond this farm, away from the children, and without him.

She gazed over her plain self, submerged in tepid water. Like her favorite hummingbird, she was simple. The little bird was all brown with a smidgen of black highlighting its textures. Nothing bright or bold or worth noticing, but Lydia deemed the sweet creature was as beautiful as any she had ever seen. Poised, yet hurried to get her fill and return to her nest to feed her young. She too rushed to tend to the young of the Graber household. That would account for her slim and dull figure.

She wiggled her toes. Her legs appeared longer under the water, and they carried her wherever she needed to be without fail. The longer she considered, the more she let vanity seep in. "I am not so plain and dull really," she said. Never had she view herself this closely, but now as she did, she realized she wasn't that simple after all. Did her dress ever sway the way Jenny's did when she walked across a room? Did Silas notice more than just the duties expected of her?

She didn't have bold curves, but Lydia did have shapes that made a woman a woman. Her hair was long, blond, and beautiful in its own way. A devilish grin crept its way onto her lips as she pondered her hidden qualities. "I'm no less than any other." She shrugged. "I do kind things and would never take for granted the gifts given me. Lord, if you find me worthy of him, please tell me now. I know what I want, and if you have forgiven me for hurting my *mudder*, I will not disappoint you."

The storm that threatened earlier now decided to become alive. Silas couldn't think of anything he wanted more right now than to speak to Lydia. To know if her heart was set on another or if she was open to other possibilities. He would offer it all to her if he had to—he wanted to—if she would not run off with Andy Weaver. The *dawdi haus* light flickered. Lydia was still up.

His heart pounded as thunder crashed in the distance. He could say he was just checking on her, seeing they were fine, considering the storm. Yes, he would do that, he motivated himself, walking closer to the front entrance. Pulling his hat down firmer on his head, he stood outside the little built-on addition, mapping out his every word. Should he ask if she found the books? *Of course, she found them. You laid them on her bed.*

Pebbles underfoot teased. He could toss one at her window just as he would have if they were courting. It was tempting. He shook his head at how nervous he had become. When he looked up again, this time Lydia herself filled the window. Long blond hair reaching further than he could see, bare shoulders with soft flesh. She must have been bathing. He took a breath and averted his eyes to his boots. What he had to say would have to wait.

"She needs curtains," he chuckled, turning back to the main house.

CHAPTER TWENTY-ONE

The next day, Lydia had started out of the barn, returning the last of the folding chairs used for Aiden's birthday gathering, when she spotted Silas and Jenny heading her way. Did the woman not have chores? She hedged.

"Jenny, I have to get Cage ready to show his owners, who are on their way now. I have no interest in taking a walk when there is work to be had."

Silas stepped across the yard, but Jenny trailed him like a predator. His voice sounded angry. Lydia couldn't help but find it a good sign that Silas wasn't happy. She hoped God wasn't displeased at her selfish thought.

Lydia slipped into the stall with Aiden's pony, Penny, to avoid dealing with either of them. *What a stupid move.* She scampered into a corner. Penny was a bit anxious most of the time, but the old girl seemed to be just as surprised as Lydia that they were both trapped in the enclosure together.

She pushed away some of Penny's unpleasant droppings with her foot and crouched farther into the corner. *Please do not let her go crazy and stomp me to death.* Hands trembling, she faced the boards and forced herself to pretend Penny wasn't there behind her, contemplating her death. It had worked well on Cage, and they had become friends after all.

Footsteps entered the barn. She considered sending up another prayer, one that included her not being forced to witness Jenny stealing a kiss but figured by now she was running low in things to ask the Lord for. "*Gott* isn't a wish giver," *Mammi* always said.

Too bad. That would solve a lot of problems.

"Silas, you need a *fraa*, I need a husband. I have been patient long enough."

Lydia peered through the wooden slats and noted Silas's abrupt halt.

Pushy woman. Did women often propose marriage instead of the man?

Lydia felt her heart gather momentum as she awaited Silas's response. This was it. She'd asked God for a sign, and he was delivering.

"A woman should not speak in such a way. A man who is interested should lead. He pursues what interests him." His tone was sharp. She had felt the sting of it a time or two herself, but found it rather amusing to watch Jenny's head drop in regret of her actions.

"But you have not said anything. It has been almost five years, Silas. It is time you move on. Even the Bishop agrees."

Silas's feet began moving again, this time stopping just inches from Jenny's black shoes. "I am moving forward. I have an interest, and she knows of it. There is no reason for you being here. A proper *maedel* should know this."

Lydia could hear the sobbing. She placed a hand over her mouth, breathing through it and muffling her gasps.

"She does not love you. She loves no one." Jenny stormed out.

Lydia held her breath as Silas stood idle for the longest time.

He loves someone.

Had he lied about Mary and just did not want her to know? Silas Graber had an interest, one who knew his feelings. If life hadn't already taught her heartbreak aplenty, Lydia would have been sick, right there next to Penny. God had just answered her.

Cage had shown himself rather badly when the owners came this evening. Poor Silas, and all that hard work he had put in. There was nothing she could do for the man. Not now that she knew he had an interest, that someone had captured his heart. While he read to the children after supper, she slipped out of the house to check on the beast. Something had caused Cage's sudden change, and she wanted to know what that was.

The horse snickered at her approach, and she scolded him. "You have not been a *gut bu*. Why be stubborn?" She spoke soft words as she rubbed his head. Sensing his fuss was over, she climbed the gate and made herself comfortable. She had been coming closer each time. Cage didn't frighten her any more. fact, talking to him was much easier than *Mudder* or Hannah, in truth. Cage didn't tell her to have faith, trust in God's plans. He simply listened.

"You made him look bad, which made you look bad. Now how will you be of use like that? Do you know what happens to ornery old horses?" Cage backed away, pranced, and bucked. "Show-off. If you keep doing this, I will not come see you no more, and if you make him look bad again, you will be glue, I tell ya. We must all be useful." The horse was enjoying her teasing.

Two hands surrounded her middle, and she was falling through the air until her back hit against something hard. Before she could cry out, she was dropped and turned sharply. "Silas." She squealed out.

"I told you not to be around him. Didn't you see how he acted tonight?"

He scolded her as if she was but a child.

"You could have just…"

"*Nee*, he is not safe. You could have been hurt." His voice wobbled this time.

Lydia tilted her head as far as it would stretch to glare at him. When she opened her mouth to remind him of the last time he had thought her unprepared and foolish, surprise in her own reaction seized her words.

Silas was afraid. His rapid breaths, his iron grip on her arms indicated he was afraid, for her. What could she say to him now?

A warmth came over her like she had never felt before. She, too, was breathing hard. His eyes trailed over her and his hold loosened. Strong hands slid down the length of her arms, leaving sparks in a path until they settled on both wrists.

"Why can't you trust me?" Silas stared at her, his gaze searching for understanding.

He was so close. All she had to do was reach up, rise on tiptoe, and there would no longer be anything between them.

But he has someone.

"You may be a father, but you are not mine. I don't have to explain myself to you." She pulled from his hold, putting some distance between them. Trusting men, especially with her heart, was the last thing she could do.

"If I was your father, you would not be afraid of horses and yet foolish enough to get close to this one," Silas said.

Lydia closed her eyes and winced. Everyone knew her *Daed* died after horses rode over him and dragged him the length of the pasture. As witness to the horror of it firsthand, Silas's words stabbed harder than she was prepared for. The tears were right there and yet she willed them to hold.

"Lydia. I'm sorry. I shouldn't have…"

"Overreacted," she said. "I am smart enough to stay away from cruel beasts. And you"—she jabbed a finger into his chest—"should stick to building your stone walls. Those children deserve a *daed*." Her façade splintered when tears spilled over, and she turned away.

"Lydia, don't go. Talk to me."

He tried reaching for her, but she slipped from his grasp. "And just so you know, Mr. Graber, I have never been golfing a day of my life." She tossed back the words before running away.

Silas watched her fly away, powerless to stop her. Lydia was carrying around something heavy in the loss of Joseph, more than just seeing her *daed*'s accident firsthand and more than Andy Weaver. He was certain of it. And if she hadn't been golfing before, then who had? He kicked the dirt beneath him. Cage snorted, knocking his hat to the ground.

"Not you too," he said. He had devastated her in the blink of an eye. Had the hummingbird in his hands and scared it away.

The next morning, Lydia set aside her quarrel with Silas and focused on what was good and perfect in her life. Right now, it was breathing in the scent of freshly turned dirt and warm hints of summer. Here in the garden, she had to offer so little, and what she would get in return was so much more. It was as if by merely being present, God gifted her.

Kapp strings blowing in the wind, the sun warming her face, she sent out a silent thank you for a much-needed perfect day. She leaned over and pulled off her shoes and thin summer socks. Sinking her bare feet into the cool, loosened soil, she relished the sensation. Here, in the garden, was the one place Lydia could be herself. No one to tell her she was doing something wrong or remind her she was lacking. From planting to harvesting and canning, it was a pleasure and not a chore. *Mudder* liked her baking, *Aenti* May her bees, but Lydia was as happy as a pig in mud in the garden.

"*Nee* shoes Lydi." Mary May demanded. With a laugh, she helped Mary May remove her shoes as well. She re-tied the matching little chore apron and gave Mary May's button nose a playful finger tap.

Without asking, Aiden picked up a hoe and went straight to making another row at the far end without being told how to measure the rows or where to begin. Like his father, Aiden worked hard, but she couldn't help wonder if his need for perfection had stemmed from Jana. Lydia remembered her well enough. Jana had been a quiet woman, always neat, tidy, and kind. Still, that didn't explain where Aiden's careful way of things birthed from.

She watched him.

He would be a great carpenter one day.

The way he studied his surroundings and his need for precise order, were clear indicators that his habit of moving things to satisfy his own view of them bordered perfectionism. Everyone had a gift worth pursuing. Maybe perfect order was his.

"That is *gut,* Aiden." Hazel complimented him from the other end of the large garden.

Her *mudder,* busy planting a row of bulbs and flowers at the easterly end, smiled her way.

Gideon had found a morsel of his brother's energy, but none of his need for perfection. Lydia laughed at the snake-like line he'd chopped the length of the garden. He was more suited to do well with animals, just as Ben Troyer had suggested he would. Something untamed and full of energy just like him. She bit the inside of her lip watching each of them with a keen eye. She would encourage Gideon to consider cattle or sheep maybe. Anything but horses. Her heart couldn't bear it.

She shook off the instinct of considering hopeful futures for each of them. How could she know how much of those futures would include her? Refusing to dwell on limits and expiration dates, savoring this warmth of family around her, Lydia prayed for just enough time to instill safe ambitions within them. Silas was indeed healing and pursuing someone. If only she knew who. Then again, Lydia didn't want to.

"Ouch," Gideon yelled, dropping his short-handled hoe used for digging weeds, not ponds.

"Let me see." He held out a hand to Hazel. "Just a blister. I can fix that."

Mudder could fix anything.

"Don't forget the honey," Aiden hollered in the distance.

Lydia shot him a frown, and he shrugged his shoulders and grinned. Like Silas, he had a silent charm that made you smile. Once you got to know him. In just a few more years some young *maedel* would be captivated by that charm.

Turning around, Lydia found Mary May at her heels again. The four-year-old had one chore: helping Hazel drop flower bulbs of gladiolas in a row. Now she was on Lydia's heels again wearing a frown as if she had lost her dolly again.

"Something wrong Mary May?"

"I *gut*," Mary May answered a bit mischievously, swaying back and forth like she was. Lydia studied her for a moment before resuming planting seeds.

"I am planting the peas, so don't touch them and I will show you how to bury them when I am done." The little shadow smiled. Lydia continued dropping a seed every few inches. "The more the better with peas," *Daed* had always told her. What a wonderful day for planting it was.

Silas released Cage to pasture and the contrary black steed

bolted to the far end of the field. He wished he had his energy after what they'd just gone through. He stared down at the red dips and grooves burning his wide palms. He had held on tight, as he was prone to do. Today he didn't feel like one of the most sought-out trainers in the area. Today he felt old. Still, it was apparent Lydia wouldn't heed his warnings, so he would put in the time. Cage was either going to be broke or leaving. That was how it had to be.

He couldn't hold on to the laugh that escaped him remembering her threats to the horse. Scolding Cage and then threatening to make him glue. It seemed her determined nature didn't exclude animals.

She had gone from fearful of horses to perched on a gate fussing at one. If he didn't know any better, Lydia and Cage had visited a time or two. It would explain the animal's calmer behavior on certain days. Cage liked her. Silas knew the feeling. She was doing so much for his family, his home, and farm. Maybe it was time he returned the goodness.

Thirsty, he took long strides towards the house, anticipating Hazel's lemonade. He was worn and dirty. His shirt was so damp it was fixed to him like an extra skin.

He spotted Lydia and the children in the garden. He was glad he'd gotten the ground turned last week. Anticipating fresh beans and tomatoes, he detoured to see how things were progressing. After what conspired between him and Lydia last night, he had decided he couldn't let her avoid him. He too had a habit of avoiding things that made him uncomfortable. Perhaps they both had plenty to face.

His daughter's head bounced up and down beyond the slats of the fence, and he slowed his approach to get a full-scale view. Aiden was hoeing ground like a man on a mission. He was a hard worker, that was for sure and for certain.

Reaching the fence, Silas leaned on it, taking it all in. A barefoot Lydia donned in her grey chore dress was straddling a row and dropping seeds closer than he preferred. He wouldn't address it. The woman would have a reason for what she was doing, and he was too tired for another quarrel even though he had to admit quarreling with her did have its appeal.

When he realized what Mary May was doing, the corners of his mouth drifted upward. On Lydia's heels as usual, but for every seed Lydia dropped, Mary May scooped it up and tucked it into her little sewn-in apron pockets. He supposed he should intervene, and then chuckled.

Not this time.

He lingered, bemused. When Lydia reached the end of the row and raised her head, she caught his gaze and the humor dancing in his eyes.

"What now?" she asked, one hip thrust forward in rebellion.

Lord, the woman was his undoing. He could imagine ten years from now her standing there, looking that way at him. He thought his heart had taken a beating last night when he found her near Cage, but that sharp glare had it all up and pounding again.

"That's not how we plant peas," he said, still holding a grin despite her. She didn't bother to pause, to glare at him with those piercing blue eyes as she often did when he questioned her methods. Rather, Lydia marched straight to the fence he was leaning on. She hadn't a clue just how her temper affected him.

"I have planted peas since I was Mary May's age. I can't possibly be doing something this simple wrong too." Chicory blue eyes sparked with temper and when he held his smirk against it, her face shifted between anger, heartbreak, and self-doubt in a matter of seconds. With so much emotion worn openly, he wondered why she even spoke at all.

"Then Hazel is a better teacher, my dear." He pointed; glad she hadn't noticed him address her affectionately. Lydia followed his finger's mark to Mary May behind her plucking seeds out of the ground where Lydia had just dropped them and sliding them into her tiny pockets.

"Mary May Graber!" Lydia scolded.

Squealing, Mary May beelined around the fence to him. But Lydia wasn't going to let her go easily.

"I'm going to tickle the peas out of you, Mary May Graber." Lydia took up the chase. Aiden fell on all fours in the freshly turned earth, laughing harder than Silas thought possible for his eldest and often too serious son.

"No, *Daed*, don't let Lydi tickle out *mei* pee." Taken aback by the quick turn of humor, Silas froze, one hand on Mary May's head as she clutched to his leg, one hand on the fence steadying himself.

Little girls, big girls, shouldn't talk this way, but for the life of him he couldn't help but burst out laughing too. Lydia rounded the fence and pulled Mary May from his leg and into her arms. The two tumbled to the ground, and Lydia started tickling her until her squeals turned to giggles. Soon after, giggles became hiccups. Between Mary May and the contagious laugh of Lydia Miller, Silas was spellbound.

"My pee! My pee!" Mary May warned.

"Okay. Okay," Silas intervened, rescuing Mary May from the ground before she really did lose her pees. Safe in his arms, Silas did well to slow his own laughter. He looked down. Lydia was still on the dirty ground, laughing, her *kapp* crooked. When she peered up, his heart kicked his ribcage with a jolt. No wonder the children adored her. *Hummingbird,* with her sweetness, her continuous energy. He reached out a hard hand, helping her to her feet.

A perfect day. How long they all had craved it. His heart raced faster than when Cage bolted him from the saddle. Pulling Lydia to her feet, he gave her small hand a squeeze before letting go. Disheveled and breathing hard from her silliness, he brushed a strand of light hair from her face. With ease, two fingers tucked the strands back into place, tilting the *kapp* to rights again. These were the same blond locks that wandered down to unimaginable lengths. He ached to have a true touch, not a simple teasing of a few loose strands, in his fingers.

Lydia ceased her joy, her fun, and her breath. Their eyes locked. A mammoth of emotions danced behind blue eyes. He had her again, right then for the briefest of moments. What was it Aiden had said? A patient man could catch a hummingbird. He exhaled his own held breath, hoping to inhale her in.

"You not get my peas, Lydi," Mary May clenched one pocket in her tiny hand while the other clung to her father's strong neck. "She not get 'em, huh, *Daed?*"

He looked down into Lydia's lavender-kissed eyes. "*Nee, my liebling.* Lydia did not get them." He forced a half-hearted laugh for the sake of Mary May and her accomplishment of keeping the peas from Lydia, but he could not ignore the obvious shudder that ran over Lydia. He had rattled her and knowing he had was enough to hope.

"Excuse me," she said in a shaky breath.

Silas stepped aside, letting her go—for now. He had no intention of doing it again if he could help it.

Shifting his daughter in his arms, he turned and watched Lydia rush toward the house where Hazel stood on his porch watching the whole intimate encounter. To Silas's surprise, an approving smile floated as soft as a dandelion seed on a summer breeze before she followed Lydia inside. Hope filled his heart as he expected a lot would be said within his four walls today.

"Let's get these picked up and planted the right way," Silas said to his children, and they began picking up the scattered peas. Hazel was right.

One day you will laugh, and it will feel gut, she had told him. *One day everything will look brighter.* And it did.

CHAPTER TWENTY-TWO

"But you know Cage," Silas said with a crooked smile.

"We are friends, *jah*, but I am not riding him. You can barely ride him." Was he crazy? Whatever possessed him to think she dare attempt such a thing?

A sparrow darted from the barn rafters, and Lydia wished to follow it out into the open. Anywhere would be better than in Silas's barn right now. Between the incident in the garden and her fear for what he had in mind for her, every quivering breath birthed from yesterday's mistakes overwhelmed her. Taking a step toward the sunlight would have been ideal, if not for shaky legs not willing to cooperate.

What if I mess up? Get someone hurt.

"*Nee*, you are not riding him. Jippy is good enough for my Mary May, she will do well for you. Besides, you will be in the buggy, not on the horse."

Like that mattered. She snorted. "I do not think this is a *gut* idea. I know you are trying to help, but I cannot do this." He could never understand the extent of her fears, but no one did, and she wasn't about to reveal them.

"You can do anything you choose to. You have nothing to fear. I will be with you, every step. Trust *Gott*, trust me, all will be well."

What a strange turn of events in such an ordinary day. She did trust him, but he was asking more than she believed she could give. Calming each ragged breath, Lydia set her shoulders and dared to try.

Gott, be with me. With us. Don't let me get him killed too.

"First, you need to get to know her. I will help you harness her. If you get scared while driving her and let go, she will just come back to the barn without you worrying things can go wrong."

It sounded all too easy. "You're mocking me. Do you think me a child needing assurances?"

His hazel eyes swept over her in careful measure from head to toe. Intense, shudder-worthy, the way he scrutinized her every detail was more intimidating than the day in the garden when something flickered in his eyes that said he saw her. Just her.

"I am most aware you are no child, Lydia Rose."

That low, gravelly tone of his voice penetrated every pore on her flesh, those eyes teasing every sense. She gripped the sides of her dress, searching for the wits and logic she lost in an instant. This would have been much easier if it were anyone but Silas Graber, a man who loved another but gawked at her with wanting in his eyes. He stepped closer and removed one hand from twisting her dress. Hands that worked hard but were tender in his touch.

"I think I will try now," she said before she kissed a man who cared for another. Last thing she needed was a man just like Andy Weaver teasing every girl in his path. No, she'd learned her lesson. She couldn't trust herself at all when it came to man or beast. Today she would take her chance on the lesser of the two evils. A four-legged beast named Jippy.

After an hour of rubbing and cooing and hitching horse to buggy, Lydia climbed up into the seat. When Silas settled beside her, she felt anxiety ride over her flesh in waves. Her heart wasn't sure it could take both driving the buggy and having Silas this close.

Just focus on the horse and lines.

Summoning her hidden reserves, Lydia put everything in motion and veered Jippy towards the driveway. Getting this over with fast was what she needed right now.

"You should relax. You seem to know what you are doing."

His confidence in her was no different than *Daed*'s had been. She would not relax until this whole crazy idea of his was over. How many silent prayers could a woman send upward before God considered it a burden?

"Not really." she said as the buggy wheel hit a small hole and bounced her bottom upward from the seat. "*Ach*," she said, settling back into place. "Hard to control if you cannot stay in the seat." Maybe she shouldn't tackle this as she did most new things.

"Cinnamon rolls," Silas said all too quickly.

Lydia knew he devoured her mother's rolls like a starved animal, but what did cinnamon rolls have to do with driving a buggy?

"Cinnamon rolls?" She shot him a quizzical look. His grin flaunted the small dimple again. Oh, what a handsome grin. She had always believed so, even the day he'd first arrived to move them from their home to his, but now she was finding it overly distracting.

"Eat plenty cinnamon rolls and that bottom of yours will stay put."

Lydia gasped at his boldness. Mouth open, she all but forgot she held the reins in her hands.

"Whoa, pay attention. I will leave my flirting for another time." He chuckled, helping her regain the road. "Now slow down before pulling out."

Flirting. Another time.

He was not making this overcoming fear easy. How was she supposed to concentrate? Then again, maybe that was Silas's plan all along. Distract her. *Not nice.* She frowned at the deception.

"I am not driving on the main road." She paused. "And stop trying to distract me. You will only make me more *naer-fich*."

"Nothing to be nervous about. I have a feeling you have never been one to take lessons for naught either. Everything you do is thought out first." He chuckled. "But it's good to know I can still be distracting."

Lydia worked to keep her composure, despite the shudders of chills running along her skin. "You're being nice. I did mess up harnessing Jippy. If you didn't help me, I wouldn't have gotten this far," she said to respond to his compliment. "And you're not that distracting." She grinned, keeping her eyes forward. This, two conversations at once, was kind of fun. Maybe she should stop now. Playing this game, the one *he* had adopted.

"You are just out of practice is all. Tomorrow is a new day with no mistakes in it yet." Silas leaned back, crossing his ankles as if it were a Sunday joy ride. "I think Mary Hicky will no longer need to take my children to school *kumm* fall."

If he only knew the mistakes she had made, he wouldn't sound so hopeful. Yet here she was, facing that fear and developing another. Suddenly driving a buggy didn't seem that scary, but the man who cared for another flirting with her did.

"If I'm here still. I don't think that it's a *gut* idea, me taking them. I would never forgive myself if the children got hurt." Silence lingered between them for a moment, and she felt his eyes on her as she focused on the road ahead.

"Things happen, Lydia. Accidents we cannot control no more than the weather. I know part of your fear of horses comes from what happened to Joseph."

Her lips pursed. He couldn't know just how deep that went. If he even knew the depths of her irresponsibility, he would keep the children as far from her as possible.

"I don't want to talk about this."

"Another time then. I'm patient," he said as if they would someday.

That wouldn't happen.

As the sun slid away in the evening, and the frogs sang their song, Silas finished brushing down Cage, who had in fact decided he might want to be worth something after all. Threatening to make him glue must have done the trick.

Today with Lydia had changed everything. Though it hadn't gone as he hoped, they had crossed a bridge. He had been correct about where her fears came from and in another lesson or two, he hoped those fears could be shelved and forgotten.

Inside, the house was quiet. Too quiet, even for bedtime. Silas removed his shoes and hat and took a moment to wash his hands at the kitchen sink before venturing farther to investigate.

In the sitting room, on the couch he once slept on, lay Lydia and all three of his children, sound asleep. An open book, Summer of the Monkeys, lay open on the arm of the couch. Silas picked it up, dog-eared the page, and set it aside.

Mary May lay on Lydia's side with her short, stubby arm around her neck. Gideon was cradled in Lydia's right arm. He smiled knowing she probably did so to ensure he didn't slip away. At the far end of the couch, lay Aiden, head back, mouth opened. His legs were outstretched with one leg dangling to the floor.

Silas lingered over them, storing the picture to memory. "So, hummingbirds do sleep," he said.

She had been holding up walls for so long and now as he chipped them away, she rested. She softly moaned, and he knelt to cradle her cheek with the touch of his hand until she slid back into slumber.

Silas still had feelings, wants. It would be easier if he didn't, but every time he tried ignoring them, she did something to ensure he felt each and every one of them.

One by one, he scooped up each child and carried them to their beds, until all that was left was a sleeping beauty who had unknowingly stolen his heart. He pulled the afghan from the back of the couch over her, and she nuzzled inside. Heart pounding, Silas leaned over and brushed her cheek with a kiss.

"*Gut nacht,* hummingbird," he whispered.

"I see you have many talents," Hazel praised him as she carried a warm bowl of oatmeal to his place at the table. "I never thought she would ever take to driving a buggy after my Joseph, and you did it. *Danki* for that, Silas."

Hazel patted his shoulder and returned to the stove. What would she think if he told her he prayed for her *dochder* each night? What was she say if she knew how often he dreamed of her?

"I think she was ready on her own. I didn't push...much." He grinned before lowering his head in prayer. After a few moments, he raised his head again and sprinkled brown sugar and cinnamon in his bowl.

He ate slower than usual, hoping to see Lydia this morning before heading out.

"I ordered the lavender from the greenhouse," he said. "I look forward to seeing the color here." He took a healthy bite.

"That's *wunderbaar.* I told you she felt lining the driveway would brighten up the place," Hazel said. "As long as it does not smell like—" She paused and turned to Silas.

Jenny, of course, was the subject in both their heads, which sent them into silly laughter.

"She is a persistent, that one." Hazel didn't hold back at the obvious. "In my day, we didn't go around acting so bold. It takes more than fine looks to earn a smile." She pulled fresh biscuits from the oven and pinched the top of one in the middle for doneness. Plating them both breakfast, she returned to the table.

"So, Joseph was handsome enough to earn your smile." Silas smothered a warm biscuit with butter and took a bite. "Love at first sight?"

He remembered the first time he and Jana had been paired together. It was all by accident. He'd come with friends for a fun game of baseball, and she needed a ride home. He liked her timid manner, the way her mousy voice sounded as she talked about her family. She was poised and gentle, and something about her struck him. Their friendship became a relationship.

He could still remember the look on Jana's face the day she introduced him to their son. Gideon had been born at the hospital by emergency surgery, and Mary May. Silas closed his eyes on that dark memory of how the light faded in Jana's eyes after bringing Mary May into the world. There were times a man felt helpless, and it was important to lean on God. Silas had and had been leaning on the Lord's good graces since.

"*Nee*," she said, matter-of-factly, an astute smile on her lips. "I did not like Joseph one bit in the beginning."

Silas raised a brow.

"Joseph was courting another and asked to drive me one *nacht* after a singing. I said *nee*, Barbra was my friend." She used her hands in the air to help deliver her point. "I found him bold and careless, but he was handsome, he was." Her smile grew wider and more confident. "I was wrong not accepting that time."

"So, Joseph Miller had been persistent and patient."

And capable of catching hummingbirds.

"He was many things more too. What do you think of

bees?" She changed the subject.

"The *kinner* keep mentioning them," he asked, a bit embarrassed, knowing Hazel would see right through him—did see right through him. Would she accuse him of trying to interfere with Lydia and Andy by enticing her daughter with things that interested her?

"I think bees would thrive here, just as many things seem to be."

Hazel returned to the counter trying her best to hide her expression. She did a poor job of it with that knowing smirk.

After a long silence, Silas pushed his bowl forward and leaned back in his chair.

"I see the way you look at her. I raised two other *dochdern*," Hazel said.

He smiled and got to his feet. "It's hard not to." He spoke honestly. "Does that concern you?"

"*Nee*. I think it *gut*. For both of ya. *Gott* promises to mend the brokenhearted, does He not?"

That He did, Silas held. "Do you ever think about…" Silas began but stalled. It was too private a question.

"To love again?" Hazel smiled.

The woman had a gift for mind-reading.

"I have little time for such thinking, but that doesn't mean one should not want that."

Hazel had a way of deflecting if she didn't want to answer a question. Perhaps love to her was seeing it in others. It did make sense, considering she liked to meddle with pairing others up.

"Did you and the Bishop plan this?"

"We hoped, but if you think me or Joshua Schwartz has that much power you are mistaken."

"You should know I have feelings for her." It was only right to be upfront and honest with Lydia's mother. "I won't let it affect our arrangement, but I felt you should know."

"I already knew."

She did?

"The moment I found you two fussing over a messy kitchen I knew." Her head cocked to one side and her grey eyes stared at him. "I know Lydia is confused, with Andy back and trying out sweet promises on her, but I also know her heart. She has feelings for you. I see them and hear them in the little things she says. I trust *mei dochder* to know her heart and do what's best for it. I hope you can trust your own and not dally too long."

Silas took Hazel's words as an informal blessing to pursue her daughter. "I will do my best."

Lydia brushed Jippy down after their trip. What had she been so afraid of? "You are a great teacher, Jippy. *Danki* for bringing me home safely." Lydia added a handful of fresh oats to her bucket as a reward.

"Always talk to old nags?"

Lydia jerked with a startle and turned to find Andy standing in the opening of the barn. She hadn't seen him in days and knowing what she did know, she wished he had stayed away.

"Easier than people most days," she said.

He strolled toward her with that same profound confidence she had come to detest. Closing the stall door, she gathered Jippy's lines and bridle and hung them on a nail nearby.

"I haven't seen you for a spell."

Maybe he had forgotten which day he was to see her and which some another poor *maedel*. How many were there? She tossed out the question, not wanting to know the answer. Her life had enough strain in it. No need to add keeping up with the lies of others to it.

"I have been looking for work. My *onkel* doesn't think I have what it takes to milk."

Maybe because you can't wake up early from all your courting.

"Gavin is probably correct. You could return to your old job. You loved working in the buggy shop. At least that's what you said to me."

"You want me to leave Kentucky? I thought—"

She knew what he thought, and it ran through her like a lightning bolt, singeing a path from her heart to her head.

"Did you enjoy golfing? You know that little place over in Mason near the big cemetery?" Lydia lifted a brow, daring him to deny it.

Andy's face shifted between three shades of red, all of which Lydia had no true name for. She crossed her arms over her chest, waiting for his excuses to come spilling out. Andy always had one ready for use. His open mouth spouted no sound. Instead, he pulled her into his arms, bent his head, and rushed his lips over hers.

Lydia shoved him back, shocked by his forceful need to have what was not his to have. She pressed her hands to her mouth in revolt. Who was he to think he could do that without asking?

"What's the matter? Don't you love me, Lydia?"

"I—" A strange thought bloomed, reaching her midsection. Andy assumed her naïve, needy for his love. As the shock of his actions pulsed through her, so did the reality of who and what he was. Anger rushed to replace surprise, sprouting with it a new and wicked temper.

"Don't you have another who would welcome your kisses?" Lydia brushed by, hoping he didn't follow.

"I came back for you. Does it matter who wants me? It's you I want. Does that not count for something to you?" His desperation hung in the still air. "I have chosen you, Lydia. It has always been you."

The first sting of tears threatened, and she forced them back until he finished his heart's wants.

"Why will you not let me hold your hand or kiss you?"

Nothing could dry up an emotion faster.

"My first kiss is for the man I plan to marry, the one I choose, and that is not for you to take. I won't compete for any man's affections." If he only knew how strongly she meant those words. "I won't settle for less than I deserve. Go home, Andy Weaver. Go back to Ohio and whoever awaits you there." She shot daggers at him with her intense look. "You should have no problem doing that—again." Hurt emptied, Lydia stormed out of the barn and away from the only future she had—gladly.

Chapter Twenty-Three

Benjamin Troyer had been welcomed home. His failing heart had slowed to a stop, and poor sweet Penny Lapp had been the unfortunate who had chosen that day to take her turn visiting with him. Penny was crying even now, but Lydia had run all out of free comfort to give as the funeral had concluded and the meal finished.

Hannah was consoling their fragile friend right now. Hannah had been good at consoling lately. She had told Hannah about Andy in the barn two nights ago. Hannah didn't hide her pleasure and even offered to pay a driver to deliver Andy Weaver back to Ohio where he belonged. It made Lydia laugh then, but today, tears were in order. Ben had been a *gut* man, his wisdom profound, and Lydia would miss their long talks.

As people began making their way home, Lydia stood still, staring at the lonely little house Ben had lived in. Heaven would hold him now, but she would much rather have kept the dear man near as opposed to letting God have him. Who else would tell tales of her *daed* and his foolish boyhood of racing buggies and hiding cigars under trap doors in old corn cribs? Who else would know what she had done and seen how it affected her?

As the sun angled right from its high place in the sky, Lydia felt the overbearing heat of the day enhance her weary mood and tired mind. As everyone made their leave from the small home and simple yard, Lydia removed the black bonnet and adjusted her *kapp*. At least that felt better. Now all that was left was tidying up and closing the quiet house until it would be needed once more.

"The ladies are coming tomorrow to tend to the *haus*. I will take the *kinner* back to the farm while you finish with the tables," Hazel said, shaking Lydia from her downtrodden thoughts.

Lydia didn't turn to face her *mudder* for fear of bursting into tears once more.

"Don't be long, my dear." Hazel squeezed her shoulders and left her to finish.

Mudder knew her too well. She did need a moment alone. So many people had left her, either for glory or by choice, and for the life of her, she couldn't adjust to the loneliness it filled her with.

"We are leaving too, Lydia," Hannah said, approaching. "Silas said he would take you home and help fold up the tables. I will be here tomorrow and help."

"*Danki*, Hannah. You have been a *gut* friend this day."

"I am a *gut* friend every day."

Hannah winked before embracing Lydia into a rare hug. Hannah wasn't one for affection. "I know you and Ben were close, but he is in *Gott's* hands now."

She knew that. She just didn't like it. Lydia watched her leave before taking to task tidying up the tables.

Folding each of the table coverings one by one, light-headedness caused her to sway. Had she forgotten to eat? After thinking on it, she realized she had forgotten in her hurry to help others.

Stupid. Stupid.

She gripped the table and closed her eyes, waiting for the

dizziness to pass. When she felt the tablecloths slip from under her arm, Lydia's eyelids flew open.

"Let me help."

"I don't need help."

"You cannot do everything all the time. We are a community, we help each other." Was Silas going to fuss at her today? Could she not even do kind, right?

"I wanted to be alone more than I wanted help." Lydia's words snapped through the air, then she gathered herself.

"Lydia, you're exhausted. Just stop. Take a breath. Have you even eaten anything today?"

"I do not want to breathe or eat. I want to be alone." Maybe that was too loud. A little spoiled child loud. It didn't affect him as she expected it would have.

"You do so much for others. Please let me tend to this much for you. It is just a few tablecloths."

Despite how kind and patient he was being, she couldn't let herself care. Silas's heart belonged to another, and regardless of her bleak future, she was not the kind to interfere with someone else's.

"I got it. You may go." *Don't look at him.*

"*Nee.* You do not have it."

Lydia stopped moving. The veneer of her busy cracked, and she glared at him for slowing her, for presuming to know her. He stood his ground. The longer they stood, the wearier she became, and soon her eyes glistened with unwelcomed tears. "I let go." Her voice trembled her weak confession in brokenness.

"Let go?" His brows furrowed into confusion.

"You should have never let me know those children. You should have trusted yourself and found someone who would be better. I am not a woman who can be trusted with such things as those beautiful children." If Silas Graber had a thought, she didn't hear it as she ran away, all the way back to the farm without looking back.

She had no plan or idea where she was going but she did know she wasn't going to stop walking until her legs ached. What better way to be forced to her knees than falling? And she was falling. Andy was returning to Ohio, Silas was a fool who flirted and teased with her when he had every intention to love another, and Ben was gone, taking her secret with him. She chided herself for almost giving that up to Silas.

Lydia stomped past the large farmhouse, past the barn with its flowerbed springing forth with life, and aimed straight for the back pasture.

Ben had told her she needed to move on, that she wasn't to blame for that horrible day, but she couldn't believe him. Who else could be blamed for letting go of the horses and causing her *daed*'s death?

No one, that's who.

The day's warmth had given way to a cool evening. She continued clomping forward without any real destination. Trudging through the tall, damp grass and uneven earth, she measured her life choices. She would live and die a caregiver or burden.

The northern pasture was a lush green and glistened in dew.

Andy thought I would kiss him even after knowing about him see-ing another woman. Silas thought he could spark flames with no inten-tion of honoring them.

A tree line came into sight and she aimed toward it.

Ben even said those children needed me. That I understood their loss.

"But I don't understand." Her voice cried out for Him. It wasn't like a single ear would hear her heartbreak out here. No one to tell her she was crazy for talking to herself or fussing with God. She spit as something flew to her lips, fearing a gnat or bug came too close.

Sounds of music slowed her pace, the kind *Englisch* kids often blared out of their cars while speeding past on the road. It wafted through a tree line of oak and poplar. Lydia stopped and listened to the twang of a man singing about his need to find a runaway woman. It was laughable. There would be no man searching for her but running away did hold some appeal right now.

Edging closer to the sounds and adopting the shadows, she stepped lightly. Concealed in thick brambles, elder bushes, and old trees knowing the earth's secrets, she spied a dozen or so Amish teenagers indulging in the pleasures of rumspringa, or their runaround years.

She had missed those years—poor choices of her own doing, of course, but she'd missed them all the same. Weekends for her were writing letters, pining over Andy Weaver, and dreaming of tomorrows, not living for her today. She had been a fool, that was for sure and certain.

A couple young *maedels* were dressed in *Englisch* clothing, but she recognized them well enough. Two boys she was certain were sons of the bank teller in town poked each other in playful fun. The sweet lady who collected deposits for the bakery had their picture displayed for all to see when you came to her counter. The mingling was worrisome, and not real smart if she did say so herself. How many more years until Aiden would be in a scene like this one? She would have to tie Gideon to the bed when his time came, that was for sure.

Another tune started, capturing her attention. Lydia swayed to a low beat. It was a dreadful tune full of melancholy, but this missed opportunity she would take. She had missed so many things before her baptism.

Did all music sound woeful? No one seemed happy, but the instruments lightened any lonesome feeling the singer's words gave. She had always imagined spinning in a circle until all she felt was dizzy, and she did.

Arms out, eyes heavenward, she spun. It was a strange

and forbidden freedom that those on the other side of the fence would never understand, or maybe they did, and she was the only one who had never slowed down to embrace it. Not a soul but God to see out here. She would not apologize for it after and do this one thing for herself.

A hand clamped onto hers, another hand captured her waist, bringing her to a stop. "Silas," she blurted out when her eyes locked on to his. Embarrassment ran hot over her cheeks.

"May I?" he asked in that deep, alluring voice that always sent her nerves into overdrive.

Flummoxed, her shock strangled any words hoping to escape. He held her so close that she could see a fleck of yellow in his right eye. How had he even known where to find her?

"I think every beautiful woman should have the chance to do that one thing they always dreamed of." He spun her once, forcing a surprising giggle out of her, before pulling her close again. Since when did Amish men know how to dance?

"Mary May told me," he confessed through a shy grin.

What a handsome face he had. "I am sorry. You must think—" He shushed her with a finger's touch and took her hand back into his.

"You have no idea what I think, but it's time you do."

He guided her into a slow dance, and she felt her mind go dizzy by his abrupt appearance, his touch, and the way he was looking at her now. There were no doubts left. She loved him, heart and mind. She loved him, his children, his life, and wanted it for herself. God must think her the worst of all.

"You defended Gideon, even after he caused you to fall at the bakery."

Seeing her shocked expression, he smiled until the corners of his eyes crinkled like a leaf to a flame. Another sound came on the old truck radio, but this time Lydia didn't hear the words sung, her focus solely on the man holding her and giving her this moment. The world was theirs, for a time, and she was dancing. Dancing with the man she loved.

"You hung the hummingbird feeders back up," she said, careful to keep her feet moving in perfect line with his. His touch was magnetic, and she felt her body relax a little as their bodies moved in sync with one another. If he only knew the thrill he was giving her right now.

"You destroyed my kitchen and cut Mary May's hair." His lips were teasing now, holding that boyish mischievous grin.

"You returned my books." She held his gaze without sway.

"They were *gut* books."

Had he read them? How many surprises did he have in him?

"I would have returned them sooner, but…" He winked. "I had to see everyone got their happy ending."

"You got my bike from a stranger's car, taught me to face my fears, and I heard you bought lavender." Now she was smiling, teasing, hoping she was doing it right. Flirting was not natural to everyone.

"And bees. You forgot I hope to add that to this life we have made."

Had they begun building a life? The knots in her stomach tightened.

"I have come to love the scent of honey. It smells just like you." He leaned forward, breathing her in. "I want that smell everywhere."

She trembled, straining to retain some sense of decency, but her weak knees had her melting deeper into him.

"I thought lavender was more your liking." She was getting better at this flirting thing. He was here, for her, and she knew without a doubt this dance was his way of telling her that.

Silas chuckled. "I will never love the scent of lavender…

that much. If you hadn't wanted to plant it, I promise you I would have never bought any." She placed her hand on his chest. Silas's heart was pounding even harder, faster than her own.

They held on tightly as if letting go would bring this precious moment to an end. With his head above hers, she rested her face on his chest and breathed in every scent that made him all man.

Moonlight was veiled behind a cloud-thick sky. For a moment, the dark swallowed them into a private haven, a safe and impenetrable place where nothing could seek them. It was a small slice of time that belonged only to them. She wanted to stay there, in his arms surrounded by night. How long she had needed arms to hold her like this. It was a feeling akin to home.

Too soon the moon returned and when she peered up again, Silas lowered his head to her. "Silas?" she whispered, recognizing he too had needs to be addressed.

"Now would be the time to argue, tell me to stop," he said. "I cannot strum up the courage to let go and walk away right now."

He leaned so close their breaths mingled. She held firm, surprised at her own strength as the warmth inside become a blaze.

"I heard what you said," he whispered.

So close. So wonderfully close.

"I know you want your first kiss to be with the man you love, the one whom you choose to marry."

His arms tightened around her. His lips a feathery touch.

"Let me be that man."

One hand slid from her waist and eased upward, cradling her cheek. Lydia leaned into his touch. He loved her, wanted her, leaving no doubts between them.

"You want me? Are you sure?"

"My sweet, beautiful Lydia Rose." His thumb caressed her jawline, the intensity causing her to shudder. The kiss dangled before her, and she waited for the man who had lost so much to want love again—and love her. Why would he want her to leave if he was looking at her like that? Could he not see she had been waiting for him all along? Why was love this confusing? It should be simpler.

"Silas, I don't want to leave."

"Then you have a choice to make. Because, if you do not walk away now, I will kiss you."

The threat, the promise of his words, only sent more shivers through her.

Please, please do that.

"I thought you had feelings for another. I heard you tell Jenny you had an interest, and she knew it."

"I have only ever cared for you," he said, desperation painting his words. "I did not want to come between you and Andy. If that is what you want, I wanted you to have what made you happy."

"We both thought wrong about the other."

"Wasted time," he said in a rusty tone.

"Silas, I only want you."

Like everything he did, Silas took control, devouring her lips so fast Lydia barely had time to blink, but her response was complete surrendering. If not for the need for air, neither would have stopped.

"Just like honey," he whispered in her ear as his lips roamed.

She held tightly. He had challenged her, and she was the better for it. His lips found hers again, and she knew she would be the better for that too.

"I am sorry." He pulled back, breathless. "I have wanted to tell you, craved telling you so long. I am not being fair. You deserve to be treated with the proper respect of a gentleman. Forgive me."

"There is nothing to forgive. I rather like that you feel you cannot have enough of me. I thought you loathed me." She chuckled. How could they have misread everything this badly?

"I never loathed you, dear." He brushed his palm along her face. "Kept my distance. Found reasons to not be near you. You have no idea how hard that was."

"I have some idea," she smiled up at him. Silas Graber was in love—with her.

"I love you. I want you to stay. Stay with me, here. I want to marry you and keep you always by me." Usually courting and a respectable amount of time passed before two people spoke to the bishop and asked to be wed. Then there was that allotted time for publication, two weeks before the wedding. Looking at this man now, Lydia felt that if he could bend the world to serve him, they would marry by tonight.

"I would love to marry you, Silas Graber. I love you too." Silas grinned happily when she wrapped both arms around his neck and kissed him. "How long before we can marry?" she said with bated breath.

"Not soon enough."

CHAPTER TWENTY-FOUR

On bended knee, Silas finished driving the first nail. Reaching over his shoulder, he rubbed the tender place the Bishop slapped this morning. Of course, Joshua Schwartz laughed at his eagerness to wed Lydia, and Silas expected nothing less but a few chuckles when he stopped by the Bishop's home before heading into work. For an older gentleman, Joshua sure packed a good wallop.

The sun rose on his back. The last day of May greeting its final good morning. Lydia would be sharing the news with Hazel this morning. Oh, how Silas wished to see the expression on his future mother-in-law's face. Hazel would probably claim them as another successful match, being as she was in part responsible. How he had earned this second chance, he didn't know, but God sure was giving him one. Tonight, they would tell the children together. His smile grew wider.

"What's got you smiling like a cat in the milk pail?"

John walked up to where Silas was bent over, working.

Pulling a nail from his leather apron and drove it into the framework for the second walkway of the new office building.

One section at a time.

He had a fondness for old brick walkways, like the one in the center of town. "I think they call it...happy." Silas grinned. His insides felt as eager as they had when he was a man of twenty.

"Happy, huh? Does this...happy involve a real *schee* blonde about way high." John held a hand just below chin level.

Silas shot up a quick look. News might travel fast, but that was not possible. "How did you..."

"We all have eyes you know." John quirked a grin.

"Are you good with that?" John might not see his moving forward as a good thing.

"Why wouldn't I be?" John stepped closer and kicked a smaller stone from his path.

"Jana was your half-sister. I thought—"

"Well, you thought wrong. Jana would want you to be happy. And I like her," John said. "Was a terrible thing losing her *daed* like she did."

Silas nodded.

"The *fraa* thinks she has been *gut* for you and those *kinner*."

"They adore her, even Aiden." It was no mistaken how far Aiden had come from first despising the idea of Lydia in his home to missing her when she wasn't there.

"I also hear you're not the only one who notices what a *gut maedel* she is. I fear if you do not do something soon, you will let a *gut* woman slip through your hands."

He had done something. Spilled his heart, danced with her in his arms, and drank in every inch of her. All in one evening. His smile couldn't be contained, and John met it with piqued interest.

"So, you didn't let her slip through your hands?" John laughed, holding his middle.

"I didn't." Silas grinned. "I had no choice. The woman captivated me."

"Captivated, huh? I didn't even know you knew such words."

John slapped his back causing the tenderness there to burn fresh.

"Well, I'm happy for both of you."

Silas started to thank him just as Toby Brown marched over, newspaper in hand, ball cap hiding the nothingness on his head. "I think they are going to shut us down, fellas. That little inspection last week didn't go so well." He tossed the paper towards Silas. Opening the disheveled mess, Silas read the front page. *Local company overlooking safety of employees.*

"What safety issues?" Toby had both men's full attention. Silas got to his feet.

"They think we are pushing the deadline and not letting the concrete set enough. My engineer swears all is well. I would never put my guys in danger."

Toby huffed, either from talking too fast or from frustration, Silas was unsure.

"Plus, some of the boys still won't wear the helmets. And there is that safety harness issue."

"What safety harness issue?" John asked as if this was the first time he'd heard anything about safety harnesses.

As head foreman for half of the Amish crew, Silas found his reaction off-putting. Of course, John wasn't the only foreman. Robert White handled the *Englisch* men and Freeman Mast handled the Amish men of Walnut Ridge.

"Well, they want me to put a safety harness on every single body above ten feet. I have over sixty men up there. Sometimes more," he said matter-of-fact-like. "How can men move around anchored down like that? It'll just slow the work and exceed our deadline finishing." Toby wiped his damp brow, his expression full of worry. "Now they want to let some reporter in here to poke about and ask questions." Toby shoved both fists onto his hips. "I'm going to have an ulcer, I tell ya, boys. Somebody is not wanting this job finished."

Silas peered at the paper again when a headline caught his attention. *Local police catch suspect linked to missing Ohio women.* Under the chilling words was a picture of a man being arrested by police officers. "*Ach,*" he said. The man had brown and silver hair, missing a front tooth, and in the backdrop, a blue car. It was the stranger. Silas took a sharp intake of air, but before his heart could react men's voices rang out, filling the mid-morning with a different kind of warning.

All eyes shot upward toward the ridge of the building still one part skeleton and one part solid. Men began scrambling towards the edges. Silas used the newspaper to shield the sun from his eyes just as a man began lowering himself out of a window frame by a rope held by another man.

"What in the…" Yells followed from all four corners and various levels. Silas made out their warnings to one another when a chunk of concrete the size of a buggy wheel dislodged mid-way on the eastern side and shattered on the pavement below.

He and John watched as a young man slid over the side of the structure in a panic. At forty-five feet from the ground, what urged the man over, he hadn't a clue. Until he did. That's when he felt it too. The earth was moving.

"Get out of here!" someone screamed, the bone-chilling warning echoing.

Men on the ground began scrambling out of the structure, putting as much distance between what was coming as their feet would allow.

"Hold on to something!" screamed another man from somewhere above.

"Oh Lord be with us all," John said seconds before yanking Toby and Silas from the walkway by their sleeves.

The sound of five stories of concrete, iron, and wood

crashing to the earth had no comparison in words. The earth below them shook, alerting the whole town that disaster had come to the small town of Pleasants. One minute the earth was moving beneath a Kentucky blue sky. The next moment, skies turned gray, and the sound of a disaster aftermath rang.

Silas shook his head, slinging chunks of debris and dust from his hair. Once his ears stopped ringing, screaming replaced it. At least those begging cries held life. He struggled to free himself from the heavy weight of debris as reality hit him with a jolt.

Through a thick cloud of dust, he could see the two far walls of the five-story building had collapsed into entrapping arms of suffering and pain. Men had been working each floor at a hurried pace after all the rain that had fallen recently which put the deadline for completion further behind schedule. The newspaper article ran through his mind as a fog of thick grit clouded his vision. Toby had pushed limits and now they had shattered at the expense of innocent workers.

Silas reached out an arm. He knew John was nearby. He could feel his brother-in-law's body draped across him. The moment John shoved him to the ground flashed through his mind. Silas muscled out from underneath of him just as sirens began wailing in the distance.

A few voices sounded through the dust. There were survivors. "Please let there be nothing but survivors," he pleaded with God aloud. But he of all people knew that was not always a prayer that was answered. He managed to get to his knees and gathered his senses.

"John! John!" Silas rolled him over. John groaned at the motion, and Silas felt regretful moving him, but he had to know if he was alive.

"I am okay. Something hit my head and my leg."

Silas could see darkness on his face, blood perhaps. "Let me get you farther away. Then I must go help the others."

Shock did not hide the fact that Silas knew this day death had come to Pleasants County and would stretch its cold hand even further than Miller's Creek. Many men, too many men in the surrounding area had depended on this job. He shook his head, pulled John away, and did what he had to do.

Help as many as you can, the Lord did whisper in times such as these.

CHAPTER TWENTY-FIVE

Lydia ran her fingers through the soft dirt of the garden. To her left Mary May mimicked her. Glancing at the sky, she realized it was almost noon, time to prepare lunch. This morning she couldn't stop smiling, her life wasn't changing, only growing. *Mudder* had cried tears of happiness with her. She and Silas would share the news with the children tonight.

So why on the happiest days of her life did she feel off-kilter? Had life showed her how easy it was to forget despair was always around the corner?

She shuddered as if the earth below her had shifted. Something was wrong. Something somewhere was out of time, off, and she felt the urge to move or fix it. Only she wasn't sure what *it* was.

When she heard the buggy race down the lane, she sprang to her feet. "*Mudder?*" It was hours before her day at the bakery would be over and who was helping *Mammi?*

When Hazel brought the buggy to a hard stop, Lydia noticed muddy tears streaked down her mother's face. Her clothes were covered in a white dust but not flour. Her instincts had to be right. Alarms rang in her ears, piercing her lungs and stabbing her chest. Something was terribly wrong.

"Oh Lydia," Hazel said in weary sobs. Taking her mother's arm, Lydia helped her down from the buggy.

"What is wrong, *Mudder*?" Lydia felt her own tears spring forth. The last time her *mudder* had shed tears like this, *Daed* had been hurt.

"It was so loud, knocking everything in the bakery over. Glass windows broke all up and down the streets." Hazel was hysterical.

"*Mudder*, calm down. What has happened?" She held her by both shoulders to help steady her.

"The construction crew at the new office building." Hazel couldn't keep her breath steady.

"*Mudder*, you are scaring me. Where is Silas? Is Silas safe? What of Thomas and Matthew? Oh no, and Gracie's Matthew?"

"It…just…fell." Hazel gazed through her before blinking back to reality. "The building fell down."

Lydia gasped.

"Men are dead. Many men are…gone."

The weight on her chest was unbearable. This wasn't real. This could not be real. Looking over her shoulder Lydia sucked in a much-needed breath as she looked out toward the garden where Aiden was sheltering his siblings under each arm.

Turning back to her mother, she knew what she had to do, and she didn't hesitate longer. "Keep them inside. Let no one speak to them." Lydia kissed her mother's cheek before climbing into the buggy. "I will find him and bring Silas home." She nodded. "I have to, for them."

She had to. The children had already lost one parent and Lydia couldn't believe God would take Silas from them. Or her. Silas loved her. She loved him. They were to be married and live a long life together.

"Jippy. Go!" She slapped the reins as if she had done so a million times. Despite his lathered-down body, Jippy understood the urgency and turned them both around and aimed for town.

She was more than five miles out when the cloud of dust came into view. Shock seized her. Eyes blurred with tears, she was blessed Jippy knew the destination without being maneuvered.

Nearing town, the air grew thicker as sirens screamed in various directions and volumes. Sirens from the firehouse to emergency vehicles and even the tornado tower siren over toward the Greenbrier area of the county, they were deafening. Roads were cluttered with abandoned vehicles. At the main intersection, three men with reflective stripes tried directing traffic.

She spit out a bit of dust that had made it beyond her lips. The traces of debris, and if mother was right, death, tasted of an eerie, cold metal that stung the flesh of her tongue.

"Lord, I beg you spare him. Do not take away their *daed*. Do not take Silas from me. I beg you with all my heart."

Seeing no clear path to edge closer to the chaos, she veered left. It was still a good distance, but she pulled into the bakery, tied Jippy to the post out front, and raced as fast as her faithful feet would carry her into the fray.

Jogging past two women crying, murky streams striping their faces as dirt covered the rest of them, Lydia felt a surge of urgency and picked up her pace. Had they lost someone?

Nothing looked as it once did, but as she reached a sidewalk cluttered with people, she was certain she wasn't far from where the new office building had been. Screaming his name over all the blares of noise was fruitless, but she did it anyway. She squeezed between two firetrucks, grunted as she slipped through the small gap, and sprang out the other side. Then she froze. On this side of the vehicle was another world.

Shocked to the point of numb existence, Lydia stood peering over a sea of chaos, confusion, and what she believed was a day of utter heartbreak. Faces were dirty and wide-eyed. Some searching while others looked dazed and confused. Clenching both sides of her dress, she whispered a prayer.

Scanning the faces, no feature stood out and no silhouette belonged to her beloved. Cries and moans mingled with the sirens, but thankfully a few alarms died away into the distance.

To her left, she spotted her friend Penny, shoulders slumped and head lowered. Her fingers, black as tar, gripped a straw hat. Lydia rushed to her. Her eyes held steady on the mound of rubble before them. Penny had only just begun courting Amos Mast. Had Amos been lost this day? Called home?

"Penny."

"Lydia," Penny cried out in relief. They embraced. "They cannot find my Amos. He promised me it was safe. He promised. They cannot find him."

Penny's voice was desperate for hope, a hope Lydia had no idea how to give her. "They will, Penny, have faith. Have you seen Silas?" It felt dirty to ask about her man when Penny was still uncertain about her own. A shiver of selfish fear crawled over her, within her.

Penny nodded, focusing back on the rubble. Lydia soon spotted Karen, the *Englisch* driver many of the Amish hired when needed. She stood aside a stretcher where a large body was being lifted into the back of a dark-colored truck. Had so many been injured the use of trucks was required? The madness and overwhelming state of realness were too much to comprehend.

"*Gott,* I am getting married. I am going to be a *mudder* to those children. You cannot have him," she cried out, rushing deeper into the madness.

"Lydia! Lydia Miller!" a voice called.

Thomas hurried to her side, looking as uncontrolled as he ever had. His blue and green eyes were wild and bloody looking, his breath spent. "They cannot find my Michael."

He gripped her shoulders tightly and gave her a shake. Like Penny, he only wanted confirmation, someone to tell him if they were accounted for.

"Silas? Have you seen Silas?" She yelled back. If he replied, she didn't hear him. Thomas let go and rushed by her, continuing his search. She shot up another prayer, this time for her cousin Michael and for Thomas.

Standing at the center of the catastrophe, she stilled, taking in the full measure around her. The sheriff was moving people back away from the rubble. When they locked gazes, he nodded and then resumed his duties. A respectful gesture, acknowledging her. The last time they'd locked glances, he was helping her father into an ambulance. She didn't believe in signs and such stupid worldly things, but her heart did drop a few inches into her belly at that simple nod.

Was God preparing her for more bloodshed, more heartache?

Men in uniforms, from workers at the nearby millworks to local game wardens and those conservation guys, rushed into the heart of the disaster. Lydia stood idle, watching a small machine with a bucket attached to the front clearing their path. Somewhere to her right, she heard *Gott*'s name being called upon in a deep, strong, penetrating voice.

The preacher held both hands in the air. Lydia recognized the *Englisch* local as one who came many mornings to the bakery for donuts and an occasional pie. He was standing over a dozen long bodies. Their faces were hidden under towels and bedsheets and coats. One even had a horse blanket, blue and gray perhaps, covering him.

The preacher's words were muffled, but Lydia prayed with him, nonetheless. *Gott* didn't mind which side of the fence prayers came from, only that they shared the same fence. And it was clear that today, no fences divided the communities. Both sides shared that same desperate hope for His grace, and His mercies. Many needed both today.

Eyes stinging from all the dust, lungs too, Lydia caught a

glimpse of a womanly figure on bended knee. The bank teller woman to whose window she had delivered the bakery deposits many times. Lydia forced her feet to move forward, to offer comfort as she searched. It was a small thing, but something.

Kneeling, Lydia placed a hand on the woman's shoulder, the body before them that of Robert White, the local construction man who hired both *Englisch* and Amish. He was gone, chest crushed, legs distorted. Lydia assumed she would be sickened by such a sight, but it was not her first time seeing a good healthy man struck down by circumstances out of control.

"My boys don't know. How will I tell them?"

Tears flooded her green eyes, and Lydia had not a word to bring comfort but offered her a hand.

"Hey!" Another voice called out.

Looking up, Lydia saw the two grocery store cashiers, one she knew named Kayla and the other who she had not known by name, cradling an older woman. To their left was the Amish cheesemaker from the neighboring community—*Schwartz, was it?* Lydia had only met her once. She waved Lydia over, and she got to her feet again.

Stay busy and don't think.

It had always helped her in the past.

"I'm Elli. I need your help." Elli was leaning over a young man. A rod of iron pierced his left leg, his ankle on the right flattened and blue.

"What can I do?" Lydia asked, unsure, trembling with fear. She had no medical training, but how many emergency responders could handle such a day as this? Pleasants, Miller's Creek, and even Walnut Ridge shared the same few volunteers and few hired trained men.

Help as many as you can.

The voice came on a whisper and Lydia knew that over the sounds of so much noise, it could only be from the One who hadn't answered her once all her life. There was no mistaking when God spoke.

"Hold this here and yell for help until it comes. I must go help another. We must all help on this day."

Lydia nodded and pressed both hands over the bloody cloth wrapped in a circle around the iron rod.

"Press hard, stop the bleeding," Elli ordered before hastening away.

Lydia did just that. As she pressed firmly down, the warm ooze of his lifeblood covered her hands, and the man cried out. "I'm so sorry. I must." She winced.

"It is okay, but it does not mean it don't hurt." He blew out a hard breath, deflating his cheeks as he did. "So, I am gonna make some noise." He bit down on his own hand. "Thank you," he said before laying his head back in exhaustion.

"What is your name?" Lydia asked. An older man collapsed nearby, but she dared not raise to go to him, though her heart ached to, for fear of the young man would bleed too much before help would come to take him where he could be treated professionally.

"Kenneth," he said. "I hung on as long as I could."

He must have fallen after the two walls came down. Lydia couldn't imagine what fear had filled him in those moments. Voice scratchy, she called out over and over, eyes searching moving bodies for Silas. Finally, two firemen came to her aid and relieved her of this one duty, giving Kenneth a chance at life.

She wiped her blood-soaked hands on her apron front. The sheriff pulled another body, limp and broken, out of the rubble.

Old death, you are desperate this day.

The sheriff's face, though darkened from the muck, was set stone firm. Lydia doubted anyone had ever dealt with such tragedy before. They were working hard to rescue—or for a better word, recover as many as possible. Still, she couldn't allow herself to believe Silas was in there, lost in the rubble, awaiting recovery. He built walls and walkways. Hadn't that been all he talked about?

A nearby volunteer, dressed in bright green and stripes that made him visible in the dark, though not so in dust, yelled out the other two walls were unstable. The older man that had collapsed was gone by the time Lydia reached another cluster of volunteers.

The cries of pain in this small corner of the world Lydia felt certain were being heard across the country by now. She spotted a few people with cameras and shuddered. Reporters and photographers scavenged through the crowds like vultures capturing the aftermath.

Pushing up her sleeves, she moved around, searching. Not finding him wasn't necessarily the end. What if he had been taken to hospital? Fresh hope filled her.

You have just given him to me, Lord. His children could not bear losing another. I beg you spare him.

"Stay busy and trust in the Lord. You can do this Lydia." A few steps later she used her apron to tie a tight knot around an Amish man's arm. He wasn't from her district, but his face seemed familiar. "This will help for now. If they don't get you in ten minutes, untie the knot and then tie it back again. Trust this," she ordered and rose to help another.

After more than an hour bouncing between needs, she caught a glimpse. A tall and sturdy shadow carrying a wilted form moved towards the preacher. Lydia pivoted from a man whose face was bloody from a long gash down his right side. Recognition hit her like a slap and her breath gasped, taking in another helping of death and dust. The figure added the body to the line of covered faces, another loss, and rested on a bended knee. He bowed his head, and the preacher placed a hand on his shoulder, a comforting gesture. The man had dark hair, maybe. Who could tell with everyone so similar in the chaos? If there were two kinds of people in this world, it had fallen on this day too. One could not tell *Englisch* from Amish. Young from old. Barely could one tell death from life.

When the shadow stood, Lydia felt the magnetic pull and took one careful step forward. He started walking back towards the center of everything, and then as if feeling the same pull, he paused. In slow motion, he turned and locked his gaze on her. It was only at that moment she felt her heart start beating again.

A cry escaped her as she sprinted towards him. Silas's long strides licked up the ground between them in equal pace. As their bodies collided, two strong arms lifted her from the earth. His hold was so tight, so breathtakingly tight, and wonderful. She felt the same and clutched him tighter. His body shuddered as he buried his head between her head and shoulder.

What he had gone through, seen, and helped do this day, she could only imagine. She kissed his dirty head, his face. Sitting her down on her own two feet, he began searching her over.

"I was afraid," she said, crying happy tears.

She was here. Silas eyed her blood-soaked dress, crimson apron, and swollen eyes.

"Are you all right?" he said.

Lydia glanced down at her soiled clothes. "It's not mine," she reassured him.

He gathered her close again. Holding her soothed him.

"I prayed you were safe. That I would find you."

Cupping both sides of her grimy face, Silas felt his body shudder again. As a man, he never wanted her to see such things as what surrounded them. As a man who loved her, he'd hoped she would never know how close she came to losing someone again.

"My *lieb*, we have found each other." He swept her into a kiss right there. Three flashes of bright light disturbed their heartfelt reunion, and he blinked. They both turned towards the disruption to see that a small, rather clean-looking woman had been snapping their picture with one of those oversized black cameras. Silas didn't care a reporter took their picture. All he cared about was what he held in his arms.

ABOUT THE AUTHOR

Raised in Kentucky timber country, Mindy Steele and has been writing since she could hold a crayon against the wall. Inspired by her rural surroundings Steele writes Amish Romance peppered with just the right amount of humor, as well as engaging Suspense. She strives to create realistic characters for her readers and believes in charming all the senses to make you laugh, cry, hold your breath, and root for the happy ever after ending.

She is a mother of four and grandmother to a half dozen blessings. When not at her writing desk, Steele enjoys family, coffee indulgences, and weekend road trips. Steele is represented by Julie Gwinn and her debut novel, Christmas Grace, releases September 2020. She is also the author of A Cranberry Christmas, which releases at a later date.

Visit her website https://mindysteeleauthor.wordpress.com for more in formation on her upcoming releases.

Acknowledgements

Thank you to my family and my hometown for your continuous support and love.

Thank you to my agent, Julie Gwinn, for believing in me and all the tireless work you do.

Thank you to my Amish friends, Matt and Mirim, for all your insight, information, and for all the sweets that fed me throughout writing this series.

Thank you to my local library for letting me take up space on days when I need a fresh view.

Thank you Dawn Carrington, editor-in-chief, and the entire Vinspire team for all your efforts in turning my dreams into reality.

Thank you most to God, giver of wings and words. May I never disappoint you.

Dear Reader

If you enjoyed reading To Catch A Hummingbird, I would appreciate it if you would help others enjoy this book, too. Here are some of the ways you can help spread the word:

Lend it. This book is lending enabled so please share it with a friend.

Recommend it. Help other readers find this book by recommending it to friends, readers' groups, book clubs, and discussion forums.

Share it. Let other readers know you've read the book by positing a note to your social media account and/or your Goodreads account.

Review it. Please tell others why you liked this book by reviewing it on your favorite ebook site.

Everything you do to help others learn about my book is greatly appreciated!

PLAN YOUR NEXT ESCAPE!

WHAT'S YOUR READING PLEASURE?

Whether it's captivating historical romance, intriguing mysteries, young adult romance, illustrated children's books, or uplifting love stories, Vinspire Publishing has the adventure for you!

For a complete listing of books available, visit our website at www.vinspirepublishing.com.

Like us on Facebook at
www.facebook.com/VinspirePublishing

Follow us on Twitter @vinspire2004

Follow us on Instagram @vinspirepublishing

and follow our blog for details of our upcoming releases, giveaways, author insights, and more!
www.vinspirepublishing.com/blog.

We are your travel guide to your next adventure!

CPSIA information can be obtained
at www.ICGtesting.com
Printed in the USA
LVHW102302150422
716321LV00004B/214